Praise for

JENNY
OLIVER

'This was one of my first Christmas reads of 2014 and it was really good. Highly recommend this one!'
Book Addict Shaun on *The Little Christmas Kitchen*

'With gorgeous descriptions of Paris, Christmas, copious amounts of delicious baking that'll make your mouth water, and lots and lots of snow – what more could you ask for from a Christmas novel!'
Bookboodle on *The Parisian Christmas Bake Off*

'. . .this book had me in tears by the end.'
Rachel Cotterill Book Reviews on *The Vintage Summer Wedding*

'I really enjoyed this book and I loved how it was more focused on a family love, rather than the heroine seeking out a man to help her get over the infidelity of her husband. By the time I finished the book, I got this real "*Frozen*" vibe to it.'
Book Mood Reviews on *The Little Christmas Kitchen*

'What's not to like about Christmas, Paris and baking?!'
Sheli Reads on *The Parisian Christmas Bake Off*

'Jenny Oliver writes contemporary women's fiction which leaves you with a warm, fuzzy feeling inside.'
Books with Bunny on *The Vintage Summer Wedding*

For guaranteed sunshine all holiday long, pack your bags and escape to *The Sunshine and Biscotti Club* – Tuscany's newest baking school!

WITHDRAWN

Praise for

JENNY OLIVER

The
Sunshine and
Biscotti Club

JENNY OLIVER

CARINA™

This edition is published by arrangement with Harlequin Books S.A. CARINA is a trademark of Harlequin Enterprises Limited, used under licence.

First Published in Great Britain 2016
By Carina, an imprint of HarperCollins*Publishers*
1 London Bridge Street, London, SE1 9GF

The Sunshine and Biscotti Club © 2016 Jenny Oliver

ISBN 978-0-263-92201-1

98-0516

Our policy is to use papers that are natural, renewable and recyclable products and made from wood grown in sustainable forests.
The logging and manufacturing processes conform to the legal environmental regulations of the country of origin.

Printed and bound by
CPI Group (UK) Ltd, Croydon, CR0 4YY

Jenny Oliver wrote her first book on holiday when she was ten years old. Illustrated with cut-out supermodels from her sister's *Vogue*, it was an epic, sweeping love story not so loosely based on *Dynasty*.

Since then Jenny has gone on to get an English degree and a job in publishing that's taught her what it takes to write a novel (without the help of the supermodels). Nowadays, her inspiration comes from her love of all things vintage, a fascination with other people's relationships and an unwavering belief in happy ever after! Follow her on Twitter @JenOliverBooks or take a look at her blog jennyoliverbooks.com.

LIBBY

As the church clock struck midnight, Libby Price was attempting to haul a double mattress up a flight of stairs on her own.

Now halfway up, the decision to begin the process was beyond regretful. The night was sweltering. The stairs were narrow. She was exhausted. But she'd had to do something. Something that strained every part of her being, because otherwise she would have lain in her bed contemplating her afternoon.

Still she kept being plagued by visions of herself striding purposefully to the bottom of the endless garden. Seeing Jake lounging in one of the deckchairs. Legs up on the metal table, eyes half closed as they soaked up the sun, bottle of water in one hand, sweat trickling off his forehead.

He'd rolled his head in her direction when he'd heard her footsteps. And she knew he thought she was coming out to admire the new outhouse he'd just finished building. To admire all its sharp angles and big metal framed windows.

He hadn't expected her to swipe his legs angrily off the table. A move which, admittedly, even Libby had been quite surprised by. He hadn't expected the fury and the anger, the shouting, and the piece of paper that she'd thrust into his view.

'It's a website, Jake,' she'd half shouted. 'A website with the slogan: *Marriage is dull, have an affair!* And guess whose credit card and email address is linked to it? Don't look all innocent, Jake. It's been bloody hacked. One of my blog followers sent me the link. Do you know how that makes me feel? Do you?' She'd actually stomped her foot just for some physical manifestation of how furious she was. 'How could you do this to me? How dare you do this to me? God, I'm so angry.'

That bit she was quite proud of. It wasn't like her at all. She had somehow summoned this fiery strength from the devastation and even Jake had seemed momentarily startled by the force of it.

The mattress teetered precariously as the memory made her concentration lapse. Her arms strained under the weight as she tried to heft it onto the next step so she could take a break. Sweat was pouring off her. She was boiling hot. The hotel felt stuffy. The scent of the lemon grove next door, usually exquisite, now made her feel like she was trapped at a perfume counter, the smell too sickly and heady. She tried to get her breath back but could feel her muscles screaming. She was so tired.

The mattress wobbled. Leaning it back against the wall, Libby squeezed herself alongside it, trying to keep it in place with her bodyweight, as she decided to try and shove it up from the bottom.

With her shoulder against the shiny new material she made a move to push but it didn't budge. The top of the mattress now caught against the step.

Why had she started this? Had it been as much to stop the loop of memories as to test whether she could do all this on her own?

She put her hands over her face. The weight of the mattress was pressing against her body. There was so much that needed doing before the hotel was ready, and getting a mattress up the stairs seemed like one of the more minor items on the to do list. If she couldn't shift that, what could she do? Perhaps this was a painfully stupid exercise that would prove, as she suspected, there was simply no way she could do it by herself.

Her body slumped.

The mattress slipped a step.

She shouted in annoyance.

A mosquito buzzed around her ear.

She thought about all the plans she and Jake had made for the renovations. All their hopes and ambitions scribbled in notebooks and on napkins. When they'd first turned up at the dilapidated hotel, he'd squeezed her hand and said, 'Don't worry, we're in this together.' That was how it was meant to be. Him squeezing her hand, her squeezing his.

How was it possible that could turn so suddenly to such anger and shame buzzing like the cicadas as she'd marched down the garden path?

She squeezed her eyes shut, pressing her face into the mattress, as she thought about the moment when, after her outburst, Jake had stood up, looked down at the lush grass then up to meet her eyes and said, 'Libby.' Taking a step towards her. 'I think actually this might have needed to happen. I think actually it's a good thing, you know. For me.'

She hadn't really listened. Instead she'd replied, 'When you were doing it, when you were shopping online for a mistress, did you think about me? Did you think about hurting me?'

He'd shaken his head. 'No. Honestly, Libby, I was just thinking about me. And it seemed—I don't know—separate from you. Libby, I feel like shit but I think it's right that this has happened. This…' he'd pointed to the beautiful new outhouse, the garden, the hotel, 'is all too much. I thought I'd be OK with it, but I'm not. Living here—it's too remote. I feel like I can't breathe,' he'd added with a huff.

'You feel like shit?' she'd said. 'Jake, you've shattered me.'

He'd looked at her with pity in his eyes. 'I miss my life, Libby. I miss life.'

'But this is our life.'

'No.' He'd shaken his head. 'No. I'm going to go away for bit I think. I'm sorry.' That was when she had crumpled. When the air had been knocked out of her.

That was the reason why she was hauling a mattress up the stairs like a carthorse, arms stretched behind her as she tried once again to tug it to the top. So that she didn't have to go to sleep, so that she didn't have to close her eyes and see herself begging him to stay.

If only she hadn't cried. If only she hadn't held on to his arm and tried to pull him back.

She yanked the mattress.

Stupid, stupid Libby.

He'd paused and hugged her when she'd sobbed. Just for a couple of seconds. Enough time for her traitorous mind to think that this could all be forgotten, that they could just focus on the hotel, on the renovations and the imminent arrival of the guests.

But then he'd let her go and held her by the shoulders and said, 'Will you be OK? Should I call someone?' in a voice that suggested she was some weak Victorian maiden. With a surge of anger she had bashed his arms off her.

'I'll be fine,' she'd hissed, and he'd had the nerve to look sympathetic. 'Just go.'

She'd watched him jog up the steps to the terrace and thought, *Come back*.

Then she'd made herself remember the website, the affairs, the fact she'd found out through her own blog.

Go, you bastard.

No, stop. Come back.

Now as she stood on the staircase, the harsh halogen lights burning above her, she found herself smacking the mattress, thumping it with all her frustration, humiliation, and anger. It felt quite good until it slipped from its perch mid-step and, as she fumbled to catch it, careered down to the bottom like a sledge thumping hard on the floorboards, smashing into the side table and shattering a glass bowl filled with lemons.

'Bollocks.'

Libby sat down on the step, chaos on the floor around her. She stared at the lemons rolling along the gaps in the floorboards like trains on a track, stopping when they hit a stack of old mirrors about to be relegated to the garage. She glanced up from the lemons to her own reflection. Tired, sad, angry. Who was this person, she wondered as she stared, if she was no longer one half him?

EVE

'Do you think the kids are getting enough kale?' Eve asked as Peter walked into the kitchen having just put their four-year-old twins to bed.

'Yes. Because I don't think anyone actually eats kale.'

'But it's a superfood. I don't know if they're getting enough superfoods. A woman today said that she gets up at five every morning to make superfood smoothies for her and her kids' breakfasts and then meditates for half an hour before they wake up. I don't have the energy to get up and meditate.'

Peter was flicking through the local paper open on the table and splattered with spaghetti Bolognese. 'Is this Bolognese? Did the kids have Bolognese? Are we having Bolognese as well?'

Eve nodded.

'Excellent.'

'But what about the kale.'

'Bugger the kale. I was brought up on frankfurters and chicken Kiev. I'm OK.'

Eve rolled her eyes and went back to the washing up. Then after a minute, after she'd heard Peter get a beer out the fridge and flip the cap, she said, 'The thing is, sometimes I just want a proper chat about things like kale. I know it's neurotic so don't look at me like that, but sometimes I need to talk about it. It's important to me.'

She saw him sigh. 'Eve. I've had a really long day. I don't need to talk about kale. You don't need to talk about kale. You want to talk about kale because you don't have anything else to think about at the moment because you're refusing to think about work.'

'I am not refusing to think about work.'

'OK, well maybe if you put as much energy into thinking about work as you did about kale then you'd have come up with something new by now.'

She scoffed, indignant. 'It is not that easy, Peter. I haven't got any inspiration at the moment. Nothing. I can't do it if I have nothing.'

He took a swig of beer to mask his slight shake of the head.

'What's that supposed to mean?' she asked, referring to the head shake.

'Nothing.'

She raised a brow.

'I just reckon it's bullshit. Sit in your office, do some work. Just do it,' he said, and then the phone rang before she could reply. Peter reached round to answer it and said, 'It's for you. Libby.'

Eve frowned. 'From Italy?'

Peter shrugged, handed her the phone and walked out into the living room.

She watched him go, quite grateful for the excuse to end the discussion. There was something simmering underneath her and Peter's relationship at the moment, had been for a while. Nothing noticeable in the everyday, but just a fraction less between them. Conversations reached sighing point quicker. Less tolerance maybe for the other's nuances. Less kissing, less sex, less closeness as a couple, while still cemented as a family.

'Hi, Libby? How's it going?'

Peter was scrolling indecisively through options to watch on Netflix when Eve walked into the living room. It was by far her favourite room in the house, one she could happily cocoon herself in forever. It had taken her years to get it just right. The sideboard was her most cherished item, vintage wood laminate with a yellow Formica top that she'd got at a car boot sale in the village. She spent a lot of time artfully rearranging the little antique fair statues and old French café jugs she had lined up along it after the kids walloped into it or decided to use it for a dolls' tea party.

Peter chucked the remote down on the coffee table without picking anything to watch and said, 'What was that about?'

'She wanted me to go to Italy. Jake's gone apparently. She caught him on that affair website, you know the one on the news?'

Peter's eyes widened. 'Bloody hell,' he said, then sat back into the big grey sofa and added, 'Mind you, kind of thing he'd do, isn't it?'

Eve frowned, refolding a blanket she had draped over the armrest. 'That's not very helpful.'

Peter rolled his eyes and picked up the remote again. 'Are you going to go?' he asked, staring at the Netflix options.

'No,' she said with a shake of her head, catching sight of some rogue Lego figures and bending down to get them out from under the table. 'No, I don't think so,' she said, stretching her arm to reach the last one. 'Jessica and Dex have said they're going to go, so that's OK,' she said, chucking the Lego into the box in the corner of the room. 'I don't really want to leave the kids.'

There was a second too long a pause before Eve realised what she'd said and as she walked back to the sofa added as casually as she could, 'And you.'

'And me,' Peter said with the raise of his brows.

'Of course you, it goes without saying,' she added with a laugh, checking to see if there were any other toys lying about the place.

'It doesn't, Eve.' Peter shook his head.

'Of course it does,' she said, spotting a small plastic cow hiding behind one of her French café jugs and going over to pick it up.

'No,' Peter said, the rows and rows of Netflix options skimming past at unreadable speed.

Eve was just going over to stand the plastic cow up with the rest of the plastic animals on the toy farm when Peter said, 'I need to talk to you about something.'

'What?'

He leant forward so his elbows rested on his knees and his fingers steepled to a point in front of him.

Eve went and sat on the edge of the coffee table in front of him, the plastic cow still in her hand. 'I didn't mean to miss you off when I was talking about holidays. I really do just include you by default.' A small frown appeared on her face—that had sounded better in her head.

He took a breath in. 'Something's gone wrong, Eve. With us.'

'No, it's fine.' Eve shook her head. 'Look at us— lovely house, lovely kids, lovely, lovely, lovely.' She used the plastic cow to emphasise the point, trotting it in front of her like she might with the kids, and immediately regretted it.

She felt Peter waiting as she put the cow down next to her on the table. Then he said, 'Don't get me wrong, I don't think it's unfixable, I just know it's there.' He sat up straight, running a hand through hair that really needed a cut. Eve found herself thinking that he could take their son, Noah, with him to the barber's at the weekend. Noah would like that. 'I nearly had an affair,' he said.

'What?' Eve stopped thinking about the barber's and almost laughed. 'Are you joking? Is this because of Jake?'

Peter shook his head. 'No. Maybe. I've wanted to tell you for ages. I didn't do anything. One hundred per cent I didn't. But I thought about it, Eve. I thought about it. And in the past I would never have even considered it.' He sank against the sofa cushions.

Eve pulled her hair back from her face, holding it there as she said, 'Jesus Christ, what's wrong with you all? Why are you all having affairs?'

'I didn't! I didn't have an affair. Don't lump me in with Jake. But I feel like if I don't tell you then I am like him,' Peter said. 'Eve, the only person I've wanted to talk to about this was you—and you're the only person I couldn't talk to about this.'

'I feel sick,' Eve said. Right deep inside herself sick. Like everything precious was slithering away.

She swept the little plastic cow off the table in annoyance and for a moment sat with her hand covering her face. 'What does it mean?' she asked.

Peter sat forward again. 'I have no idea what it means. It just means that things can't go on as they are. It feels like we've got a chink. Both of us on different roads. I don't know,' he said, rubbing his forehead, 'I'm shit at explaining stuff like this. That's what it feels like to me. Like we're running parallel on different tracks.'

'Who was it? Do I know her?'

'That's not the point.'

Eve bit her lip. 'I just want to know. So I can see it, you know, in my head.'

He closed his eyes for a second. 'A supply teacher.'

Eve frowned. 'Not the little blonde one?'

Peter exhaled slowly. 'This isn't about the affair, Eve. There wasn't an affair. Shit, I shouldn't have said anything. Are you crying?'

'No.' Eve shook her head, desperately holding back any semblance of tears.

She bent down and picked the cow up, putting it on the table next to her again, feeling like she needed a mascot.

'I think maybe we just need to take some time,' Peter said. 'What do they call it? Have a break?' he said doing quote marks with his fingers. 'Sorry, I don't know why I just did that. I hate people who do quote marks. I'm nervous,' he said.

The oven timer plinked to say the Bolognese was ready.

They both stayed where they were.

'I think maybe you should go to Italy,' Peter said in the end.

Eve nodded; needing to look away from him she glanced round the living room, the timer beeping incessantly in the background, the sense of being cocooned gone, everything no longer quite so secure.

JESSICA

The hotel was exactly as Jessica had imagined it would be.

Quaint, she thought, as she stepped out of the taxi, sunglasses on, hair smoothed back into a low ponytail. There were twee green shutters on every window, flowerboxes on every balcony railing filled with gnarled white geraniums, an archway into a ground floor bar with dark wooden chairs and terracotta half pots as light sconces, a mildewed green and white striped awning. And painted down the centre of the building was a sign saying Hotel Limoncello.

'God, I can't stand Limoncello,' a voice drawled from the taxi, and she turned to see Dex, Valiumed up to the eyeballs post-flight, lying across the backseat and staring up at the same view.

'Can you walk?' she asked, glancing down at him.

'Certainly,' he said, sliding himself along the leather like a caterpillar and then stumbling out onto the warm pavement.

'Christ, even the pavement's hot. It's too hot, Jessica. I'm too hot,' he said, pulling himself up to standing.

She held in a smile as she paid the taxi driver who'd hauled the luggage round from the boot and was now looking dubiously at Dex as he tried to hold himself upright.

'This bag is ridiculous,' Dex said, leaning against Jessica's massive case. She had packed, as usual, for every eventuality.

Next to hers, Dex's bag was tiny. Hand luggage only. He had packed, he'd said, what he always packed for any holiday: three pairs of shorts, three t-shirts, underwear, one pair of flip-flops, a hat, and a book.

She could hardly believe he could remember, considering that neither of them had been on holiday for the past three years, instead chained to their desks building the recently award-winning Waverly Design Agency. Which was actually where she'd quite happily still be, she thought as she glanced back to the hotel and felt the heat already burning her hair and her skin. And where she would be if it wasn't for that Design Agency of the Year award.

Jessica had foggy memories of the ceremony, of Dex nudging her out of her seat to go up and collect the award while she was still perfecting her happy-for-whoever-won face. She vaguely remembered the surge of triumph, but then the champagne had been popped and she had nervously drunk more and more as strangers came over to offer their congratulations. Amidst it all had been a phone call from Libby that had seen Dex and possibly Jessica herself, she couldn't quite remember, shouting, '*Italy! Of course! Why not? A celebratory holiday.*'

Even while she'd sat next to Dex on the plane, his sedated charm offensive making the flight attendants giggle, Jessica was still perplexed that she had agreed to something quite so spontaneous. Part of her was wondering if Dex had filled in her inebriated memory gaps with his own Italy bound agenda.

Then a voice shouted, 'You're here!' and Jessica was forced to stop trying to decode her current predicament as she looked up to see Libby running down the entrance steps to greet them. Dressed in a striped Breton top, black capri pants, and little red ballet pumps, and her glossy brown hair in a knot on top of her head, Libby looked perfect. Certainly not like someone whose husband had just left her, Jessica thought, as she was pulled into a hug that smelt of Pantene, Chanel, and lemons.

'I've missed you,' Libby whispered into Jessica's ear. 'I've missed you so much.'

Jessica, not one for hugely honest displays of affection, tried to pull away with a laugh but Libby didn't let go, kept her captive in the hug, in the smells and scents of memories.

'I've missed you, too,' Jessica said in the end and was finally let go, as if she'd said the magic words. 'Dex isn't quite himself,' she said, pointing to where Dex was trying to pose in his aviators against the suitcase, a dreamy smile on his face. 'He's flight medicated.'

'Libby, my darling,' he drawled, trying to stand up straight and stumbling. 'Jake's a god damn fool.'

Jessica winced.

But Libby just waved it away. 'It's fine. Completely fine. Far too much to do to think about it.'

'Yes,' Dex agreed. 'We are here to work. At your service,' he said with a woozy salute. 'Though I may have to have a bit of a nap first.'

Libby laughed. 'You can have a nap, Dex. Shall I show you to your room?'

'Yes, please,' he said. Then he held up a hand and added, 'Just to let you know, the others will need rooms as well. I take it Eve's not coming? Hasn't left the deepest countryside since those kids were born.'

Libby frowned at Jessica. 'What's he talking about?'

Jessica shrugged. 'I have no idea. I think he's just rambling.'

'Come on, Dex, let's get you to your room.'

'You have to wake me up when Jimmy and Miles arrive,' he said, attempting to pick up his case.

Libby looked confused. 'Jimmy and Miles aren't coming, Dex.'

But Jessica knew that look on Dex's face, had worked with him long enough to know when he was lying, and this wasn't one of those times. She felt herself swallow down a sudden lump of worry.

'They are.' Dex nodded. 'I invited them.'

LIBBY

Libby didn't have anywhere to put Miles and Jimmy if they really did turn up. None of her rooms were ready. She'd struggled to pick the best two for Jessica and Dex. Maybe Jimmy could camp in the back garden. That was his kind of thing. Last Libby had heard he was sailing round the Venezuelan coast.

These were the thoughts going through her head as she went to pick Eve up from the airport, driving the winding roads that sliced through mountains and curled precariously around sheer vertical drops, where the sun made towering shadows from the looming cypress trees and the pale green leaves of the olive trees spread in groves as far as she could see.

Those thoughts stopped Libby from thinking about the fact that the only time she'd ever asked Eve for help—called her and asked her to come to Italy—Eve had said no. And now Eve was at the airport having changed her mind because she and Peter were suddenly on a break.

She'd half wanted to say, 'No, you can't come,' when Eve had WhatsApped to ask if the invitation still stood.

Of all the girls in the group they had been the closest. From the first day of secondary school when they eyed each other with wary interest as they sat down at adjacent desks, to arriving in London together, post-university, ready to start their first proper jobs, ready to be cool, hip, twenty-somethings who drank cocktails after work and wore pencil skirts. They had been the ones to rent the flat in South London. It had been their adventure. They had advertised for tenants and ended up with quiet, awkward, but sardonically funny Jessica who arrived at the interview flame red curls all awry with just a rucksack of possessions and five hundred pounds cash and basically begged them to take her because she needed somewhere to sleep that night.

Little did they realise then that Jessica had spent a lifetime carving out a tiny personal niche for herself in a world suffocated by strict religious parents so fearful of the world around them they had built a shelter in the garden and stocked it with six months' worth of survival supplies ready for Armageddon. At twenty-one, Jessica had finally broken free. And it was Libby and Eve who got to witness her humour, her verve, her personality as it was allowed to flourish unshackled. Watch her awesome highs as she would almost check to see if life was allowed to be this good, but then want to hide their eyes at her crashing lows as she experienced the turbulent relationship emotions that everyone else had been allowed to experience in their teens.

And then there was Dex, who pretty much told them he would be moving in because that was his way. He wouldn't be there long, he'd said, he'd go when his cash was flowing again, but at that time his father had cut him off for hacking into his university's computer system and changing his degree to a First—the result he needed to be gifted a Ferrari—and he'd been sent out to fend for himself over the summer. However, in some twisted logic, he'd been allowed to keep the Ferrari and whiled away most of time cruising the streets of Chelsea picking up rich, beautiful women and then having to apologise for the humble flat he was bringing them back to. Libby had spent many a morning having breakfast opposite a girl in some flash designer dress, It bag on her lap, tapping away on her phone while casting haughty sneers at Libby's Primark pyjamas.

But Dex didn't move out after that summer; in the end he stayed for as long as they all stayed. It transpired that his billionaire dad wasn't as squeaky clean as his punishment of Dex implied when one morning every building he owned was raided at dawn by armed police, including their flat, simply because of the connection to Dex. Libby, Eve, and Jessica stood sobbing with terrified shock as Dex went mad, desperately trying to protect them, swearing to the police that he had no clue where his dad was, the phone going to voicemail, trying to hold back tears as a lifetime of hero worship was shattered in just under an hour.

The raids turned up nothing, as his dad, on the phone from southern Spain the next day, assured Dex that they would, but the damage was already done. Dex drove the Ferrari to a multi-storey carpark and never went back for it.

For three years Eve, Libby, Jessica, and Dex lived together in their second floor flat underneath medical students Jimmy and Jake and aspiring musician Miles. And over the course of those three years all their lives intertwined like vines. But it was the link between Libby and Eve that always remained the strongest. From the first day they'd met they had burrowed beneath the other's surface. They had understood one another with a look, a laugh, an infinitesimal raise of an eyebrow.

Jake always said that Libby placed too high an expectation on their friendship. That she set the bar and waited for Eve to fall short so she could feel hard done by. But she wasn't convinced. To her, a mark of a true friend was how far you would put yourself out to help the other. And Eve, as always, was wrapped up tight in Eve world.

By the time Libby pulled up at the airport, in her mind Eve had become a giant monster, so it was a surprise when the car door yanked open and instead of the vivacious, effervescent, self-absorbed blonde she was expecting, there was Eve. Tall, willowy, tired-looking. Shaggy pale hair. T-shirt half off her shoulder. Bulging handbag.

'God, I always think I'm going to get done at airports,' Eve said, breathless, chucking her bag into the backseat. 'It's my parents' fault. Do you know what they used to do? Bags of weed in my teddy bear. Of course you know. I must have told you? Have I told you that? Can you imagine doing it now? Can you imagine if I was like: Maisey, Noah, just so you know, there's a couple of hundred quid's worth of drugs in your teddy. God, now I get nervous if I forget to even turn my phone off. Shit, that reminds me, I need to turn it back on.' She rifled through the contents of her bag at top speed. 'I think I've lost my phone. No, here it is.' She dropped it back into her bag and then sat back with a sigh, her eyes closed for a moment. 'Sorry. Hi,' she said, clicking her seatbelt and leaning back against the headrest. 'Sorry. I get so nervous at airports.' She breathed out. 'How are you, are you OK?'

Libby felt suddenly a bit shy. Sitting next to her once best friend. Acting over-polite as a result. 'Yeah, fine. Are you OK?'

Eve blew out a breath that flicked her fringe out of her eyes. 'Fine. Apart from the on-a-break thing. We're like a bloody sitcom, aren't we? Although less funny.'

Libby couldn't laugh along. It embarrassed her that they were both facing the same challenge in their relationships. It wasn't meant to happen like this. Libby was always the together one and Eve the shambles.

Eve tied her hair up, half of it immediately falling out because it was too short for a ponytail. 'God, I'm all over the place. I feel really weird without the kids. No one has dropped anything on me or whacked me in the face. You know, that's what they don't tell you about kids. How often you get unintentional injuries. They sit up and whoomph, their head has smashed you in the jaw.' She toyed nervously with her phone as she spoke. 'Sorry, I won't talk about the kids. I know it's really boring.'

As Libby pulled out of the maze of airport roads and onto the motorway she couldn't resist a glance across at Eve's profile. She was fascinated by how many lines she had round her eyes and the grey tint to her skin. Eve used to glow, that was her thing. Her skin shone like a mermaid's. Her hair was the envy of everyone. She'd do those big messy plaits in her hair, all intricate and knotted, that would have taken Libby two days to achieve while Eve would do it watching *Countdown*. Now she had almost half a head of black roots and it looked as if she'd done the blunt chin-length cut herself.

Eve seemed to sense the scrutiny and redid her ponytail self-consciously. 'It's all a bit shit really,' she said, and Libby turned back to the road ahead saying nothing.

JESSICA

While Jessica waited for Dex to wake up so they could finish a work project they were meant to have done before they left, she decided to go for a walk. First she explored the local town which took mere minutes as it consisted of a shop, a church, and a square, but then she found the lake—the main attraction. An epic expanse of blue that stretched like a mirage out towards the Tuscan mountains in the distance, their peaks jutting into the horizon like fat kings on thrones.

Jessica stood and watched the glassy water from a slatted boardwalk that seemed to run the circumference. The wood was warm beneath her bare feet, like walking on soft leather; the water lapped gently against the pebbles and shivered through the reed beds, and the shimmer of the sun made her shield her eyes.

She knew she should be thinking that this was paradise. It was paradise. But Jessica had never been particularly good at relaxing. She could feel her hair starting to curl annoyingly in the humidity, her skin smelt overpoweringly of coconut suntan lotion, and her mobile kept losing reception.

She knew she should enjoy the fact that she was unreachable. Even though she loved her job, thrived on it, she knew that just for a week she should wallow in being decision-less. But she liked the routine of work, the purpose it gave her. Every time she went away she would draw a blank at what exactly she was meant to do. In the back of her mind was always her mother's voice as they arrived at the Isle of Wight caravan, never wearing anything less than skirt, tights, and blouse, refusing ever to be seen without her shoes on, sitting in a deckchair saying, 'Well what's the point? It takes a week to settle in and by that time I'm ready to go home.'

All that on top of the fact that Miles was or wasn't about to appear made it almost impossible for her to relax into the moment. It made the view feel like a canvas rather than reality, like the screen at the front of her spinning class that was meant to make it feel like they were cycling a lush mountain road rather than pedalling in the sweaty old gym. It made her barely acknowledge the beautiful old white boathouse when it rose before her like a floating castle as she walked further along the boardwalk. It was only the stone-spitting skid of a motorbike drawing up at the front that made her stop short and take notice.

The building shone with fresh white paint, the windows gleamed with diamonds of stained glass like boiled sweets, and a huge, green wooden door was propped open with a beer barrel. From the soft chill out music wafting her way and the white cushioned couches she could glimpse, she deduced it was some sort of languid café bar full of people posing with martinis—not really her thing.

'You are lost?' the man on the motorbike said, lifting one leather-clad leg over his great red Yamaha. He was fractionally taller than her, cropped haired, receding slightly, week old stubble on his jaw, nose like a Roman soldier.

Jessica glanced surreptitiously behind her to check he was talking to her before saying, 'No,' and pulling her sunglasses off her head ready to slip them on and walk away. But she'd forgotten her hair had started to curl, had forgotten that sunglasses caught in curly hair. And as she tried to untangle them she fumbled her hold and they dropped to the ground. Taking a step back to pick them up from the gravel she lost a flip-flop and had to steady herself on the barrel propping the door open as she slipped it back on again. The fumes from the bike were making the sun somehow hotter and she had to fan herself as she finally stood up straight and pushed her sunglasses on.

There was a smirk on the guy's lips as he watched the whole little routine while pulling one leather glove off, then the next, and tucking them under his arm. 'You're not looking for the bar?' he said.

'No,' she said, retying her hair. 'I'm just walking. This way.' She pointed ahead about to walk away but she was caught by his expression; his eyes looking her up and down. Never before in her life had Jessica felt someone so clearly imagining having sex with her from just a look. She was momentarily stunned. Felt like she should tell him to stop looking. And then to her horror she found herself blushing.

'You want to come in for a drink?' he asked, his presence like a looming shadow beside her.

'No,' she said, annoyed with her blush, annoyed that he'd had any effect on her at all.

His mouth quirked as he watched her with his lazy gaze. 'Do you ever say yes?'

'Yes,' she said and then turned away to carry on along the boardwalk.

She felt him still watching.

It was like being stalked by a tiger. He was somehow primal. The word made her snort as she strutted away.

Primal. It was a word her mother had used once about the new postman. She would refuse to open the door to him when he knocked. Jessica had never understood what she was on about.

'Are you staying at the Limoncello?' she heard him call after her but she didn't reply.

She heard him laugh and kicked herself for not just saying yes.

She could hear her mother, 'Say one thing to him and he'll be in your bedroom window at night.'

Jessica hadn't thought about her mother so much in years. But it stood to reason that as soon as she lost her sense of self the insidious voice would creep back in. All her good work ruined. She caught sight of one of the bright red curls that had come loose from her ponytail, remembered her mother pulling one like a spring when she was naughty and telling her it was the devil inside her. She pushed the curl back into the elastic band and blew out a breath.

It was holidays. She blamed holidays entirely. They made the mind run wild with too much free time. Really, she hadn't allowed her mum into her head since she'd walked out of the door to the sound of her pleading, 'You can't leave, Jessica. You can't leave us.' Then, 'You always were a bad girl. We tried. Leave and you won't be coming back. You hear me? You won't be welcome.' To finally, 'I'll pray for you.'

Jessica shuddered. Then to make matters worse an image of Miles arriving popped into her head and was only dispelled by the guy shouting, 'It was a pleasure to meet you. Hopefully I will see you around.'

Jessica turned and walked backwards a couple of steps on the boardwalk. 'Not if I can help it,' she shouted.

And he laughed, loud and booming, hard enough for her to see his shoulders shake.

EVE

Until she saw it again, Eve had forgotten how much she adored the Limoncello Hotel. If, at that moment, she had been asked to list her top five places in the world the Limoncello would fight for one of the top spots.

She remembered the summers she'd spent here with Libby, as she followed her up the steps to the entrance hall. She could picture the red and gold wallpaper, dark and imposing, the wooden chandeliers flickering with fake candle lightbulbs, the blackened oil paintings of shipwrecks. She remembered the wide-armed welcome from Libby's eccentric, outspoken, lovely aunt Silvia who was desperate to know the gossip, to know who they were having sex with, what their ambitions were for the future—always probing, always pushing. Here they played at being adults. Straight out of school they sipped Campari on the terrace and pretended to like it.

Eve knew that for Libby it was a welcome escape from the chaos of her family, a chance for her to lie on her back in the lake and talk to no one, to spend evenings in the kitchen with her aunt as she worked—hissing up clams and squeezing lemons so the pan smoked—to make a spaghetti vongole that left diners lifting the bowls to their lips to drain the last of the sauce, or preparing tiny tortellini packed with sweet tomato ragu.

But, for Eve, it was a wonderland. A lesson in possibilities. They trawled antique markets together, lazed in the sun by the lake getting drunk, swam into the derelict boathouses—the water pitch black and the broken rafters filled with bats. Eve would stroll the corridors peering at the art on the walls and Silvia would appear by her shoulder saying, 'I won that in Monte Carlo, idiot couldn't pay his debt. Do you want it? Take it, I've looked at it for far too long.' Eve would never dream of taking anything. It belonged there, at the Limoncello. But it wasn't just the art, it was the smells; the scents of the place. Silvia would lead them into the lemon grove and make them smell the bark of the tree, the leaves, the fruit as it hung gnarled and pitted on the branches. She would give them neat lemon juice to drink that made their eyes water. She would wake them up in the middle of the night when it was raining and make them stand on the terrace to sniff the air. Everything was a sense: a taste, a smell, a mood. Silvia would waft down the corridors, the scent of warm wax polish and lemons heady in the air, the dust swirling in the sunlight and say, 'If I could bottle this, girls, I'd be the happiest woman alive.'

Now, though, when Libby pushed open the big wooden front door and said proudly, 'So here we are,' Eve found herself rigid, frozen to the top step in horror.

What had they done?

'Little bit different to how you remember it, I think,' Libby said with an expectant smile.

Eve felt her hand go up to cover her mouth.

White walls, white tiles, no pictures.

'It makes such a difference, doesn't it? Opens the place up. Makes it look much bigger, don't you think?' Libby went on, seemingly talking until she got a reaction from Eve. 'Just all clean lines. That's what we were looking for. Why are you looking at it like that? Don't you think it's lovely? We really like it.'

We.

We. We.

Eve knew it wasn't we. This was Jake. It was Jake all over. If Jake could whitewash the whole bloody world, he would. He hated mess. He hated clutter. He had to have everything just so.

'Yes, it looks lovely,' Eve said with as much enthusiasm as she could muster when all she really wanted to do was shout, *What have you done? You've ruined it, you idiots!*

Libby tipped her head, could clearly sense Eve's reticence. 'Eve, look at it. Come further in. It was so dated before. No one had touched it in years.'

'I believe you, I know. I said, it looks lovely.' Eve nodded and smiled. 'Really lovely.' She didn't need to look at it. She knew what it looked like. Cold and white.

'Honestly, Eve. It needed freshening up,' Libby pushed. 'People don't want that kind of décor any more.'

Eve nodded but all she could hear were Jake's opinions in Libby's voice. 'Libby,' she said, 'if you're happy with it, that's all that matters. You don't need to persuade me. And I really like it, anyway,' she added, an unconvincing afterthought.

Libby swallowed and turned away. 'Well, yes. Yes, we like it,' she said and started to walk forward, leading Eve to her room.

They walked up the stairs in silence, Eve staring at the walls willing the pattern of the wallpaper to come out from under the paint.

'Where are the pictures?' she said.

'In the garage,' Libby replied. 'With the carpet.'

Eve could concede on the carpet. It was old and swirly and fairly hideous, but the rest of it... She looked up at the light fittings and winced when she saw long metal strips of halogen bulbs. The surfaces were bare, trinket free. The windows were curtainless, now just covered with simple white blinds.

'I put you in your old room,' Libby said as they reached the furthest room along the corridor. She put the key in and turned the door handle. 'You'll be happy—it hasn't changed.'

Eve could remember it perfectly. Lying on the bed like a penniless monarch, her grandeur falling down around her. She'd left the plaster bare in her ramshackle conservatory at home and let the ivy grow in through the roof to conjure up the feeling of this room.

She glanced inside and breathed a sigh of relief at the sight of the huge wooden wardrobe, the damp patches on the peeling wallpaper, the big bed with the chipped gold paint, and the heavy brocade curtains. And then the wind rustled the trees and she smelt the lemons waft in through the open window.

'Libby, I'm sorry if you think I've offended you somehow,' she said. 'I do really think it all looks nice.'

'But…?' Libby said, arms crossed.

'But nothing,' Eve replied. Then when Libby looked at her, almost willing her to carry on, she couldn't stop herself adding, 'Just remember that people don't always know what they want, what they like, until it surprises them. I agree it all needs updating but this place always had character. Style. You know, just maybe you don't need to get rid of it all.'

She walked over to the window when Libby didn't reply and looked out to see the lemon grove, the familiar image of the waxy leaves winking in the sunlight. She wondered how it was that people could be so close at one point in their lives and then become so distant. Eve was as wide open as they came, but Libby, she took some chipping away to get beneath the polish. Especially now that she too had a great stamp across her saying, 'Jake'.

Sometimes, when Eve had put the kids to bed, she would sit down with a glass of wine and read Libby's blog. There was always some gorgeous looking lemon and basil drizzle cake to salivate over or a plate of something delicious that Libby said she'd thrown together because she was feeling peckish but would take any normal person hours.

Eve knew it was all gloss. All shine. But slowly she would feel herself prickle with jealousy, like pins and needles starting in her neck. She found herself jealous of the life made quirky and cool through the many filters of Instagram. Of the parties Libby catered, of the selfies with famous guests, of the Rainbows and Roast Beef Supper Clubs that she held at her flat with Jake there sipping red wine from a glass as big as a bowl.

Eve had lived in the flat below Jake for three years. She knew he was an arrogant pain in the arse half the time; she had eaten batches of Libby's mistakes, she had been to the pillar-box tiled kitchen and seen the beautiful hand-thrown bowls the colour of oatmeal and the lovely little white enamelled saucepans and thought they were lovely, if a bit impractical, but, in the pictures, in the lifestyle, she coveted them like no other.

Because they seemed to symbolise this other life—where everything went right.

And over the years it had made Eve start to stay away. Because somewhere along the line, her friend Libby had become lifestyle blogger Libby Price, while Eve was a scruffy, haphazard mother of two who struggled to run a business and fit into her countryside lifestyle and be an interested wife and not believe that everyone else was doing marvellously while she was just keeping her head above the surface.

So in the end there was no point seeing Libby because, while it was all aesthetically lovely when she did, they never had the time to get beneath the facade to make it worthwhile. It was all just too nice and polite to bother.

But what was so frustrating was that she knew the truth of Libby. Eve knew what was under there, had seen her drunkenly dancing in her bedroom at three in the morning, had seen her laughing so hard that she snorted lemonade out her nose, had seen her stuffing her mouth so full of chocolate that she couldn't breathe, had seen her sobbing on the doorstep because she couldn't take the pressure of all her brothers and sisters and her mum out of a job, but over time the walls had gone up and now it was just that bit too high to reach.

Peter had done this whole lesson at school on entropy. He used pictures of the crumbling disused ballrooms of Detroit to show that everything falls into disorder in the end. The walls always came down. It was just a case of how long it took. And how much one was willing to try.

'OK well…'

Eve turned to see Libby backing out of the door.

'Anything you need just let me know. I'm thinking drinks on the terrace at seven and we can work out a plan,' Libby said, starting to pull the door closed behind her. 'I'll leave you to settle in.'

Eve turned so her back was against the view and watched Libby leave, nodding at the instructions.

JESSICA

Jessica arrived back at her room slightly sunburnt and annoyingly still replaying the meeting with the cocksure Italian at the bar. She had planned on having a shower and doing some work to rebalance, but when she opened the door she found Dex sitting at her dressing table working on his laptop.

'What are you doing in here?'

'Work,' he said without turning round. 'I thought we were working.'

'We are, but why do we have to do it in my room?'

'Because I've got no WiFi in mine. Yours is bad enough—it only works here,' Dex said, pointing to the dressing table. 'Come on,' he said, 'let's get it done then we can be on holiday.'

Jessica frowned. She wasn't used to sharing her personal space. She remembered the early days when Dex had shown her the plans for the new office—all inclusive and open plan—and she'd said, 'No, this just won't work. I need to be able to shut a door.'

He had prattled on about the merits of sitting together as a team, exchanging ideas, laughing together and building bonds.

'My brain doesn't work well as a collective force, Dex,' she'd said. 'It works well on its own. I am anti-social. I like to be on my own.'

Dex had stalked away with a shake of his head, rolling his eyes at the architect as they fudged a small office into the sleek design plans.

Now she wished she could portion off a section of her hotel room.

'Come on, chop chop,' said Dex, pulling over a spare chair so she could sit down next to him. 'Get your laptop.'

'OK, OK, hang on.' Jessica took a minute, standing in the centre of the room, to get herself in the right mode. She went into the bathroom and splashed some water on her face—saw the extent to which her hair had frizzed and curled in the humidity and the pink tinge to her cheeks, and tried to channel First Day Holiday Jessica back into At Work Jessica.

She poured herself a glass of water then walked out of the bathroom, went over to her bag, pulled out her laptop, then set it up next to Dex.

'You look very relaxed, by the way,' said Dex as she booted up. 'Very earthy.'

She glanced across at him with a raised brow.

'What? That's a good thing. It's a good thing. I promise. Very…' He looked her up and down.

'Don't go on.'

He laughed. 'Very pretty.'

She shook her head. 'No I don't.'

'You do, it's a compliment. Take it as a compliment. You're terrible at compliments.'

Jessica scoffed. 'Because most of the time people say them to mask something else.'

Dex looked perplexed. 'Like what?'

'I don't know.' Jessica shook her head. 'Like you think my hair looks bonkers but you can't say that so you say something nice instead.'

Dex snorted a laugh. 'You really are an idiot sometimes. Anyway, right, enough of this nonsense, there's a sun out there just waiting for me.'

Jessica took a sip of her water and then started to work. Her laptop was taking longer than Dex's to open the files.

Dex glanced over. 'It's so slow! Seriously, I've told you to get a new one.'

'I don't need a new one. This is fine.'

'It can't cope with the software update. It's too old.'

'It's fine.'

He peered over. 'Do you still have that bit of plastic film over the screen, Jessica?' He turned to look at her, aghast. 'You're meant to take that off when you buy it.'

'It keeps it protected.'

'Oh my god.' Dex smacked his forehead. 'We need to get you out of that office. You are getting away with some ridiculous behaviour.'

She allowed herself a little laugh when she looked at the plastic film. 'I just like to look after my things.'

'Your laptop is ancient, Jessica. If you're not going to buy a new one, I'll buy you a new one, for the sake of the company.'

'You aren't buying me a new laptop.'

'Well, you buy it then.' He got his wallet out and handed her a platinum card. 'Charge it to my dad.'

'I didn't think you used this any more?' she said, taking the card and holding it tentatively between finger and thumb as though it might burn her.

'I don't. But you can.'

'You should cut it up,' she said.

He shook his head. 'Then I'd want it.'

'I don't understand.'

'Like ex-smokers. Better to have a pack to hand just in case.' Dex shrugged. 'Makes me want it less knowing it's there.'

Jessica narrowed her eyes. 'I think you should have more faith in yourself, Dex. You can't carry it around forever. I can't actually believe you still have it. You've kept that really quiet.'

'Well, you shouldn't spend so much time in your office, should you?'

She sighed. 'You don't need his money, you know that. You've totally made it on your own now. Cut the card up.'

Dex shook his head.

'Dex! Cut it up.'

'No.' Dex stared at the card with a longing fondness. 'I don't think I can.'

Jessica widened her eyes at him. 'Cut it up.'

Dex shook his head.

'You cut it up and you can peel the protective film off my laptop.'

He raised a brow. 'That sounds like some kind of kinky computer geek fetish.'

'OK, you can't do it any more.'

Dex laughed. 'Oh please.'

'No. You've made it too sexual.'

He snorted.

Jessica turned to her screen and started to do some work. Dex did the same, leaning over every now and then to see what she was doing.

The sun was streaming in the window. Dex kept yawning. Every time the WiFi dropped out he sat back on his stool and peered round the room.

'What are you looking at?' Jessica said in the end, unable to hold it in any longer.

'Nothing. It's just funny, that's all.'

'What's funny.'

'That we've been here mere hours and you've managed to make your room exactly the same as your office. Like, exactly the same. The books, the scarf, the make-up bag, that hand cream, the way the glass is on the coaster.'

Jessica looked around and realised he was right. It was pretty much the same as her bedroom at home as well. She hadn't realised she needed such familiarity and structure around her to feel comfortable. It was as if she had become so self-sufficient it was to the point of robotic. Carrying her life around like a snail. She frowned. 'Well, that can't be good, can it?'

Dex shrugged. 'I think it's sweet. A bit anal, but sweet. But that's what you're like, isn't it?'

Jessica made a face. 'Don't say it like it's a given.'

Dex looked confused. 'Well it is, isn't it?'

'No it's not. Anal but sweet? That's not how someone wants to be described.'

'Why not? It's what you are.'

'It's not a fact.'

Dex shrugged. 'It kind of is.'

'Well, I don't want it to be.'

He half grinned. 'Well do something about it then.'

Jessica shook her head and, ignoring the challenge in his eyes, went back to her computer.

They worked again in silence.

After a couple of minutes she said, 'Oh, and what's this about Miles coming? Is Miles coming? Have you invited Miles?'

Dex smirked, keeping his eyes on the screen. 'Maybe.'

She saw the delight on his face reflected in his laptop screen and kicked herself for asking. She looked back at her own without saying anything more, refusing to give him the satisfaction of asking again.

After a couple more minutes Dex said, 'It's fun working next to you. I like it. We should do it more often.'

'No we shouldn't.' She shook her head. 'You breathe too loudly.'

He snorted a laugh. 'I do not breathe loudly. I breathe. I have to stay alive.'

'It's distracting.'

'Remember that whole anal but sweet thing?' he said.

Jessica turned to look at him, one brow raised.

'Perfect example.'

She scoffed.

'I'm just telling it like it is,' Dex said with a grin, then he leant forward and peeled the film straight off her laptop screen before she could stop him.

Jessica gasped. Dex laughed, waving the sheet of plastic triumphantly. So she reached over and, grabbing his dad's credit card from the table next to him, she chopped it up with the scissors from her makeshift pen pot and chucked the four little bits into her waste bin.

Dex jumped up from his seat and stared down at the bin, his hand on his chest. 'I can't believe you just did that.'

'You're much better without it, Dex.'

He looked forlornly at the quarters of credit card.

Jessica patted him on the shoulder. 'You're much less vacuous without the money.'

He glanced up at her, then laughed. 'It's all coming out today, isn't it?'

'Let's finish this work,' she said.

When they'd wrapped it all up and sent it off, Jessica turned to Dex and said, 'I don't really think you're vacuous. You used to be, but you're not any more. You're probably the most solid person I know. Like, inside,' she said, 'you're good.'

He looked at her, surprised.

She shrugged. 'I just, you know, thought I should say that.'

Dex nodded. 'Thank you, Jessica.'

'You're welcome,' she said, closing her laptop. 'You're now welcome to say that I'm not anal and sweet. If you wanted.'

Dex thought about it for a bit, studying her with narrowed eyes. 'No,' he said. 'No, I don't need to say that.'

'Oh for god's sake,' she huffed, bashing him on the arm. 'Take it back.'

He laughed. 'But then I'd be lying.'

'That's fine.'

'OK, Jessica, you are not anal and sweet.'

'Thank you.'

'You're welcome,' he said, picking up his laptop and standing up. 'Although really you absolutely are,' he added, before jogging out of the door with a grin.

EVE

Alone in her old lemon scented room Eve checked her phone. A text from Peter saying 'That's good' in response to her previous 'Landed safely x'. He hadn't put an x. But then Peter never put an x. He had whole dinner party discussions about the fact it was an x not a kiss and that it was completely unnecessary and ridiculous to include on a text message let alone an email. She often wondered if the script he was writing was full of rants about the misuse of letters in instant messaging. He'd asked her to read it once a couple of years ago and she'd been so sleep deprived and so stressed with the twins that it had taken her two weeks to get round to it by which time he'd changed his mind and gone into her email and deleted it from her inbox and then her deleted items.

She wanted to write something back; her fingers hovered over the keys of her phone, but she didn't know what.

In the end she thought it best to leave her phone where it was, get changed into more weather appropriate attire, and get outside to stop herself from dwelling on it all.

Wearing a pair of skinny blue jeans cut off at the knee, a yellow vest top that was showing its age, and an equally dilapidated pair of espadrilles that her daughter Maisey said made her feet look like lumps of cheese, Eve made her way out of the hotel, across the terrace, and down through the lemon grove in the direction of the lake.

The scent of citrus intensified the closer she got, the huge waxy great lemons hanging heavy from the branches, all knobbly and pitted. She wanted to reach up and take a bite straight through the skin; feel her eyes water as she squeezed the juice into her mouth.

It made her think of the first perfume she'd ever made—from a bag of Limoncello lemons Silvia had sent as congratulations on having the twins. There was a note that said, 'The beautiful thing about women is they can change as many times as they like. You're already a wonderful mother. Who will you be next?'

Eve had stood staring at the lemons. These wonderful fat things that weren't to do with feeding babies or trying to work out why they were crying, or why she was crying as she sat alone in the draughty, crumbling cottage they had bought after she'd got pregnant. After she had been seduced by a photo in a *Homes and Gardens* magazine in the doctor's waiting room of a picturesque village where everyone had chickens and rose gardens and muddy wellington boots at the front door.

The lemons connected her back to the world. Not the pre-pregnancy one where she worked in marketing for a massive beauty company in the city. Where so many people wanted to talk to her every day she would sometimes put her Out of Office on and go and sit on the fire escape with her laptop just to get some work done. But the one before even her marriage, where she smelt the rain in the middle of the night and the bark of trees.

So she had sliced the lemons and she had squeezed them and she had gone outside and chopped all the heads off the roses in the rose garden, and then she had found the unused wedding-present pestle and mortar in the back of the cupboard and started to see if she could capture it all in a fragrance. She had got to work on who she would be next.

Now, as she popped out from the lemon groves and onto the lakeside shore, she was suddenly stopped short by a voice saying, 'All right, Eve.'

She had to take a second to get her breath back from the shock.

He knew her name.

The guy got up from where he was sitting cross-legged on the pebbles. 'Didn't mean to scare you.'

Eve turned. The sun was in her eyes.

The voice made her expect dreadlocks, an arm almost covered in ink, and eyes that could spear a person from a hundred paces.

A wisp of cloud passed in front of the sun.

Holy shit. The dreads were gone. The eyes were still the same.

'Hello, Jimmy,' she said, her mind almost short-circuiting at the sight of him.

LIBBY

From her seat on the terrace, Libby watched Jimmy and Eve approach, the air between them like firecrackers popping in the sky.

Next to her, Dex and Jessica glanced up, saw Eve laugh at something Jimmy said, and then exchanged a look. Libby knew they were all thinking about the same thing. The casual flirting, the lazy hand-holding. How they'd roll in from some club together, Jimmy, with his arm slung casually round Eve's shoulders, drunkenly rambling about getting free of the rat race, concocting starry-eyed visions of the two of them backpacking the globe, while Eve nodded along, fanning the flames of his dreams.

They were dangerous together; made more than the sum of their parts. Already Eve seemed to be burning brighter as she pulled up a chair, her hair glinting in the sun.

'OK, so here's the deal,' said Libby when they were all seated. 'I'm fully booked for the summer. I have just over a fortnight before the first customers arrive.'

Dex glanced around him and did a low whistle, his eyes taking in the lichen covered terrace, the rusted wrought iron tables, the chipped paintwork, the overgrown garden.

'I know, it doesn't look great,' Libby went on. 'And we certainly weren't expecting it all to be perfect, but cash flow meant we had to open before we were ready. The main thing is that the outhouse is built. That's where the courses are going to be.'

'What courses?' Jimmy asked, lounging back in his chair.

'Cooking courses, for the moment,' Libby said.

'You should do yoga courses,' he said.

Libby made a face to say that was the last thing she needed. 'For the moment, Jimmy, I need to stick with what I know best and that's baking. It'll work as an extension of the blog and the supper clubs—you know, so you can come out here and have a slice of the life you read about. Soak up a bit of sun, learn to cook your favourite Italian foods, and go home relaxed and rejuvenated. It's called the Sunshine and Biscotti Club.'

'Very nice,' said Jimmy, almost taken aback by the fact he was impressed.

Jessica nodded. 'I came up with that. We're in charge of design and marketing.'

'Didn't I come up with it?' Dex said with a frown.

'No.' Jessica shook her head.

'I really think I did,' Dex said, leaning forward, elbows on the table.

'You so didn't.' Jessica was aghast.

'OK, OK, look, maybe you both came up with it. The important thing is that it's going to happen in a couple of weeks,' Libby said.

But Jessica wasn't happy about letting the matter lie and was about to say more when an angry looking waitress appeared, arms crossed over her chest, and said, 'Drinks?'

Jessica swung round in surprise.

'Oh yes, that'd be lovely,' said Libby, half standing in her chair. 'Giulia, these are my friends, they'll all be helping to get the place up and running over the next couple of days. Everyone, this is Giulia.'

Giulia stared at them all, her expression unchanged.

'Giulia's been here for years, worked for my aunt,' Libby carried on brightly. 'She's a rock, I couldn't do it without her.'

Giulia made a noise that could have been interpreted as a scoff of disdain. Libby could see the others glancing down at their laps or across to the lemon grove, as though the awkwardness in the air was something visible to look away from.

Libby kept smiling.

It had come as quite a shock when Libby and Jake had realised that, to all intents and purposes, Giulia had been inherited along with the hotel. There was no getting rid of her. She turned up every day at the crack of dawn to clean and polish, then at midday she opened up the bar. The idea that they might close the restaurant for any length of time had been actively laughed at by the residents of the village—all anyone wanted from the Limoncello was the food. Jake and Libby could mess about with their renovations all they liked as long as Thursday to Saturday the restaurant opened. Dino the chef trotted up in the afternoons to start prepping with or without Libby's say so. Jake had been happy to let them get on with it as long as the money came in and he got a bowl of spicy tortellini soup or thick tomatoey fish stew at the end of the day.

To Giulia, the Sunshine and Biscotti Club was some ridiculous whim of Libby's that she had absolutely no interest or belief in. Left to her, not an inch of the place would change.

'Maybe a bottle of Prosecco, Giulia? So we can toast everyone's arrival?' Libby said, glancing round the eyes-averted table and then back up to Giulia who shrugged and stomped back inside.

'She's a keeper,' said Dex with a raise of a brow.

'Well, to be honest, I don't actually know what I would do without her,' Libby said. 'I mean I don't know how to run a bar or a restaurant.'

'But you can learn though,' said Jessica.

'Yeah.' Libby nodded emphatically, half in an attempt to convince herself.

'And what about money?' Dex asked, leaning forward, his elbows resting on the table as he looked at her. 'Are you OK for money?'

'I think so,' Libby said.

Dex frowned. 'Think so doesn't sound that certain.'

Libby glanced away from any direct eye contact. 'Shamefully, Jake's looked after all the money. I just need to get a clear handle on things, that's all.'

'Do you need to borrow any money, Libby?' Dex asked, looking concerned. 'I can lend you money if you need it, just ask.'

'No, no, no.' Libby waved a hand, 'Absolutely not, I can't take your money. And I don't think I need it, I just need to sit down and sort it all out.' She paused and blew out a breath.

Dex sat back again, his expression unconvinced as he kept close watch on her. Libby caught Jessica's eye who made a face of pity and next to her Eve looked down at the floor.

Don't cry, she told herself.

'So anyway…' she said, with a little shake and a huge smile. 'What I need from you guys is just help with the cosmetics. The house, some of the rooms, the garden, that sort of thing. Just to make it presentable.'

They all nodded.

Libby nodded too. Then she smiled again. 'Fab. Great. I think it might be fun. And also, it would really help me if just once a day we did some baking.'

'Baking?' Dex frowned. 'I'm not really into baking, Lib.'

'Don't worry, it won't be hard. That's the whole point. It's for everyone.'

'I reckon you could bake, Dex, if you put your mind to it,' Jimmy said with a grin, his big muscly arms locked behind his head.

'I'd like to see you bake,' Dex scoffed.

'I could bake,' said Jimmy. 'What is it? Just flour and sugar, that sort of stuff.'

Eve rolled her eyes, half obscured by messy blonde hair. 'You are unbelievably arrogant.'

'That's why you love me,' Jimmy said with a wink.

Eve smiled then sat back, running her fingers along her bottom lip as she watched him.

Giulia arrived with the bottle of Prosecco and a tray of glasses.

Libby wanted Eve to stop looking at Jimmy the way she was looking at him. She wanted her to stop creating distractions. She was still annoyed at her for her earlier implied comments about the décor, annoyed at the gnawing feeling of regret, guilt even, that it had conjured inside her as she imagined her aunt nodding along with Eve about the changes. It made her want to suck all the white paint from the walls. But instead she focused on the planning. 'Perhaps we could portion out the jobs now. Just so we've all got it straight in our heads. Maybe, Jimmy, you could do the garden?'

'Aye, aye.' Jimmy nodded. 'Plants love me.'

She rolled her eyes. 'Dex, could you take the terrace? And the outside walls?'

'If I must,' said Dex, reaching forward to swipe the Prosecco from the ice bucket.

'And, Jessica, perhaps you and I can make a start on the rooms?'

'I can help with the rooms,' said Eve.

'No, I think it's fine with Jessica and me. Is that OK, Jessica?'

'Yep.' Jessica looked up from reading an email on her phone and nodded. 'Whatever you need.'

'And, Eve, you could smarten up the area round the pool?'

'There's a pool?' said Dex, glancing around trying to find it.

'Behind those olive trees,' Libby said, pointing to her right. 'It's tiny and really shabby. Is that OK, Eve?'

Eve shrugged a shoulder as if it had to be. 'If that's what you want, Libby,' she said, her expression in the dim light of the terrace almost challenging.

Libby ignored it. 'Yes,' she said. 'I think that would work.'

Dex popped the Prosecco cork, splashed the frothing bubbles into the five glasses, and then raised his for a toast. 'To Sunshine and Biscotti,' he said with a grin.

As Libby chinked her glass she remembered Jake making exactly the same toast when they had arrived in the spring, and wished for a moment that he was there. That it could all just have carried on exactly as it had been. She didn't care what website he'd been using, just wished that she hadn't found out.

When she saw all the others smiling at her, she forced a big smile in return, refusing to acknowledge quite how lonely she felt. Taking a huge gulp of bubbles, she picked up her phone and made them all chink their glasses again so she could snap it for her Instagram.

'Hold it there. Jimmy, just move your glass up a bit. Dex, out the way. Yes, perfect. Brilliant.'

Perfect summer night toasting the Sunshine and Biscotti Club, she titled it.

And as the evening wore on and the sun set around them, the moths starting to flutter around the outside lights, the Prosecco oiled the chat and the Instagram likes came rolling in, the perfect distraction from her worries.

JESSICA

'So, what do you think? We paint this white or we keep the wallpaper?' Libby was standing with her hands on her hips, staring at Jessica, the morning sun shining bright behind her.

Aesthetically Jessica was a minimalist. She had grown up dusting a house rammed with knickknacks—little ornaments, crucifixes, cross-stitches—and in retaliation kept her décor to the absolute minimum. Her artistic talent was in graphics and was predominantly computer based. She spent her spare time redesigning album covers to suit her own vision. Home furnishings were not her thing. 'I don't know really. I like white, but the wallpaper's also quite nice. Quite authentic. Libby…' Feeling herself starting to sweat in the searing morning heat, Jessica paused to undo the top half of the boilersuit overalls that Libby had lent her for decorating. 'I'm not sure I'm the right person for this. I really think Eve might be better suited—'

'No, you're fine,' Libby said, only half looking in Jessica's direction as she struggled to tie an old scarf around her head. 'We'll paint it.'

'How's it going?' Dex popped his head round the door and snorted a laugh when he got a glimpse of their outfits.

'I was just saying that I think Eve would be better for this job,' said Jessica.

Dex took one look around the room and said, 'Oh yeah, definitely. Jessica's crap at interior design. If she had her way we'd all just be in pods plugged into our laptops.'

Jessica shook her head at him pityingly. Dex winked at her.

'Why don't you get Eve to help?' Dex said. 'This is just her thing, isn't it? She was always wafting about with rugs and scarves and things at the flat.'

'No, it's fine,' Libby insisted.

Dex glanced down the corridor. 'Hey, Eve! Come over here,' he shouted.

'Dex, what are you doing,' Libby said, a little panicked.

'What's wrong?' Eve asked, appearing in the doorway, one earphone in as she commented on some Lego construction one of her kids was showing her on FaceTime.

'You have to swap with Jessica—she's way out of her depth,' said Dex, ushering her inside.

'You're so sweet together, you two,' Eve said as she hung up the phone. 'You've become like her big brother.'

Jessica snorted.

Dex puffed out his chest with pride. 'I like to think I keep an eye out for her.'

'You are unbelievable.' Jessica sighed as she walked over and handed Eve her paintbrush.

Dex ruffled her hair.

'Get off me,' Jessica said, laughing, taking the opportunity to dart out of the room and down the stairs in case Libby somehow managed to get her way and summoned her back again.

The sun was burning bright as Jessica sauntered out onto the terrace. She breathed in the scent of the lemons, delighted to be working on her own in the seclusion of the pool area.

There was a bucket, soap, and a scrubbing brush ready and waiting by the gap in the olive tree wall that led to the pool area and she went over to pick it up. But, just as she was bending over, all her elation at having got away from the decorating was instantly dissolved by a voice saying, 'Jessica?'

She paused where she was, her fingers gripping the handle of the bucket.

He was here.

She looked down at her outfit and thought, *Why do I have to be wearing a boilersuit?*

'Miles!' she said, standing tall, the water in the bucket sloshing slightly.

He looked exactly the same but completely different, standing there in a white linen shirt, top button undone, khakis, and navy espadrilles. His black hair was scruffy but in a way that suggested it wasn't usually like that; as though he'd had a long journey and no mirror to check it in. His cheekbones were less visible, less sunken, like he probably ate better than he did but, from the fit of the shirt, he clearly worked out rather than lay on his bed for hours with his guitar scribbling down lyrics.

Her brain tried to superimpose the old Miles over this version. The black skinny jeans, the black t-shirt, the cigarettes, the dirty hair, and the sneer, but it was almost impossible.

'You all right?' he said, running a hand through his hair.

'Yeah, fine. You?' she said.

When Jessica had thought about seeing Miles again she had envisioned it for some reason at her office, where she was immaculate, groomed, sleek, successful, and emotionally untouchable.

Now she stood in a bright blue boilersuit, the arms tied around her waist, wearing a black vest, pale skin untouched by sun, hair curling of its own accord. And she found she had nothing to say. No casual chitchat. Just an overriding desire to back away.

Rescue came in the form of Jimmy, who loped up the garden, rake over his shoulder, and shouted, 'Miles, mate! How are you? Christ I haven't seen you since New York.'

'Hey, Jimmy! Good to see you.'

Jessica watched them for a second, but the mention of New York left her wanting to escape even more, so, with a back step and a small wave of her hand, she walked quickly to the shelter of the pool.

She took the few steps down past the olive trees, and came out in a courtyard pool area that looked like it had been bottom of the list of priorities for some years. The crumbling patio floor was filthy, sticky with sap and lichen, with tiles missing like pieces of a jigsaw. The rusted table and chairs were strewn with olive leaves and spiders' webs that looped from the metal to the olive tree branches like Christmas lights. The sailcloth shades that cast a triangle of relief from the sun were green at the edges from mould and mildew. And the tiny pool looked as if no one had swum in it for decades, probably preferring the wide expanse of lake just a stroll away.

Jessica stood for a moment, letting her heart rate get back to normal, her hand resting on the rusted table. She could feel the sun beating down on her bare arms, singeing the skin. She needed a hat but it was inside and she couldn't go back while Miles was still talking to Jimmy on the terrace.

She crept over to the row of rangy, unkempt olive trees in an attempt to peer through the gaps to see what was going on.

She could see Miles's khaki clad legs. They made her think of all the unsuccessful dates she'd had over the years, no candidate matching up to her vision of him.

She could hear Jimmy as she peered through the leaves, unable to get a very good look, the branches all overgrown. Then Miles's deep laugh.

She reached up and moved an olive branch out the way as surreptitiously as she could. Then she caught Jimmy say something about Flo, and Miles saying, 'Yeah, it's better.' And she immediately let go of the branch and stepped away.

Flo.

Flo Hamilton was a friend of a girl who'd been on Jimmy's university course and had taken Jimmy's room in the boys' flat when he'd left. She'd bounded in, all white teeth and American confidence. Jessica had made the mistake of not taking much notice.

Jessica heard Dex come out onto the terrace, and the sound of more back-slapping and guffawing. Then obviously Miles must have been shown inside and it all fell silent.

She rubbed her face with her hand and stood for a second before retying her hair and taking a proper look at the pool area.

It was an unloved little hideaway, enclosed on every side by olive trees whose branches snaked out in search of one another. Taking her bucket, Jessica went and sat in a big wicker chair in the one shady corner and stared across at the pool. It was just about long enough for two strokes of front crawl and was tiled in pearlescent black stones that made the water green and dark. It would be like swimming in twilight as the sun blazed overhead. Olive leaves scattered the surface like little boats.

She wondered if she could hide there forever.

It was the dirt that made her get up in the end. The desire to make this little area shine to its full potential.

She got to work with the scrubbing brush, the hard bristles scratching over the lichen-coated tiles. And the more she scrubbed, the more she fell into the monotony of the noise. It made her think of her parents' house where she'd lived with sweeping and scrubbing as a background noise for years. Polishing and hoovering. Constant tidying. The dull thumping sound of the living room doors as their glass panels were dusted; the smell of white vinegar on surfaces and the sight of cloths soaking in bleach.

It was almost impossible to believe it had once been her life. Every time she thought about growing up in that house, which was as little as possible, she'd be astonished by her younger self, by her resourcefulness. Shut up in her room, every second of her life was accounted for. She was confined by the overwhelming fear her parents had of the world and the people in it. The mistrust of society. Straight back from school, straight back from work. Jessica had waited years to squirrel away the cash to leave.

As the sun blistered down, the sound of her scrubbing was interrupted by a familiar voice saying, 'Ah, you have been put to work.'

She stopped to look up and saw the guy from the bar standing with his arms crossed over his chest, dressed in leather motorbike trousers and a bright purple t-shirt, a smirk on his lips. 'This outfit, it is very flattering,' he said, pointing to her boilersuit.

Jessica raised her brows. 'Are you stalking me?'

'Ha, no.' He shook his head, then took the couple of steps down to the patio. 'I am looking for Ms Libby. I help her out a bit last week and I am free today so I thought…?' He shrugged. 'She might need more help. I am Bruno by the way.'

'Libby's inside,' Jessica said, starting to scrub again.

He cocked his head, his eyes narrowing as he studied her. 'You know in most cultures it is polite to return a greeting. A person might even say their name.'

She paused, wiped her brow, and then leant her hands on the edge of the bucket. 'I'm sure they might,' she said, one eyebrow arched. 'But I think it would also depend on whether that person wanted the other person to know their name or not, wouldn't it?'

Bruno held his hands up to object. 'I don't know what that person's problem would be with just wanting to know someone's name.'

'Jessica?' Miles's voice called from the terrace and he jogged down the steps to see if she was still by the pool. 'Jimmy said you had the bucket. Oh…' He paused when he saw Bruno. 'Sorry, I didn't realise you were with someone. Hi.' Miles held out a hand. 'Miles.'

'Bruno.'

Jessica stiffened and she could see Bruno notice.

'You are all friends?' Bruno said as he looked between them.

'Kind of,' said Jessica.

'In a fashion,' said Miles at the same time.

Bruno nodded.

The sun seemed like the fourth person in the conversation, beating down on them all, firing up the unescapable cicadas, a tinnitus hum in her ears.

'Yes,' said Miles. 'Yes, we're all friends.'

Bruno had his eyes still on Jessica, absorbing her reactions. She looked down at the dirty tiles.

'Well, I erm…' Miles pointed to the bucket. 'I just came for that. I'm giving Jimmy a hand.'

'I kind of need it,' Jessica said. 'Isn't there another one?'

Miles frowned. 'I don't know. Jimmy just said there was a red bucket.'

'OK, fine,' she said. 'You have it. I'll find another one.'

Miles looked a bit hesitant.

'Seriously, have it, I can do something else,' she said, pushing the bucket his way.

Miles walked over and picked it up, the water sloshing over the sides in what seemed to be his haste to leave.

Bruno watched him go and then said, 'I'll go and find Ms Libby.'

At the top step he stopped and glanced back. 'I've never met a Jessica before,' he said.

'Well, now you have,' Jessica said, pushing herself up to standing, still distracted by the arrival and departure of Miles.

He nodded. 'You look like a Jessica.'

She put her hands on her hips and sighed. 'What's that supposed to mean?'

Bruno shrugged. 'An interesting challenge,' he said with a smile, and sauntered off in search of Libby.

LIBBY

The sun was low in the sky, just brushing the line of trees as it tipped into late afternoon. Everyone was exhausted. The heat had sucked them dry of energy. Libby and Eve had done some fractious decorating, unable to agree on almost any of the renovation choices. In the end they had focused on ripping up the carpets with Bruno.

Jimmy and Miles had slashed half the garden. It looked like a first day haircut, no one quite sure whether it would settle into something good or bad. She was amazed Miles had flown all the way from the States to be there. He said he'd been due a holiday but she wondered if really he'd been craving something familiar. He hadn't mentioned Flo so neither had Libby but in retrospect she wished she had. It was weird though, to know what to say to him, because he looked so unlike himself nowadays—all polished and smooth-edged.

She'd wondered what Jessica had thought when she'd seen him. But then she'd seen the sparkling poolside patio and, putting two and two together, Libby had presumed she'd been in need of hard-work distraction.

The terrace, on the other hand, was practically untouched, Dex having had a snooze in a lounge chair for most of the morning.

Now as Libby stood in front of them all in the outhouse she suddenly felt a bit stupid for cajoling them into a baking class. They were all there, standing reluctantly behind their benches like school children. Jessica had her phone on her table and was trying to surreptitiously scroll through her emails.

'OK, so, what I'm thinking is that there will be scheduled baking times every day throughout the week. So, one day we'd make muffins and things for breakfast, another day bread for lunch, and then in the afternoon, like now, we'll make a dessert or *petit fours* for after dinner with coffee. That's how I planned it. It might change. That's why you're here. Guinea pigs. OK.' Libby gave a small laugh and tied up her hair.

Miles tried to stifle a yawn behind his cup of coffee. 'Sorry, jet lag,' he said.

It was much easier when she did it to camera for her YouTube videos, with no one watching her.

Dex was leaning forward, chin cupped in his hands, elbows on the table, staring unblinking at her. The not-concentrating looks between Eve and Jimmy were equally distracting. All that as well as Jessica unsubtly tapping away on her phone. The worst, however, were the glares of complete disdain from Giulia at the back, who Libby had roped in to up the numbers and to try and win her round to the concept.

'OK,' Libby said again, then she felt her cheeks start to flush. She couldn't work out how to start without clapping her hands together like a strict Home Economics teacher. These were her peers, not people she could teach. They were people she had lived with, laughed with, fled the pub with after Jimmy was caught cheating in the quiz, sat in the hospital with when Dex got run over on his bike, lazed on the roof with as Jake's barbecue puffed with plumes of smoke, squirmed with as the boys tried to convince Jessica there was a ghost knocking on her window at night, sat in darkness with as Eve hid from a pestering one-night stand, exchanged sniggering glances with as Miles took the stage in some grimy club. How could she now tell them all what to do like a teacher?

She looked down at her workbench—at the little bowls of flour and sugar that she'd measured out and prepared like a TV chef. 'Oh god, now I'm getting hot.' She pressed her hands to her face.

'It's all right, Lib,' said Dex. 'It's only us. Just do it however you like.'

Libby exhaled. 'You're making me more nervous than strangers,' she said, then she laughed.

In her head, in all the planning sessions, Jake had been in the room, maybe leaning against the wooden mantelpiece, a cup of tea in his hand, a cocky smile on his face. He was the chatter. The one who made people feel instantly at ease.

Supper clubs had got much better when he'd stepped in to help. On her own they'd been a complete disaster. The first one she held, her fingers had shaken so much from the pressure that she'd barely been able to prepare anything. Smoke from the sizzling chorizo had set the smoke alarm off. The kitchen had gone from boiling hot to arctic cold when she'd had to throw all the windows open. Then the boys upstairs had thrown an impromptu party—Miles's decks in situ right above her beautifully laid table, the thumping of feet on bare floorboards, the wine running out, her beef overcooking, her cream over-whipping, and the stem ginger ice cream refusing to set. It had been an all-round disaster. The three couples had sloped out before the coffee had bubbled up on the hob.

The door had closed on her overly effusive goodbyes, and, needing to take it out on someone, she had stormed up the stairs, thrown open the door of the boys' flat, pulled the plug on the speakers, and shouted, 'Well, thank you very much. You destroyed that for me. I hope you're proud of yourselves.' All the achingly cool party-goers had stared with disdain and she'd wished she hadn't gone upstairs at all.

And of course Jake had come downstairs after her, because that's the kind of thing he did. He took control of situations. He smoothed over cracks. He'd leaned in the doorway and said, 'We're sorry. We're thoughtless, pig-headed arseholes.'

She knew he didn't really mean a word of it but it had made her feel better. It had made her smile when he'd taken a seat and looked down at the plates in front of him with a frown—at the split cream; the burnt, cracked pavlova; the liquid, unset, failed ice cream—and said, with a quirk of his brow, 'This all looks excellent.'

'It's been a disaster,' she'd said.

'Nah.' He'd sat back in his chair, hands behind his head, a grin on his lips. 'It's just the beginning. Teething problems,' he'd said, then he'd taken a swipe of the melted ice cream and popped it in his mouth. 'Might look like shit but it tastes amazing.'

She'd frowned at the half-compliment. He'd sat forward and tucked her hair behind her ear in the kind of clichéd trademark move that Jake managed to pull off to perfection, and said, 'You're going to be amazing, Libby. Because it will never be worse than this,' and she had felt for the first time that someone completely believed in her. In retrospect she realised it was probably just a line to get her into bed. But from that moment on, she had felt stronger when he was next to her.

And there had been more supper clubs. Hundreds more. They'd built a business out of it. And Jake had taken over as host—greeting the guests, entertaining them over canapés, topping up wines, tipping back in his chair and observing as she put the plates down in front of them, detailing the subtle touches that gave her mini venison wellingtons their hint of caramel, or explaining the origin of a bouillabaisse and how hers also included the often overlooked sea urchin and spider crab. He would subtly nudge her on the thigh if he thought she was going on too much and say something like, 'We're here for the food, darling, not the science bit.' And the guests would chuckle as he winked at her or gave her a quick pat on the bum.

Libby was better when she could do things in her own time. When she could delete and edit. She wasn't a spontaneous ice breaker or joke cracker.

'Ready when you are, Libby,' Jimmy said, snapping her into the present. 'I can't actually remember the last time I cooked anything.'

'What do you eat?' Jessica asked, glancing up, perplexed. 'Do you gnaw on raw fish grabbed with your bare hands from the ocean?'

Jimmy did a self-assured chuckle. 'I grab them, CeeCee cooks them.'

Jessica sighed. 'Oh god, who the hell's CeeCee?'

'She lives with me on the boat.'

Eve reached forward and picked up the laminated recipe sheet Libby had laid out on every bench. She glanced casually over the type as if she wasn't really listening but gave herself away by saying, 'As in, she's your girlfriend?'

Jessica glanced from Eve to Jimmy, a brow raised, a slight smile on her lips. She moved her recipe to the side so she could perch up on the bench.

Jimmy tilted his head to one side. 'We have no need for formal ownership descriptions.'

Jessica snorted. 'Oh, Jimmy, you're not serious?'

'I am!' He grinned. 'We have a boat, we live on it, both of us are free to come and go as we please.'

'Who owns the boat?' Dex asked.

Jimmy paused. 'She owns the boat,' he said with a shrug.

Jessica laughed. 'I bet she does.'

Libby found herself anxious to stop the chat, unable to enjoy it because this was meant to be a class. She could see Giulia tapping her fingers on the surface at the back.

'So if this CeeCee wasn't there when you got back, you wouldn't mind?' Eve asked, putting her recipe sheet down on the bench, unable to hide her interest.

'Well, technically he'd have to mind because the boat would be gone too,' said Jessica.

Jimmy shrugged. 'As I say, free to come and go as we please.'

'No ties,' Eve said.

Jimmy shook his head with a smile. 'None. At the moment we are in each other's lives. In six months maybe we won't be. Come on,' he said, holding his hands out wide, 'you gotta admit that's a more interesting way to live?'

Eve's phone rang. She looked surprised by the interruption and then started to rummage through her bag on the floor. 'Oh, that's me. Where is it? God. Hi, Noah! Everything OK?'

As Eve admired another Lego dinosaur on FaceTime, Jessica took the opportunity to get her phone out again, saying, 'I just need to reply to a couple of emails.'

Jimmy leant back on his stool and started saying something to Dex that made him laugh loudly. Miles turned to see what was being said.

'Are we going to cook or not?' snapped Giulia, and they all seemed to remember where they were.

'Yes! Yes, we are, sorry,' Libby said, cringing at what it all must seem like to Giulia. She imagined Jake watching, rolling his eyes. She was confident that he would have somehow effortlessly combined the cooking and the banter.

Eve whispered goodbye to Noah and hung up the phone. Jessica, never good at being told what to do, sucked in her cheeks as if she'd been reprimanded by the head teacher and gave Giulia a glare before putting her phone back in her pocket.

'OK, something really simple today, nothing taxing at all. We're going to start with the humble biscotti.'

'Oh, I like that,' said Jimmy. 'Ties in nicely with the name. Good one.'

Libby nodded. 'That's what I was hoping. You know, people would arrive, maybe be a bit tired, and it'd be a nice introduction to the whole thing. Not daunting.'

Giulia sighed from the back row. 'The baking. Yes. More baking, less talking. We get it done, I get back to work.'

Eve giggled under her breath.

'Yes, sorry,' said Libby. 'Sorry, Giulia.' She made a mental note to try not to include her in any of her future classes. 'Right, so you've got a choice here. I've given you the basic ingredients but you can flavour your biscotti however you like. I like dried apricots but you can use chocolate, pistachio—traditionally it was aniseed and hazelnut—it's completely up to you. Or just make it plain. The main thing to a biscotti, and actually the meaning behind its name, is that it's twice baked.'

'Do I like biscotti?' asked Jimmy.

'Yes,' said Eve, without looking up from where she had started to break her eggs. Libby caught Jessica's eye. Eve glanced up and caught them sharing a look. She raised a brow in silent question and both Libby and Jessica looked away.

'Hang on, Eve's started.' Jimmy frowned. 'How has Eve started? Are we meant to have started?'

'Well, you can start, Jimmy, because there's a recipe, but I'll talk you through it.'

'Jessica, have you started?'

'No.' Jessica was eating an apricot.

'And I am almost finished,' added Giulia from the back. 'This is very easy. Too easy I think. Far too easy.'

'It is?' Jimmy looked confused.

'OK, right, everyone, go with me on this. We're mixing flour, baking powder and sugar. The measurements are on your recipes and the ingredients are under your benches.'

Jessica leant forward on the bench, resting on her elbows, and perused the recipe. Next to her Eve had already started mixing in the eggs. Jimmy was looking perplexed at the ingredients and, without consulting the recipe at all, ripped open a bag of flour so it mushroomed out like a cloud in front of his face.

'Suits you,' Dex said, nodding towards Jimmy's white face.

Jimmy groaned and wiped the flour away with a tea towel. 'Libby, it's no good. I don't think I'm cut out for this.'

'You'll be fine, honestly, I'll come and help,' Libby said, coming to stand next to him. Jimmy pulled up his stool and she realised, as she started to measure out his ingredients, that he had no intention of doing any more himself. 'Jimmy, what flavour do you want?'

He shrugged. 'Don't know.'

She rolled her eyes. 'Look, you have to help me.'

'I'll just mess it up,' he said with a twinkling grin.

'But the whole point is that you learn. Here, get your hands in and mix this into a dough,' she said, sliding the bowl over to where he was sitting.

Jimmy made a face to suggest he was being hard done by.

In front of them Miles rubbed his eyes, stopped what he was doing, and said, 'Libby, I'm sorry but I think I'm going to have to go and sit down. I feel rough.'

Libby nodded. 'OK, that's fine.'

Jimmy followed him out of the door with longing eyes.

'I'm quite tired, actually,' said Dex. 'Can I go outside?'

Jessica scoffed. 'Tired? You didn't do anything today.'

Dex ignored her.

'Look,' Libby said, tearing off some baking parchment for Jimmy's biscotti. 'No one is forcing you to be here. If you don't want to do it, you are more than welcome to go outside.' She didn't mean a word of it. She was hoping that they would stay just because they knew it meant something to her.

But Jimmy and Dex immediately abandoned their posts, ditched their aprons, and raced out of the door, throwing themselves onto the pink metal chairs next to Miles.

Libby took in a breath. It was fine. She scooped out Jimmy's mixture and smoothed it onto the baking tray in little strips.

'I actually have an email that I have to answer so if we're not carrying on with this then I just need to go out and, you know, answer…' Jessica said, untying her apron and leaving hesitantly, unsure if it was allowed or not.

Eve had gone back to her workstation and Libby could feel her watching. She did everything she could to hold in her disappointment. And, in an attempt to overcompensate, her voice came out far too sweet as she said, 'Seriously, it's fine. Go. No probs at all.' Then she did a big wide smile as she slotted Jimmy's biscotti into the oven.

Eve stayed where she was but her phone was buzzing on the table with another FaceTime.

'Noah, I can't talk right now,' Libby heard her whisper. 'Yes, it's very nice. Very good. You're very clever.'

Then there was a slam of an oven door and Giulia marched to the front, muttering, 'I am finished with this. A complete waste of my time. There is no cooking being done. I have work to do. My biscotti are in the oven.'

Libby felt the same crushing disappointment of that first ever supper club. 'OK, well, probably best to just end it there, don't you think? Call it a day,' she said, keeping her voice emotionless and breezy even though Eve was the only one left in the room to hear.

Then Libby pulled her phone out of her pocket and took a couple of snaps for Instagram. Of Jimmy's biscotti in the oven. Of them all lounging outside soaking up the late afternoon sun: *A well-earned break while the biscotti bake.*

EVE

'So what the hell's Jake playing at?' Eve asked. They were still sitting on the pink metal chairs in front of the outhouse. Dex had been to the bar and come back with a bottle of vodka, ice, and some glasses. The biscotti that Libby had made for Jimmy sat on a plate in the centre of the table. Libby wasn't with them. She hadn't come back from the main hotel since the class had been cancelled.

Eve knew she should have gone to find her. She knew she was upset. But the idea of it felt awkward, like she'd pat her on the shoulder and not quite know what to say. She wasn't confident enough that her presence would be of any comfort at all.

Dex sat back with his vodka, the ice chinking in the glass. 'Jake will do whatever he thinks he can get away with.'

Miles sat forward, elbows on his knees, his fingers steepled in front of him. 'I just can't believe he was stupid enough to do it online.'

Jimmy huffed a laugh. 'Oh, come on, this is Jake.'

Eve reached to get her drink from the table and brought it back, her hand resting a whisper away from Jimmy's thigh. There was something intoxicating about having him back; she could stare at his face all night and it still wouldn't be enough. It wasn't even that she fancied him, which she did because it was hard not to fancy Jimmy—all tattooed tanned muscles, hair shorn close to his head, skin radiating vitality, white t-shirt so threadbare you could see his skin through it, low-slung green combat shorts—but more that she couldn't bear to have him out of her sight. Looking at him was addictive.

'It's exactly the kind of thing he would do,' Jimmy went on. 'Every time he doesn't get caught he'll push a little bit harder.'

Eve frowned, remembering the Instagram pictures of Jake carrying a massive Christmas tree on his shoulder or giving Libby a piggyback on a country walk. 'You think he's done it before.'

Jimmy almost choked on his swig of beer. 'Are you serious?'

Eve looked at Jessica who shrugged, equally nonplussed. It felt weird talking about Libby and Jake like this at their place.

'Of course he's done it before. The guy's the ultimate player,' Jimmy went on. 'He can't sit still. Never could. Christ, he's shagged people left, right, and centre over the years.'

Eve paused with her drink up to her lips. 'Wow,' she said, before taking a little sip, the vodka coursing cold through her body. Poor Libby. For a second she thought about her life envy. Even their infidelity was bigger and bolder and more media friendly than her and Peter's quiet little bust up. 'Do you think she knew?' she asked.

Jimmy held his hands up. 'I don't see how she didn't know. He's been—'

He was cut off by Jessica doing a really loud cough and they all turned to see Libby standing at the gate to the lemon grove. She had a bottle of ice cold vodka in her hand and a couple of spare glasses. All around her fairy lights sparkled in the leaves.

Everyone was silent for what seemed like hours.

Jimmy looked down, rubbing his hand over his forehead.

'Giulia said you were all on vodka,' Libby said, trundling through the silence as if nothing had happened. She swallowed. 'So, erm, I brought this.' She held up the condensation covered bottle. 'But I think, though, I think I've just forgotten something. I'll be back in a tick,' she said, then turned and took a couple of paces, then turned again and added, 'I'll leave this here.' She put the vodka bottle and glasses on the ground by the fence then disappeared back through the grove.

'Shit,' said Dex.

Eve put her hands over her mouth.

Jessica narrowed her eyes. 'You knew,' she said to Jimmy. 'You knew and you didn't tell her.'

Jimmy shook his head. 'It's none of my business.'

Miles raised a brow.

'Are you kidding?' Jessica said. 'She's your friend.'

'So was he. Is he.' Jimmy made a face. 'Come on, why would I get involved in this? Dex?'

Dex shrugged. 'It's messy.'

Jessica rolled her eyes.

'Never get involved.' Jimmy held up his hands. 'People's relationships are their own business. They choose what they want and what they want to see.'

'That's such a cop-out,' Jessica stood up and walked over to the gate to pick up the vodka.

'Oh, and you're the expert?' Jimmy said, and they all suddenly became fascinated with their drinks.

Jessica huffed, jaw clenched, and bashed the bottle down on the table.

Jimmy shook his head and sat back in his chair, taking a swig of his drink probably to stop himself saying any more.

'One of us should go and find her,' Eve said, knowing that it should be her, but something was holding her back. Pride, perhaps. The feeling of being the outsider. The fact that all this had been going on in Libby's relationship and she hadn't told her.

She glanced around for a possible candidate. Miles was still battling the jet lag and had sat back with his eyes closed. Jessica was clearly quietly fuming about Jimmy's comments and not about to get up again. It was Dex who paused as he was refilling everyone's glasses and, looking up at Eve, said, 'Give me one sec and I'll go.'

When Dex stood up Jimmy did as well but, as Dex strode off towards the hotel, Jimmy took his drink and wandered down to the very bottom of the garden. Jessica kept staring moodily down at her glass.

Eve was about to follow Jimmy when her phone rang. She glanced at the screen to see Peter's name flash up for FaceTime and was hit by a confusing mishmash of feelings. An excitement that Peter had broken their agreement not to talk for the first half of the week so that it was a proper break, but also a desire to keep hold of the slight flicker of old Eve that seeing Jimmy had dusted off and was bringing back to light.

She went over to the lemon grove to answer, pushing her hair back before she did, rubbing her cheeks and positioning herself so she wouldn't look like she had a double chin or big bags under her eyes when her image came up on screen.

'Hello,' she said, almost sultry.

'Muuuummmy!' Noah and Maisey yelled simultaneously.

'Oh, hi, guys,' she said, smiling, relieved, a tiny bit disappointed that Peter hadn't even been there to say hello.

They chattered away about their day, oohing at the big lemons and the fairy lights when she turned the camera round.

She heard Peter shout, 'Two minutes till bath time,' and found herself wanting to tell him about Libby and Jake. Like she was holding a balloon that just got bigger and bigger the more she didn't tell Peter.

He'd never met Jimmy. Dex and Jessica he knew to say 'Hi' to, but Libby and Jake they had spent time with when they were first dating. Peter had walked away from their first meeting shaking his head. 'He's too good-looking for his own good. I can't talk to him.'

'Does he make you shy and nervous?' Eve had sniggered as they'd stumbled drunkenly into a taxi.

'No.' Peter had shaken his head. 'It's like he's not really the one talking. It's like… Yeah, Claremont Road, it's the block of flats—you can't miss it, by the railway. Yeah? Great. It's like he's a guy playing him in a film.'

'What? Sorry, I got confused about who you were talking to,' Eve had said, laughing.

'I've got to give the guy directions. You're coming to mine aren't you?' Peter had frowned, clearly suddenly remembering that it would have been polite to ask first.

'And they say chivalry is dead?' Eve had said, as coy as she could be after most of a bottle of Australian sauvignon blanc, picked without consultation by Jake.

At the time she'd been more interested in the fact that she was about to have sex with Peter than with anything he had to say about Jake.

But now, when she couldn't talk to him because of their agreement, now she remembered what he had said, she wanted to tell Peter that she knew exactly what he'd meant. That the idea of Jake being like a man in a film playing the part of Jake was a very clever observation. The kind of thing that she hoped was in the script he was writing. But if she said that now, in the current state of their relationship, it would sound patronising and if she told him what had happened he'd find out that Jimmy was there and that would lead to a whole other set of problems.

But he wasn't talking to her anyway, so it didn't really matter.

'Night, Mummy,' said Noah. 'We missed you but then Daddy took us to the pet shop to look at the puppies and that made it go away.'

'That's a lovely story, sweetheart.' She laughed and then wished them goodnight and they all three kissed the screen and then the kids hung up.

Dex was just coming back down the garden and she waited for him to draw level with her.

'She says she's fine.' He shrugged. 'I didn't push it.'

Eve nodded. As they got back to the table Dex returned to his seat, pouring himself another vodka, but Eve didn't sit; instead she carried on down to the end of the garden where Jimmy was still standing.

'Everything all right at home?' he asked as she came up next to him.

'Yeah. Just the kids going to bed.'

He nodded.

'You like it there? In the country?'

'Yeah.' Eve nodded, looking out into the falling darkness, at the forest of pine trees rising like witches' brooms that started at the bottom of the garden and stretched out until they fringed the edge of the lake. Through a gap she could just make out the water, black and shiny like tar.

'I can't imagine it. You in the countryside. Someone said you have chickens,' he said, laughing. 'I told them they must be wrong. Eve would never have chickens.'

'I do have chickens. I think I'm a chicken person.'

'You weren't a chicken person when I knew you.'

'Well, we grow up, don't we?'

'And you've grown up into a chicken person?' he asked.

'Yes,' she said with a firm nod.

Nothing had ever happened between her and Jimmy. They had sort of danced around each other like storks on a nature documentary. All show and bluster. All long lingering looks as they lay in bed together, the light from the TV flickering across their faces. Jimmy was a player. He liked fun and he liked women. But where other girls came and went, Eve stayed. She was the one he couldn't have. Because Eve too was a player. In a different way to Jimmy—more coquettish flirt, more of a tousled blonde-haired, big-eyed fun lover who boys followed like the Pied Piper. And she loved it. Like a big game. At the time Jimmy was still at medical school and she'd come back from work, all stilettoed up thinking she was it, and they'd go out together to see what havoc they could cause, what fun they could have. And more often than not they'd come home together, a trail of longing behind them; they liked to leave people hanging. Leave them wanting more.

Eve's mum and dad were the kind of parents who took her to Glastonbury every year from toddlerhood. And she would dance with flowers in her hair and appear on the front page of the papers like an angel in a field. They were the kind of parents who wanted nothing more than for her to have fun. And Eve liked to have fun. But quite often Eve had also lived with her grandparents, dropped off when her parents needed some together-time. They'd drive off in their van and get so high they wouldn't sleep for a week. For Eve, her grandparents became her safety net—the safe, predictable harness that underpinned all that fun.

And as a result she went through life always just checking behind her for a similar net in whatever shape or form it might take. When she moved into the flat, the tether was her job in marketing at a top cosmetics firm.

A job where she shone, where she rose fast, where she had a nice, familiar routine to fill her days so her nights could be filled with fun.

But then Jimmy had packed in his course to cycle round the world. The moment he told her was like a photograph stamped forever in her mind. 'Come,' he'd said.

She'd stared at him.

The paths diverged in her head.

She saw herself on a rusty old bike, untethered, freewheeling down some dirt track, flowers in her hair.

But she had to go to work the next day.

'No,' she had said.

She had lived since then wondering what would have happened if she'd said yes. Like a dull background noise. Now, though, as she stood at the bottom of the garden next to Jimmy it was beeping like a metal detector, stronger than it had ever been.

'And marriage?' he said. 'That's good?'

'Yeah, fine.' Eve nodded. She picked at the leaves of an olive sapling. 'It's not fine actually. We're on a break.' As soon as she said it she knew she shouldn't have. Shouldn't have entrusted her secret to this other man. She shouldn't have casually handed him something so precious—because just him knowing their weakness made it infinitely weaker. It felt immediately disrespectful of Peter. Making him, them, foolish.

Jimmy had turned to look at her, his eyes bright in the darkness. 'Are you happy about that?' he asked.

'No.' Eve shook her head, pulling another leaf off the olive tree. 'I don't want it to end, especially not for the kids.'

Jimmy shrugged. 'I think kids adapt. I did. You shouldn't stay just for the kids.'

'I'm not.' Eve threw the leaves on the ground and brushed the tree where she'd absently plucked its branch bare in an attempt to make it better. 'That came out wrong. I'm not at all. I just…' She paused. 'I shouldn't be talking to you about this.'

Jimmy made a face. 'Why not?'

'I don't know. It feels wrong.'

'You liked marriage?'

'It's not over, Jimmy, it's not past tense, it's just a little break.'

He shrugged.

'And yes, yes I did, do, like it. I love it.'

Jimmy didn't reply; he just laughed lightly before finishing his drink.

Eve turned her back on the view and suddenly saw smoke filling the outhouse. 'Shit, did anyone take that woman's biscotti out of the oven?' she said, jogging over to the glass door.

'What woman?' Jimmy asked.

'The moody one. Giulia. Her biscotti,' Eve shouted. And the rest of them sprang up from the table and followed her into the outhouse as she ran to the back of the room and yanked open the oven. A cloud of smoke engulfed her as she pulled out the baking tray.

She felt Jimmy's hand on her shoulder as she started coughing.

'Open the windows,' he called, and Dex pushed the handle and the whole front wall concertinaed open. The smoke escaped like a trapped animal, streaming out into the fresh evening air.

They all peered at the tray of blackened biscotti.

'Well, they're definitely twice baked, aren't they?' said Dex, picking one up and then dropping it, his fingers burnt.

Eve looked at the little charred biscuits and thought about Libby alone somewhere in the hotel. There couldn't have been a more obvious symbol. 'We shouldn't have cut that class short,' she said.

'No,' said Miles solemnly.

They all stared at the tray.

Then Jimmy laughed and said, 'They're only biscuits.' And Eve nudged him because he was ruining the moment.

LIBBY

When Libby couldn't find any of them at breakfast the following morning she asked Giulia who said that she thought she had seen someone go into the outhouse. When she walked down the garden to have a look she found them all in there, standing to attention like soldiers behind their stations.

Someone had made coffee, there was a fresh cup on her table, the steam catching the rays of the rising sun. She looked from the cup to the group to see Dex raising his mug to his lips, scrolling through something on his phone. Eve had her hands wrapped around her mug, blonde hair all awry; she looked like she'd either slept really deeply or not at all. Jimmy was bent forward, elbows on his table, his fingers toying with a teaspoon. Miles was reading the paper. Jessica had retreated to the back, to Giulia's previous workstation where the smell of burnt biscotti still lingered.

Libby had remembered about the biscotti in the middle of the night and gone running down to the outhouse in a panic, only to find them in the bin, black and burnt, the oven off. Wide awake, she'd stood alone knowing she wouldn't be able to sleep if she went back to bed. So instead she'd done her make-up, styled up her silk kimono dressing gown, and decided to record a midnight feast video for the blog. The garden outside, silent and eerie in the moonlight, was the perfect backdrop.

She made biscotti because she could make it with her eyes closed and wouldn't need to rehearse. She flavoured it with liquorice because it always split opinion and that would make for good comments. To camera she explained her decadent love of liquorice, the tangy bitterness that fizzed on her tongue. She talked about how they always caused a stir at the supper club, some guests devouring them with their coffees, others too scared to even give them a nibble. She dropped a casual mention of a celebrity wedding that she had catered and how they had insisted on pink and white striped sweetshop bags of the liquorice biscotti as the favours.

She didn't mention that it had been her aunt Silvia who had taught her to make them here at the Limoncello Hotel. She didn't mention that she had made them when she got home and how her younger brother had spat his out on the table, making all the other younger ones spit theirs out too. How they had then thrown them at one another, a big biscotti fight across the table. How her mum had come in from work and gone mad about the mess. How her youngest sister had then been sick on the floor and Libby had cleared it up, along with all the biscotti everywhere. How she'd got annoyed with them all and her mum had told her to go and calm down while she made the dinner that Libby was meant to have made for the little ones. How when she sat and looked at herself in the mirror she saw her dad's face and wondered if that was what her mum saw and whether that affected the way she felt about her.

She never talked about her family in her videos. Never talked about its crazy, hectic boisterousness. She never talked about how she would be given a reprieve every summer when she was sent to the Limoncello where she would cook in the restaurant and read books in the shade of the lemon grove. Where she would take herself off on her bike and scour the local flea markets and buy old Italian enamel saucepans and flour jars. Where she was just Libby and allowed to exist as just Libby rather than as one of the mass of chaos where she was sister, half-sister, step-sister, nanny, daughter, peace-keeper. A chaos that often left her unable to breathe, with a tightness in her chest and a desperate need to escape.

In the videos she didn't talk about any of that. She talked about her life in the present. All polished up, her lips always red, her hair always shiny. She could edit it down nicely to portray exactly the life she wanted.

After she'd taken the biscotti out of the oven she had a piping hot bite for the camera; she'd hidden the burn

of the roof her mouth with a laugh. She'd staged it so
her followers would think she was taking the rest of the
plate to bed with a cup of hot chocolate but, in reality,
she'd turned the camera off and sat for a minute or two,
her mind straight back to that haphazard family kitchen
table. Straight back to the noise and the bluster. She'd
realised she hadn't made liquorice biscotti for herself
for years. Jake hated liquorice.

She'd sat in the darkness and wondered where he was.

Every time the bell rang on the front door of the hotel
she found herself catching her breath thinking it might
be him. Equal amounts hope and alarm.

Dex clicked his phone off and straightened up.
'Listen, Libby, we're all sorry. We shouldn't have been
talking about you last night. It was completely out of
order.'

She saw Eve nod in agreement.

'And rest assured, from this moment on, we are all
fully committed bakers. Aren't we?' He glanced around
the rest of the group.

Everyone nodded really earnestly.

Libby felt herself blush. She wanted to say something
but was a little overcome. They had surprised her by
being there without any cajoling.

By being there for her.

And the sight of them all standing there was much
nicer, more comforting, than she could ever have
imagined.

In the end she simply said, 'Thank you,' and then busied herself handing out new laminated recipes.

Jimmy frowned at his. 'A *cornetto*? Isn't that an ice cream?'

'No,' Libby said, passing out the rest and going back up to the front. 'It's like a croissant but Italian. Which means less butter, more sweetness, and an egg to give them their sunshine yellow. *Cornetto*—it means little horn.'

Libby held up a picture of the finished product. 'Now it's heavier than a traditional croissant and usually has a slight hint of orange but we're going to substitute the orange zest for lemon—mainly because we have so many but also to tie it back to the region.'

'It's never really occurred to me that you can make a croissant,' Jimmy said, picking up one of the lemons on his counter and giving it a sniff.

Eve frowned. 'Where do you think they come from?'

'I literally have no idea. I just see them as sort of appearing,' he said with a shrug.

'I hear you on that, mate.' Miles nodded, frowning down at the recipe as if it was algebra. 'I mean, how do you get all those layers?'

'That's part of the pastry.' Eve shook her head like they were complete idiots and turned to roll her eyes at Libby. It was only after she'd done it that she seemed to catch herself in the gesture. Without thinking about it, she'd thrown a ball on the assumption of their friendship.

Libby smiled.

Eve half smiled, and looked shyly down at her bench.

Just that one tiny piece of shared communication had Libby's confidence spreading through her like one of those fancy Japanese flower teabags that unfurls with hot water.

'OK, first thing we need to do is make friends with our yeast,' she said, picking up her little bowl of yeast and holding it so they could all see what it was.

'Why?' asked Dex, peering into his bowl with distrust.

'Because it's alive.'

'Like an oyster, Dex,' Jessica said from the back.

Dex narrowed his eyes, unconvinced.

'Your yeast is what's going to do the work for you on this one so you have to treat it well. We're going to dissolve it in warm water—not too hot or you'll kill it and there'll be no layers in your croissant. Use your thermometers,' Libby added, holding up the vintage metal kitchen thermometers she'd lovingly sourced from various flea markets.

'These are nice,' said Eve, and Libby nodded, unexpectedly pleased at Eve's approval.

The kitchenware had been Libby's vision entirely. Probably because it wasn't something that interested Jake. He had involved himself in the symmetry of the building design, in sourcing shiny metal sheets for the work surfaces and stainless steel shelving. It had been him who'd painted the whole thing white and hung huge burnished metal ceiling lamps over the workstations. Libby had worried it was a bit clinical but he'd said it was cutting-edge and thrown her one of his patented 'leave this kind of stuff to me' looks before giving her a hug. The type that always felt like a boy hugging his teddy bear.

'This is like a physics lesson,' Miles said, running his eye down the recipe.

'Don't read ahead.' Libby went over and took the recipe out of his hands, laying it down on the counter. 'Just go with what I say.'

Miles laughed like he'd been told what to do for the first time in years and Libby felt herself soften. Seeing him again was like watching her younger brother grow up. Gone was a tall, gangly, sullen dude who went to gigs and played in a band and chain smoked Marlboro Reds. He'd been replaced by this quiet man who'd filled out and bulked up; his jaw had sharpened, his features had all found their place and settled into being not bad looking.

She glanced behind him and saw the same in Dex, both of them finally fitting their skin. Trying less hard and being much better for it. She remembered how nice Dex had been when he'd come to find her the night before, hovering on the threshold of her room, clearly awkward as he politely checked if she was OK.

If she lined them all up next to Jake there would suddenly be a battle for chief that there never was in the past—Jake ruled the roost with his king of the jungle swagger.

But then she realised there would be no battle at all. Miles wouldn't care, his strength was already too hard won. And Dex wouldn't compete. He was probably the natural born leader among them, but Dex simply wouldn't want it, giving him a silent power that Jake had never had.

She was talking about yeast as all this was flowing through her head. The group were measuring and stirring and then covering their bowls with cloths so the yeast could do its stuff in the comfort of darkness.

All the while Libby was thinking about Dex and Miles and how she never would have expected them to be the yardsticks against which Jake could be measured and found wanting.

'My water's too hot,' Jimmy said, struggling with his thermometer.

Dex was peering under his tea towel. 'Bubble, you little buggers.'

'OK, put the yeast to one side and we'll move on to the egg.'

'But I haven't done mine yet,' said Jimmy, looking worried.

'What have you been doing?' Dex shouted. 'It's just stirring the stuff in water.'

'I've got some leftover water, Jimmy.' Eve went over to his bench with her saucepan and poured her perfect-temperature water into his bowl.

Jimmy had his hands on his head, flustered. Libby paused where she was, not quite ready to help him, not quite able to forget what she'd overheard him saying last night about Jake. So it was a relief when Eve showed him what to do with his yeast. Libby watched him laugh at something Eve said, saw her reach right over past him and him maybe smell her hair—or just conveniently inhale—as she grabbed an egg from the packet and broke it into another bowl. She wanted to warn him off. Didn't want Eve led down that path. But she knew it wouldn't make any difference. It would play out whether she wanted it to or not.

The thought had echoes of Jimmy not telling her about Jake. And she realised that it wasn't that he didn't tell her about the affairs that bothered her. It was the fact that he knew.

And that made her feel stupid.

Embarrassed.

It undercut everything that she had thought she had.

'See, now you're level with the rest of us,' Eve said. Jimmy nodded and turned cockily round to Dex to say, 'I'm up to speed, I'm with you.'

Dex rolled his eyes and went back to beating his egg.

'What next?' Jessica called from the back.

'So now your yeast will be ready so it's flour, yeast, egg into your mixers.' Libby strolled up and down the central aisle as she spoke.

'Mine doesn't work,' shouted Jimmy.

'Plug it in, you doofus,' said Dex.

Eve laughed.

'Add a pinch of salt,' said Libby, trying to remain the in-control grown-up. 'And then it's the butter, vanilla, and the zest of your lemon.'

'OK no, mine's a disaster. It's like sick.' Jimmy clicked the head of his mixer up and stared down at his mixture.

Dex peered over his counter. 'It is like sick. Exactly like sick.'

Miles turned around to have a look, gave a wry snort of laughter, and turned back to his own dough.

Libby walked over and looked into Jimmy's bowl. 'OK, it's just a bit curdled. We'll fix it.'

Jimmy took a step back as she started to rescue his mix, instinctively putting space between them.

She felt him watching as she pulled it back to a smooth consistency. When she slid the bowl along the counter back to him he stepped forward with a nod. 'Thank you,' he said.

'You're welcome,' she replied, but neither of them quite met the other's eye.

JESSICA

They sat outside in the morning sun as the dough rose. Libby brought out little honey cakes and some liquorice biscotti that she'd somehow managed to knock up the night before, while Jessica made coffee.

Dex was meant to be helping Jessica but he was just leaning against the counter eating biscotti, saying, 'It's exhausting, this cooking. I am exhausted.' As he popped another into his mouth he added, 'So how are you doing with Miles?'

'Awkwardly.'

Dex snorted.

'It really would have been nice if you'd told me he was coming before we arrived,' she said, pushing the plunger down on the cafetière.

'You wouldn't have come if I had.'

Jessica didn't reply.

'It'll be good for you,' Dex said, and then poured himself a coffee and strode outside saying, 'So what are you up to these days, Miles?'

Miles had his eyes shut leaning back in his chair. He rolled his head round to answer, shielding his eyes from the sun with his hand. 'Still at the label,' he said.

'Doing well?' Dex asked with a little smirk on his lips.

Miles shrugged. 'Pretty well,' he said, his eyes narrowed slightly as he waited for what was coming next.

Dex nodded. 'And you're not doing any of your own stuff any more?'

Miles shook his head, holding in a smile. 'No. No, I'm not.'

'No gigs?'

'No gigs.'

'Well, thank the Lord,' Dex said with a grin as he plonked himself down in his seat. 'I think that makes the world a safer, more melodious place.'

Libby gave him a little thump on the arm.

Miles closed his eyes again, refusing to rise to the bait any longer.

Jimmy chuckled as he soaked up the sun.

Jessica watched from the doorway. She remembered so clearly the evening that Miles had got the call from the record company to say they were interested in his stuff. To ask him to come in for a meeting. He'd walked into the living room, all of them sitting round about to go out, and mumbled the news. Flo had jumped up and made a massive fuss, run to the fridge to get a bottle of champagne. Miles had waved it away, awkward from the attention.

Jessica remembered being so amazed. So in awe. She'd asked all sorts of really serious technical questions, trying to prise out the answers in between Flo popping the champagne cork and sloshing it into glasses.

At the time it had never occurred to her why there had been a bottle of champagne in the fridge ready and waiting. Or why none of the others shared her amazement. She'd caught Dex rolling his eyes as he'd drained his glass.

She couldn't understand it. Jessica had spent hours lying on Miles's bed listening to him strumming on his guitar, soaking up all his chat about the venues he would one day play.

For a girl who had spent most of her life sitting in her bedroom alone listening to music she'd managed to borrow from friends at school, Miles was akin to suddenly waking up and finding herself living with a bona fide superstar. She was living in this flat where everything was allowed and no one was afraid. No one locked all the windows and the doors at half past nine. No one shouted. No one had even read the Bible. People touched, they snuggled, they kissed. It was the world in all its technicolour. And Miles was everything her mother warned her about. He was sullen. He sneered. He liked to lie in the dark and stare at the ceiling. He liked to listen to obscure new music. He liked to do all of those things, with her. And in her naivety, Jessica had been certain Miles had what it took to be the next big thing.

The thought of it now actually made her have to stifle her own smile as she slid the tray of coffees onto the table, the sharp, bitter tang twining like smoke with the sunshine scent of the lemon groves.

She'd never laughed at anything that involved the two of them before and it was quite liberating.

Miles opened one eye. 'Thanks, Jessica,' he said.

'No problem,' she replied, taking her mug and going to sit in one of the chairs furthest away from him on the opposite side of the table, snatching up a couple of biscotti before Dex demolished them all.

Jessica had been no match for Flo. She was tall and confident, spoke exactly what was in her head, she was funny and charming with hair the colour of ebony and an innate cool that came from growing up in New York with music industry parents. She knew all of Miles's adored bands and then some—she'd met them, she'd smoked cigarettes with them on the tour bus, she'd danced at their house parties. Did she like their music? Sure, why not... The thing was, Flo liked everything. She knew about everything. She could lounge on the sofa playing PlayStation wearing cashmere and hundred-dollar foundation as coolly and comfortably as she could fly out of the door in a gifted designer dress to the BAFTAs because her dad was in town and had got her a ticket.

And the thing about Flo was she got what she wanted, whenever she wanted it. And her sights, at that time, were set on bagging herself a British bad boy with razor sharp cheekbones and a tortured soul.

It had transpired that the record exec who'd called was a friend of Flo's dad and the meeting had never gone any further. But it was enough to start the ball rolling between the two of them.

And gradually Miles's soul became less tortured as he adapted to Flo's lifestyle.

The business class flights back to New York, the backstage passes, the Ralph Lauren clothes, and the job at the record label. All while Jessica watched from the sidelines unable to get in.

EVE

They ate their *cornetti* straight from the oven. Like lemon candyfloss the layers pulled on and on with every bite, the piping hot pastry burning their chins. But they'd barely finished their last mouthfuls when Libby said, 'We should probably get to work.'

Eve internally sighed. She couldn't bear another afternoon arguing with her about furnishings so, as they all heaved themselves up the path, she stopped Miles and said, 'Do you think we could swap? I'll do the garden.'

Miles frowned. 'You sure? It's really hot.'

'Yeah, I'll wear a hat.' Even the midday sun was preferable to watching her beloved wallpaper disappear under a coat of white emulsion.

'OK.' Miles nodded and jogged up to join Libby who glanced back over her shoulder when she heard the news but didn't object.

Eve knew it was dangerous working with Jimmy. She could feel her mind wandering. Could feel a prickle on her skin whenever she was with him. And, because he'd hardly changed one inch, being with him made her feel younger. Made her forget about the new lines on her face and the dark circles under her eyes.

He slung his arm around her shoulder, a pair of secateurs in one hand and an electric strimmer in the other, and she felt engulfed by the strength of him. Couldn't help comparing him to Peter who was slim built and slight—had never set foot in a gym or on a court in his life. They were exact opposites in every way. And being so close to Jimmy now, seeing how he strolled through life without a care, ignited something within her, some sense of wrong that was yet to be put right. Something completely other to the Eve she had become and right back to the core of who she was.

'Right then, Evie. We've got work to do,' he said, and they spent the next couple of hours hacking away undergrowth.

As the early afternoon sun raged above them, Eve looked at her arms and realised she was starting to burn. 'Jimmy, I'm going to go and get some more sun cream,' she said.

'OK, no worries,' he called, lopping off a frond of exotic cactus.

When she came back out, however, she couldn't find him anywhere. The garden tools were all leaning neatly up against the outhouse alongside the wheelbarrow.

'Jimmy?' she called, and when there was no answer she started walking further to the bottom of the garden. She peered into the shadows of the forest, inhaling the sharp smell of pine and lemon and lake. The sliver of lake she could see was glass flat, the occasional dart of sunlight bouncing off the surface. All around her the sound of cicadas buzzed like white noise. Jimmy's t-shirt was slung over a fence post, still warm to the touch.

She stood on tiptoe to see further and caught sight of him right in the middle of the forest, sitting legs crossed, his hands on his knees, back straight, bare chest, staring out towards the water.

The idea of him meditating made her do a little snort of laughter to herself as she climbed over the old wooden fence and walked over to join him. The trunks towered above her, the odd pine cone falling with a thump from up high. White pigeons cooed from their perches.

She pulled off her hat as the canopy of branches shaded the glare of the sun.

'Is this mindfulness or meditation?' she asked as she got close enough, fallen pine needles crunching underfoot.

Jimmy didn't turn. 'I prefer not to label it.'

Eve laughed. 'Of course you do.'

Still he didn't move. 'Take a seat. I think it'd be good for you.'

'Oh you do, do you?' she said, with no intention of sitting down.

'Get rid of some of the tension.'

'I'm not tense.'

She saw his shoulders shake slightly with a laugh. 'Eve, you're so tense you're like a spring.'

'I am not.'

He gave a tiny shrug. 'Suit yourself.'

She walked past him to look out at the water. 'What are you looking at?'

'I was looking at the water. Now I'm looking at you.'

She turned and realised she was completely blocking his view. 'Oh, sorry.'

'Seriously, come and sit down,' he said, shifting over to make room for her on his towel.

'No.'

'Why not?'

'Because it's weird.'

'What happened to the hippy in you?'

'I was never a hippy.'

'You used to try things.'

'I still try things.'

'Well, sit down then.'

She stood for a minute, contemplating the suggestion. The idea of meditating made her feel foolish but Jimmy didn't seem to have any intention of doing anything but.

She folded herself down so she was sitting on the ground cross-legged. Glancing over to him for pointers she couldn't help but notice all his muscles, the tattoos snaking down one half of his torso.

He glanced over and caught her staring. Smiling, he said, 'Now just sit and let your mind become quiet.'

'Don't I need a mantra?' she remembered her dad with all his hippy cronies sitting on the hill at Glastonbury chanting but, in retrospect, that was probably more to do with the drugs than any form of meditation.

'Do you want a mantra?'

'Do you have a mantra?' she asked.

'I prefer not to have a mantra but I can give you one if you'd like.'

'No, no. If you don't need one, I don't need one.'

Jimmy laughed through his nose.

They sat together in silence.

Eve kept glancing across at him without moving her head.

Jimmy was completely still.

She looked out at the sun. It was bigger here than at home, dangling like a Christmas bauble from the thin wisps of cloud, teetering on the verge of plunging straight into the lake.

She looked at the water; rays of sun reflected like landing strips in the blue.

She looked at the trees; the shadows danced on the rough, ridged bark.

She looked back at Jimmy.

There was so much she wanted to say. A blob of bird poo had fallen from the tree and she wanted to laugh. She wanted to make sure that underneath it all Jimmy thought this was all a bit ridiculous. She wanted to know if they were going to go for a drink afterwards or carry on with the garden. At the very least she wanted to make some funny quip about the fact that his *cornetto* hadn't risen at all, coming out of the oven more like a pancake.

'So what do you think about?' she said into the silence.

'I try not to think about anything.'

'Nothing? I can't think about nothing.'

'Well, try to let your thoughts just flow past you,' he said without moving his head. 'Observe but don't get involved.'

'Like a conveyer belt?' Eve said. 'Like the *Generation Game*?' she added with a little smirk.

Jimmy didn't reply.

Peter would have laughed.

Peter would have laughed at the whole set-up. Rolled his eyes at the very notion of sitting in a pine forest meditating.

And somehow, while that made her miss him, it also hardened her resolve to sit in the pine forest and meditate, purely because he wouldn't have done it. Because they were on a break and this was the time to do all the things she didn't do as one half of their couple.

But it was so boring.

'I think there's an ant trying to get into my pants,' she said after a minute.

'Probably.'

'What if it's a poisonous red ant?'

'Eve?'

'Yes.'

'Be quiet.'

She made a face but, chastened, sat in silence staring at the sun. Then she shut her eyes and watched the bright blue stain on her retina play on her closed lids. She could smell the pine. She could smell the lemons. It had been months since she'd come up with a new fragrance. She should have had a new drop for summer but she hadn't been satisfied with anything and had instead gone back to her archive and rereleased a classic—geranium and white rose. She had assumed the inspiration would come, but for five months she'd been staring at her notebook trying to think of something that excited her.

The previous year she'd been giddy with excitement, overflowing with it, because she'd been approached by a department store for a brand partnership. In her haste to secure the deal, terrified that they might come to their senses and choose someone else, she'd misunderstood the contractual small print and handed over almost complete exclusivity which, in the end, had come close to breaking her. She had watched her name and her beloved brand suddenly skewed and morphed to whatever the store wanted. She lost the majority of her other stockists, had to renege on smaller deals and all fledgling projects, while her life became a constant publicity campaign for the brand partnership events. All while juggling the twins. A lawyer she drafted in too late confirmed that she could do nothing but sit and wait it out.

And when the term ended at the beginning of the year she had been expecting, alongside her new freedom, a giant wave of creativity. But instead she had found herself frozen rigid. Her creative spirit flattened. Her muse squashed. Preferring to skirt the issue completely she poured more and more energy into the kids. Into the kale. Or lack thereof.

Now as she sat, her life moving slowly past her eyes on a supermarket conveyer belt in her head, she found herself thinking about fragrance. About the pine and the lemon and how it was sweetened somehow with the freshness that came from the lake. To recreate it, she maybe needed a herb. Thyme, perhaps, or bay. And something to replicate the warmth. A sliver of chilli or maybe amber oil. Honey could work but might make it all too sweet. She narrowed her eyes as she tried to imagine the smell.

Then the silence was broken as Jimmy said, 'So you're on a break, then?'

Her head flicked round, the perfume ideas gone; she hadn't expected him to be the one to speak first. 'Not so much a break as just a bit of thinking time,' she said, a little bemused that he'd interrupted the silence.

'Oh, right.'

'I was deep in conveyer belt thought just then, you know.'

Jimmy chuckled. 'Sorry.'

Eve closed her eyes again to try and reclaim her scent.

'So tell me about these chickens.'

Her eyes flicked open and she sighed, her fragrance gone. 'Actually I hate the chickens.'

Jimmy laughed. Deep and loud, it echoed through the trees.

Eve lay back and laughed as well, staring up at all the millions of pine needles above her and the cracks of light peeking through.

'They came from Noah and Maisey's school fair,' she said snapping a pine needle between her fingers. 'They used to be battery chickens. We were new to the area and all the other parents were going on about bloody chickens and what good pets they make and I wanted to look like we fitted in so I said we'd have them.' She rolled her head to look at Jimmy and saw amusement dancing in his eyes. 'Don't look at me like that. No one had talked to me for two weeks before that. And it worked, they let me in the gang. Probably because I was suddenly saddled with two bloody annoying chickens just like all of them. They don't do anything except squawk and peck and poo everywhere. They don't even bloody lay eggs. But Noah and Maisey love them. I sometimes think about just leaving the door open so the foxes can get them but I can't do it. They look at me with their ugly little eyes and guilt overtakes me.'

Jimmy laughed and lay back next to her. 'So you think you shouldn't have moved?'

'I don't know. I don't know. I thought that it would be all idyllic but I think maybe it's just lonely. In my head I'd go on long country walks and come up with ideas but I don't walk anywhere. I go in the car.' She snapped another pine needle between her fingers. 'I miss being able to walk to things. To shops. To life. I suppose it makes me feel a bit trapped.'

'And that's why you're on a break?'

She paused; they were lying with their heads turned so their faces were a few inches apart, and she could see all the lines and marks on his face. The little scar across the bridge of his nose from when he'd been punched for getting off with some bloke's girlfriend. Eve had held the frozen peas on his face.

'Maybe that's why,' she said. 'I hadn't really thought about it. But yes, it could have something to do with it. It's all much more concentrated. Like everyone knows everything about me and I'm not very good with that. It makes me too self-conscious. I want to be able to choose if I want to be part of the gang, you

know? I don't want to have to be part of it just so I have
someone to talk to in the day.'

Jimmy blew out a breath and said, 'Eve, I live on a
boat away from all civilisation. Of course I know. It
sounds horrendous.'

She smiled.

She saw his eyes light up.

He sighed. 'I wish you had come with me.'

Eve tried to play it cool. It took every muscle in her
body to keep her lying where she was and not to jerk
upright.

'I knew from the moment I picked up my bike it
was a mistake.' He propped himself up on his elbows,
looking up at the sky rather than at Eve. 'It's pretty
damn lonely cycling round the world on your own,' he
said with a sad little laugh.

The sun flickered between the pine needles above
them like a reel of old cine film. The pigeons cooed at
each other.

Eve tucked her hair behind her ears and then toyed
with another fallen needle. 'So why didn't you come
back?' she asked.

He sat up and looked down at her. 'Because I'd
already gone,' he said with a shrug. 'Never go back,' he
added, as if that was explanation enough.

Eve sat up as well. 'That's not a real answer,' she
said, running her fingers through her hair to brush out
the needles.

'I suppose I'd told everyone I was going so I thought I may as well get on with it.'

'What, so it was pride?'

He laughed. 'Don't get me wrong. It was really good fun, but—well, I just shouldn't have left you behind,' he said, jumping up and swiping the pine needles from his shorts.

She didn't correct him. She didn't say, 'But you didn't leave me, I chose not to go,' because Jimmy was reaching out a hand to help her to standing and the sun was dancing in the air between them and he had a big, wide grin on his face. She knew that saying anything more would spoil the moment. Would make him frown and go back to tearing the garden apart when actually he was pointing towards the white boathouse on the shore, saying, 'Fancy a drink?'

And she wasn't ready for it to end.

So she said, 'OK,' and he slung his arm across her shoulders and they started walking in the direction of Bruno's bar.

In her flip-flops with her big hat, sun-kissed skin, and pine-needle-tousled hair, Eve had a flash of her twenty-something-year-old self, bubbling with nervous energy and uncertainty, skipping through life making mischief with Jimmy. And the memory of it made her spine tingle. It made her thirsty for more. It made her want to drop everything and cycle round the world if it meant she could just hold on to that feeling.

JESSICA

Jessica had been working in the pool area when she'd heard Libby broach the subject of Flo with Miles. The conversation had floated down through an open window as the two of them ripped up carpet together.

Jessica had scrubbed harder at her patio tiles hoping to drown their words out but it didn't work. Every time she'd paused, her arm muscles aching, snippets of conversation had filled the air.

So in the end she had chucked her brush into the brown soapy water in the bucket and walked through the lemon grove to the boathouse bar, where she had snuck herself a corner table in the shade to avoid being spotted by Bruno.

The bar was more relaxed than she'd given it credit for. All around her on the decking were white and blue deckchairs and huge stripy sun umbrellas. Her table was metal with a matching chair and a blue umbrella. There was a foosball table under a huge towering plane tree and a toy car that kids could sit in and ride for a euro. The waiters were the only drawback, all achingly cool with hipster beards and dreadlocks, clearly just there for the summer, and oozing the kind of entitlement only the young millennials could pull off. She'd been sitting there for half an hour and still no one had taken her order.

It reminded of her of New York. Of sitting on her own in cafés trying to kill some time. Of knowing that it didn't matter if no one took her order because she just wanted somewhere to sit, but the lack of order-taking somehow highlighting her aloneness. She was unnoticeable.

Thinking of New York made her think back to earlier, with Libby asking Miles about Flo. It made her think about the email invite from Miles to his and Flo's wedding at The Plaza. How he'd added a postscript to say that they didn't have to come, that he knew the flights were expensive. Jessica had presumed that was the get-out clause. That none of them were going to go and would just wait for the photographs. She knew Eve wouldn't go; she'd just had twins. Jimmy was off somewhere round the world. Jake was a junior doctor so had no money and no time, and Libby, trying to build her catering business, had even less of both. Jessica was in a fairly crap design agency job, broke, and certainly not going to go out of her way to watch Miles marry Flo. It was only Dex who'd championed the trip; who'd emailed them all asking how long they were all going to stay in the States and should they plan some sort of road trip. When he was met with a string of Reply All rebuffs he'd taken matters into his own hands and bought them all, except Eve, return tickets to New York. Accommodation, he'd said, was no matter, his parents had a place overlooking Central Park.

'You've been waiting long to be served?' Bruno's voice broke Jessica's concentration.

'Oh, Jesus Christ, you gave me a shock.' She had to put her hand on her chest to steady her heart.

Bruno stood back, both hands in the air. 'I am sorry. Sorry.' Then he laughed and summoned one of the waiters. 'Why haven't you got her a drink?' he asked the young hipster who said something back in Italian and was given a long rebuke before Bruno turned back to Jessica and said, 'What can he get you, my darling?'

She wasn't sure. She'd waited so long that now she had no idea. 'Just a water. A sparkling water, thanks.'

Bruno beckoned for the waiter to go and sort it out quick smart and then pulled up a chair at Jessica's table, sitting back, ankle crossed over his knee, familiar knowing smile on his face. 'You look very serious. Far too serious for someone who is on holiday. You looked…' He seemed to play around in his head for the word, then said, 'British.' He laughed.

Jessica raised a brow. 'And you're seeming very… Italian,' she said, looking him up and down as if to question why he was sitting at her table.

A smile stretched over Bruno's face. Jessica turned away and looked out at the lake. The waiter came over with her water, placed it down delicately on a coaster, and then sloped off, all the while under Bruno's scrutiny. After a moment's silence as Jessica stirred her water with the straw, Bruno said, 'Do you want to go on my boat?'

'No.' Jessica shook her head.

Bruno laughed, unfazed, clearly very much enjoying his time sitting with Jessica if the big smile on his face was anything to go by. Jessica had been quite keen for him to leave but, as she turned to look at him, one aloof brow arched, she was now having to stop herself from cracking even the merest hint of a smile. His grinning amusement was infectious. She bit the insides of her mouth as she turned away, looking out at the lake again, which, knowing he was sitting there watching her every move, suddenly seemed sharper in her eyes. The whiteness of the parasols seemed more blinding; the hiss of the cicadas more incessant; the clinking of the ice in her drink almost ear-splitting.

'Do you want a game of foosball?' he persevered, angling his head towards the battered wooden mini-football table in the corner by the bar.

Jessica found herself laughing. 'No,' she said, with a shake of her head.

'You can't play?'

'Oh, yeah, I can play, I just don't fancy it now,' she said, taking another sip of water, the bubbles fizzing and popping on the surface.

'You are worried you'll lose?' he said, leaning forward so his arms were crossed on the table.

She closed her eyes and shook her head, as if his childish reverse psychology was beneath her. She was torn between wanting him to give up and leave and thinking she might miss him if he was gone.

He shrugged. 'Suit yourself,' he said, and was just pushing back his chair to stand up when Jimmy and Eve appeared at the table.

'Don't leave on our account,' Jimmy said, looking inquisitively between the pair of them.

But Bruno stood back and gestured for one of them to take his chair. 'No, I'm going,' he said. 'The lovely Jessica cannot be convinced to play at the table.' He nodded towards the foosball.

'Really?' Jimmy frowned. 'I'll play.'

Bruno cocked his head, semi-interested.

'Eve, do you want to play?' Jimmy asked. Then he turned to Bruno and said, 'Sorry, I didn't catch your name.'

'Bruno. This is my bar.'

'Very nice,' said Jimmy. 'I'm jealous.' Bruno shrugged as if he wasn't surprised.

Eve meanwhile was looking at Jessica, clearly wondering what had been going on between the two of them before they turned up, and when Jessica wouldn't catch her eye, said, 'Why not? I'll play.' And then with a teasing little tap on Jessica's shoulder added, 'If you play we can have two teams.'

Jessica rolled her eyes. Eve was always like that, always up for the next thing, for anything that caused a bit of mischief. She'd been the one small enough to climb through the boys' bathroom window directly above Jessica's bedroom and tap on the window with a ruler, convincing her she was being haunted. She'd been the one to make them hitchhike to the South of France and camp for a week on the beach. She'd always been the one that needled them all, pushed them out of their comfort zones. But when Jimmy had left it seemed to take the edge off Eve's verve. She had been more than happy for Flo to move in and pick up the mantle.

It was the sliver of familiarity in Eve's playful goading that made Jessica push back her chair and stand up, trying to ignore Bruno's satisfied smile. 'Boys against girls,' she said, determined not to give him any more encouragement by partnering with him.

'If you want,' Jimmy said, striding towards the table. 'Except you'll probably lose.'

'Why would we lose?' Jessica said, marching towards the opposite side of the table to Jimmy. 'Because we're girls?'

'You're always so easy to wind up,' Jimmy said, laughing, pouring a couple of euros into the slot so the little white ball dropped into the hole at the side of the table.

Jessica glared at him. She heard Bruno chuckle as he took his place next to Jimmy.

Eve stood next to Jessica. 'I'm not very good at this, Jessica,' she whispered.

'Just guard the goal,' Jessica replied. 'I'll do the rest.'

When Dex and Jessica had moved into their first office space, a big draughty room that had once been an old hat factory, Dex had been so excited by the huge expanse of empty wooden floor he had gone out and bought a table football game, a basketball hoop, a pinball machine, Lego, and loads of multi-coloured beanbags. He'd read somewhere that it was all meant to encourage creative play and free imagination. Except, gradually, as they employed more people and the company grew to what it was today, all the creative paraphernalia just got on people's nerves. The noise of the basketball bouncing was so annoying it had had been locked in a cupboard; the beanbags were too squishy and made people feel stupid as they tried to hold serious meetings; the Lego was ignored from the moment Dex strode through the office in a foul mood one day, saw an assistant building a tower, and said, 'Working hard I see,'; the pinball was disabled because the banging was too loud; but the table football, which lived in the kitchen area, was such a success they had set up a league. It had been topped two years in a row by Jessica and a guy in web design called Karl. By chance, as she waited for the microwave to heat up her soup one day, Jessica had found it to be one of the most brilliant cures for stress and, from then on, if she ever had a problem that she couldn't fix, a couple of rounds with her little blue-shirted players and without fail she had a solution.

Three games later in the bar and Jimmy was beginning to realise that girls against boys wasn't such a good idea after all.

'What? What? That was a foul!' Jimmy slammed his bar of players hard into the table.

'You can't foul, it's table football,' Jessica scoffed.

'You were spinning. You're not allowed to spin them.'

'I wasn't spinning, Jimmy, I was just moving them really quickly,' Jessica said with a look of pity in Jimmy's direction.

'It was spinning.'

Bruno coughed. 'I actually don't think it was. I was watching and it wasn't spinning.'

Jimmy gave a big sigh. 'This is a farce.'

Jessica made a face. 'Just because you're losing.'

Jimmy didn't reply but sulked his way through one more game before saying, 'I think I'm going to get a drink.'

Jessica licked her lips. Her eyes met Bruno's across the table and his were alight with laughter.

Eve stood back as well. 'I don't think I've got any better,' she said, then looked out at the lake, the water glistening in the sunshine, and added, 'I wish I could go for a swim.'

'There are towels for guests in the beach house,' Bruno said, pointing towards the white wooden hut midway down the jetty.

'Oh, really?' Eve looked to where he was pointing. 'That's a really clever idea.' Then she paused. 'But I don't have a swimming costume on.'

Bruno shrugged. 'So go naked.'

Eve snorted with surprise. Then said in a half whisper, 'I can't go naked. People might see.'

'So?' Bruno looked unperturbed.

Eve giggled.

The wind blew, gently rustling the leaves of the plane tree overhead, and rays of sun dappled the shade of the table.

Jimmy came back from the bar. 'What are you talking about?'

'Bruno is trying to convince Eve to swim naked,' Jessica said, leaning against the handles of her foosball players.

'I'm game,' Jimmy said.

'I'm not sure.' Eve shook her head.

'You don't have to swim at the end of the jetty. There is a lovely spot just up the path. Very private,' Bruno added.

Jessica glanced to where he was pointing.

'You want to swim?' Bruno said, and Jessica realised he was talking to her.

'Me? Oh no. There's no way I'm swimming naked.'

'Oh, come on,' Jimmy chivvied, still clearly riled by Jessica's foosball win. 'Live a little.'

Bruno was already walking round from his side of the table assuming swimming was a *fait accompli*. Jimmy followed him in the direction of the more private part of the beach.

'It could be fun?' said Eve to Jessica, back-stepping out from the shade of the plane tree and into the sun to join the boys.

Jessica shook her head. 'No way.'

'Come on,' Eve said, with a hesitant little shrug. 'I think we'll regret it if we don't.'

'I won't.'

Bruno turned to look at her. 'You are stubborn, aren't you?' he said, narrowing his eyes, trying to get the full measure of her.

'God, yeah, Jessica's always been stubborn,' said Jimmy with a knowing grin.

'I have not.'

'Yes you have. Ask anyone. Ask Miles. He'll agree you're stubborn.' Jimmy was walking backwards and nodded towards the entrance to the bar as he spoke. 'Hey, Miles,' he shouted, and Jessica swung round to see Miles strolling in.

'Yeah?'

'Is Jessica stubborn?'

Miles frowned, trying to work out what he'd walked in on. But Miles didn't have to reply because he was closely followed by Dex, who shouted, 'Of course she bloody is, she's like a mule.'

'A mule?' Bruno looked confused.

'Like a donkey,' Dex clarified.

Bruno laughed. 'A donkey, I like that.'

'I am not like a donkey.'

'So come skinny-dipping,' Jimmy goaded.

'Are we skinny-dipping?' Dex asked. 'Brilliant. I'm in.'

'Miles?' Jimmy asked.

Miles tipped his head to one side, considering. Then said, 'OK,' as if it were no different to going to the bar to get a beer.

'Right then,' said Jimmy, 'Let's go. See you later, Jessica.'

Jessica stood where she was for a second as they all trooped forward towards the olive grove to the left of the bar. Eve next to Jimmy, her blonde hair, pulled into a scruffy ponytail, somehow already brighter and lighter and shinier than it was when she arrived. Dex like a puppy bounding up towards Bruno so he was leading the way. Miles at the back, hands in his pockets, sunglasses on, sauntering with the casual ease of someone at peace with themselves. And Jessica, staying where she was, heart hammering, feeling frustratingly gutless.

It reminded her of the time they all went skiing. Dex and Flo, who'd both skied from practically the moment they were born, threw themselves down the mountain wearing just t-shirts and salopettes and then got absolutely smashed at lunchtime and did it all again. Miles of course was fearless and followed as best he could on his snowboard. Eve, after taking one look and deciding it wasn't the sport for her, drank vin chaud and soaked up the sun all day in a deckchair. Which left Libby and Jessica in the baby class. Libby, a natural competitor, picked it all up fairly quickly, but not Jessica. She stumbled and she fell, unable to get up, one ski lost, impeded by Dex's huge jacket that she'd had to borrow because they'd lost her luggage at the airport. Dex and Flo would come flying past with their ski poles in the air clapping at her attempts to snowplough. For Jessica, it was all very embarrassing and humiliating. But she didn't give up. In the end she made it almost to the top of the mountain and all the way back down again, covered in snow from all her falls, but she got there. And the reason? The words in the back of her mind through it all?

Because Flo can do it.

Now, as they all strolled off together towards the private beach for skinny-dipping, it was only as Jessica watched them disappear into the olive grove that the badgering thought popped into her mind, making her suddenly break into a little trot to catch up. Flo would do it.

LIBBY

Libby knew they had far too much to do to take a break but everyone had been so good, worked so hard—even Dex who'd come up from the terrace to help shift the old carpets downstairs—that when they'd suggested a quick beer down at the boathouse bar to cool off she'd nodded and sent them on their way.

'You coming?' Miles had asked from the doorway.

'Yeah, I'll be there in a bit. I have some blog stuff to do.'

He'd nodded and jogged away down the stairs.

Alone in the shabby, carpet-less bedroom, Libby had got her laptop out to check her blog and YouTube channel, to answer questions on the liquorice biscotti post which had been one of her most successful to date, and that was when she'd seen the massive screed written by the person who'd initially sent her the link about Jake's infidelity, which she had subsequently deleted from her comments. This time, though, they were focusing on Libby, asking who she thought she was—trying to hide details of her marriage from the fans who'd supported her over the years. Making comments about her face, her figure, her manner, and deciding, in the end, that it wasn't a surprise she couldn't keep her husband. Other people had started commenting on the comment—some good, some bad, some plain horrible.

Libby had stared at the screen with her hand over her mouth for what felt like minutes but could only have been a few seconds, because suddenly Dex was standing behind her, having gone to grab his sunglasses from his room, saying, 'What the hell is that?'

'Nothing.'

He bent down to read it all over her shoulder and when she tried to shut the laptop he swiped it from her. 'Libby, this is abuse.'

'It's not abuse. It goes with the territory.'

'You've had this before?' he asked, holding her laptop in one hand and looking across at her.

'No.'

'Well, it doesn't go with the territory then.' He scrolled through and checked the other comments. 'You want me to shut it down?'

'The website? No!' Libby pushed herself up off the bed and tried to take the laptop back but he wouldn't let her.

'Not the website, the comments. I'll disable them now.' He went over to the dresser in the corner and took a seat, checking details on her computer she didn't even know existed. 'I'll do the blog and the YouTube channel.'

'No, Dex, don't, it feels like running away.'

'Lib. It's not running away, it's giving yourself a bit of a break. Shit's gone down. You're allowed a break, you know. And it doesn't have to be forever.'

She covered her face with her hands and exhaled.

'You don't have to carry on like some superwoman,' he added, tapping away, his back to her.

She pinched the bridge of her nose.

Dex glanced over his shoulder. 'Are you going to cry?' he asked.

She shook her head. 'No.'

He nodded. 'You want me to do this?'

She thought how the blog was the one place that had stayed normal throughout all this. How, whatever was going on outside, she could dive in there and be in complete control. The idea of more and more insidious comments seeping into her little haven made her feel like it might capsize the already rocking boat. 'OK. Turn the comments off,' she said, feeling immediately as though she was building herself a bubble, one that she could hide in for the time being, but, at some point soon, it would hit the floor and burst into thin air.

'What's going on?' Miles was in the doorway. 'Dex, you coming?'

Dex turned to look at Libby and she gave him big wide eyes back to make sure he didn't say anything about this. 'Yes, he's coming, he was just sorting something quickly for me. Go,' she said with a big smile at Miles.

Dex got up slowly, looking like he was trying to come up with some reason to force her to come with them.

'And you're sure you're not coming?' said Miles.

'Yeah.' She laughed, looking round at the newly exposed dirty wooden floors. 'I have loads to do.'

Dex looked anxious.

'Honestly, go!' she said, getting up and shooing them out of the door.

She hadn't moved from her spot back on the bed when Giulia appeared ten minutes later with a stack of post, mainly bills.

'You need to pay for this, it's red,' she said, thrusting the electricity bill in Libby's direction.

'OK.' Libby nodded.

'And this, it's red also.'

Libby took the gas bill.

'And this one is quote for the roof.'

'OK.' Libby took the letter.

'And this is the hotel inspector.'

'What inspector?' Libby frowned.

'From the very good website. He comes every year. But every year it is a no.' Giulia shrugged. 'Your aunt, she was always very upset.'

'Oh.' Libby looked down at the envelope with Hidden Gems stamped on the front.

'He could be very important for the business,' Giulia said, tapping the letter in Libby's hand. 'And the shower in room five leaks through the ceiling this morning.'

'Oh god!' Libby put her hands on her head, the cellophane windows of the letters crunching against her hair.

'You want I can call Dino?' Giulia asked, hands on her hips.

Libby looked puzzled. Why would she call their chef? 'Does Dino know a plumber?'

'Dino is plumber, too.'

'Fine.' Libby held up her hands. 'Call Dino. Do whatever you can to fix it,' she said, standing up and following Giulia down the stairs, but, as Giulia turned in the direction of the lobby, Libby dipped out the back door and into the hot, fresh air, tucking the bills into a cubbyhole on her way out.

*

'They went that way.' One of Bruno's achingly cool waiters nodded in the direction of the olive grove when he saw Libby looking confused as she scanned the bar for her friends.

'Oh right, thanks,' she said, unsure as she walked away about both why they would be in the olive grove and why there had been a sly little smile on the waiter's face.

The olive grove was dense and cool. The funnel webs of spiders crisscrossed every pitted groove in the bark of the trees; a sea of black nets carpeted the ground either side of the path to catch the olives but seemingly everything else as well—the leaves, broken twigs, ice cream wrappers, and a couple of old Coke cans. Every step she took hushed the nearest cicadas, like chasing the gold at the end of a rainbow, always a step away. She got to a point in the path that always reminded her of her aunt. One direction led towards a goat farm on the hill but the other wound down to a deserted section of lake that was her aunt's favourite for swimming, just the two of them. Only the locals knew about it because to the casual observer it seemed there was no direct access to the water, except through a rather perilous-looking sliver of rock fall that was littered with debris and big broken tree branches. It was a precarious scrabble down but worth it for the isolated beach where the water lapped gently against the pebbles and the ducks waddled along the shore. There she would lie flat in the water for hours, floating as she stared up at the vast expanse of blue, and her aunt would tell her stories of her debauched trips across Europe in search of antiques and gambling haunts.

She hadn't been back there since they'd moved into the hotel. Something had stopped her taking Jake; perhaps the idea that he'd turn his nose up at the deserted little inlet. Jake liked the wide stretch of white pebbles on the beach directly in front of the hotel where there was always someone to chat to, usually female, and he didn't see the point in trekking to find somewhere different, especially if it was Libby leading the way.

Concluding that Bruno would probably not have led them to a goat farm, Libby stepped off the path and weaved her way through the undergrowth in the direction of the fallen rocks and the beach.

She thought about her aunt managing the hotel alone. The haphazard style, the leaks, the much needed renovations, but still the guests returned year on year, unable to get enough of the food and the eclectic hospitality.

As Libby squeezed her way through the gap between the rocks she remembered a conversation with her aunt when she'd ask what her father was like and she'd said: 'Libby, the thing with me and your dad was that we were so very alike in every possible way but in every possible way we were different. Let me tell you,' she'd said. 'You can't trust us. We're selfish.

We're lousy with money. We're very unkind when we're angry. But the difference is, my dear girl, the difference is that I had no one to look after apart from myself and this pile of bricks. That's the difference.' She'd paused, taken a swig of her gin, and added, 'And I can hold my drink.'

When her dad had died they'd had to prise a bottle of Jack Daniel's out of his hand after rigor mortis set in— that was the myth Libby'd grown up hearing.

As her only blood relation, Libby was adored by her aunt Silvia and, while Libby had loved her back, it was only now, when she too was shouldering the hotel alone, that she wished she had given her more credit, wished she had said congratulations just once, especially as it had been her aunt's skill and praise that had forged Libby's own career path. It was the tutorage—sharp but fair—that she had given Libby as she'd stood next to her in the kitchen, helping create the famous Bolognese or the exquisitely simple truffle oil pasta that brought people from miles around, that had made Libby believe she had a talent worth nurturing. She had said thank you to her aunt, but she hadn't said congratulations, only rolled her eyes at the lack of order.

She stopped thinking about her aunt when she skidded down the short sheer drop, took the final few metres of shingly path, and was met with the sight of Bruno's impressively tanned bottom as he ran down the sand and dived into the water with a splash. Dex was already out swimming, beckoning for the others to get a move on. Eve was hurriedly changing, clutching her clothes close, and, when she was bare, she ran with Jimmy—almost but not quite holding hands—through the shallows and out to join the others. Miles was undressing with an amused confidence, yanking his polo shirt off to reveal an unexpectedly impressive set of sinewy abs.

'Libby!' Dex shouted from the water. 'Take all your clothes off, we're skinny-dipping.'

Libby cringed, regretting what she'd walked into. She was and never had been a naked in public person. She didn't even sleep naked. Jake did.

She reached the shore in exact step with Miles as he ambled towards the water's edge, bare as a button. 'All right, Libby?'

Libby swallowed. 'Fine, thank you.'

He chuckled. 'See you in there,' he said, and then broke into a jog, flinging himself into the crystal clear water with a splash.

Libby turned to see Jessica sitting on a rock. In the sweltering heat she suddenly looked completely overdressed in her shorts and vest.

'Are you not swimming?' Libby asked.

Jessica made a face. 'I am,' she said with an unconvincing nod. 'I'm just not.'

Libby smiled and went and sat next to her. 'You don't have to. I'm not taking my clothes off.'

Jessica sighed. 'I do have to, though. I do because I know otherwise I'll regret it.'

'Really?' Libby frowned. 'It's only swimming.'

'Yeah, but it's being in the moment, isn't it? It's existing. Look at Eve, she's in there.'

'I think at the moment Eve is just doing anything Jimmy's doing.' She stared out at Eve cavorting in the water, splashing around and yelping when she got a dunking.

'What's she playing at?' Jessica said, shielding her eyes from the glare of the sun.

'I think she's just putting off thinking about what's going on at home.'

Jessica turned to look at Libby. 'Is that what you're doing? Always working rather than hanging out with us? I've hardly seen you since we got here.'

'No,' Libby said, laughing, then she sucked in her top lip and stared out at the group splashing about in the water. 'Maybe,' she said after a second or two.

'Are you angry with him?' Jessica asked.

'Who?'

'Jake!'

'Oh right, yeah. Erm.' Most people asked if she was upset, if she'd be OK, they said that he'd come back and it would all get back to normal. The presumption was that he'd just momentarily lost his way. That was the thing about Jake; he was so charming that he'd been forgiven everything all his life.

'I'm angry for what he's made of me. You know? I feel ashamed that I wasn't enough, which I know is stupid and unfeminist, but it's so embarrassing.'

Jessica laughed, soft and comprehending.

'Come on, you two!' Dex shouted from the water. 'Get in here!'

'Do you think anything is going to happen between Eve and Jimmy?' Jessica asked, looking towards where they were racing each other to one of the buoys further out in the lake.

Libby shrugged. 'I hope not.'

Jessica picked up a fallen twig and snapped it a couple of times, then, throwing the pieces onto the sand, she said, 'You can do it without him, you know that, don't you? You don't *have* to be in a relationship.'

Libby had been in a relationship since she was fourteen years old. The longest she'd gone without a boyfriend was two weeks when she'd been dumped just before her A-levels and was revising too hard to get another one. Even when she'd come to the hotel for her summers she would find herself a cool young local or a lazy, fun-loving tourist. Someone, anyone, just so she wasn't on her own.

'I hate being single,' she said to Jessica.

'I know you do. But I promise, it's not that bad. I'm single. Dex is single. We're OK.'

'Dex isn't single. Dex just doesn't settle down. There's always someone on the go.'

Jessica shrugged. 'Not so much nowadays, you know. I'd count him as single.'

'Well, I hate it. It makes me feel lopsided.'

Jessica snorted. 'That's ridiculous.'

'I know,' Libby said, looking out at the water. 'I suppose I've never said it out loud before.' But it was true. Without Jake by her side it felt like there was a hole she was dragging along next to her. Her brain had settled comfortably into being a two. She made decisions as a two. She laughed as a two. She couldn't work out what pace to eat at now she was on her own. She didn't know what was funny on the TV.

Her stock line to herself had always been that she was used to having someone around. She wasn't used to being on her own. But that didn't tally because more often than not, in the event of all that chaos, she had found herself terribly lonely.

'What I don't understand about you,' Jessica said. 'Is that you're always so capable. You're so good at what you do and you soldier on despite whatever anyone thinks. I don't understand why you don't think you can do that on your own.'

She looked at Jessica, all crazy curls and wide-open face, and said, 'It's hard. You're good at being single.'

Jessica laughed. 'No,' she said. 'I'm not. I just think I have a lower tolerance threshold than you.'

Libby pulled her legs up, resting her feet on the rock, and wrapped her arms around her legs. 'You know what I hate is that if he comes back I'm pretty sure I'll take him back.'

'Then you're the stupidest person I've ever met,' said Jessica. And suddenly she pushed herself off the rock, yanked her top off and then her shorts, kicking off her sandals at the same time. Standing in just her underwear she said, 'Now we have to go swimming.'

'Why?' Libby frowned.

'Because we're the fools, Libby.'

Libby was unconvinced.

'We're the watchers. The ones waiting on the side lines. The losers in the story that no one wants to be. You've just admitted that you'd take your idiot husband back after he's publicly shamed you. If that's making *me* want to swim it should certainly make *you* want to. Libby Price,' Jessica said, unhooking her bra, 'take all your clothes off and get in the god damn water. Because I'm not doing this on my own.'

Libby was so shocked that she laughed. Jessica suddenly reminded her of her aunt. She would have made her strip and get in the water, no excuses. Jake on the other hand would have let her stay back, would have been more than happy with her just watching him swim.

She realised then why her aunt would always sigh at the idiot tourist boyfriends that Libby would end up with. Because what she didn't want from Libby was congratulations for how she ran the hotel, she wanted her to be as free and unencumbered as she was. To find herself and have fun while she was about it.

*

They dried off in the heat of the sun, Bruno happily lying completely starkers, giving Dex and Jimmy the confidence to do so too, while Libby, Jessica, and Eve pulled on underwear with awkward haste in order to bask in the warmth. Miles put on boxers and his t-shirt and went climbing across the rocks to explore.

Libby had never felt so invigorated in all her life. She had never done anything quite so out of her comfort zone, ever. She felt refreshed, changed, as though she could cavort in the shallows naked every day for the rest of her life. But was also secretly quite pleased to have her underwear back on.

The sun was hovering like a tennis ball mid-play, wisps of cloud just taking the edge off its afternoon heat. Libby rolled her head to look at them all, lying like seals on the beach, and suddenly wished that they were never going home. There was a comfort and familiarity of having them here that took her back to the safety of the flat. To when everything was just possibility. To the safety of their early twenties when she didn't have to think about things like the frown lines that were starting to stay long after she stopped frowning, trolling internet comments, her bloody biological clock, and whether she could run a hotel on her own. Then she remembered her aunt and thought about her rolling her eyes at her now—a cigarette between her lips, a gin and tonic in her hand, a bathing cap over her sleek silver hair—pointing towards the sun and the sea and telling her to just live in the god damn moment. She'd have waved the cigarette and said something like, 'You could be dead tomorrow and where would all this worrying have got you? Dead, that's where.'

So Libby rolled over towards Eve who was lying on the sand next to her and said, 'What are you thinking about?'

Eve opened one eye. 'I'm thinking about the fact that my back doesn't hurt. Ever since having the twins, when I lie on my back in Pilates it really aches down one side but right now it doesn't hurt at all. Like it's resetting itself.'

'Have you had any time on your own since having your kids?' Jessica asked.

Eve shook her head.

'Wow.'

Eve propped herself up. 'I think most mums don't get any time on their own.'

'Yeah, and I think some do,' said Libby. 'My mum shipped us off every summer. To pretty much every relative we had. I don't think she would have survived otherwise.'

'I don't really have any relatives,' Eve said with a shrug. 'Not ones that would take the kids for more than an hour anyway. My mum and dad are too old now— they couldn't handle them. And I'm not sure they'd want to.'

'What about Peter's side?' Jessica asked, raising herself up so she was resting on her forearms.

'Yeah, his mum has offered but I don't know. She feeds them loads of crap and, well, she's babysat a couple of times and they're always up watching TV when we come home. God knows what would happen if they stayed the night with her.'

'But isn't that the whole point of grandparents?' Libby said, glancing at Jessica for support, who shrugged like she had no idea. 'To let you stay up late and eat crap? When I came to stay here I remember having to remind Aunt Silvia that I was only thirteen. She was plying me with sloe gin and asking me if I fancied any of her friends.'

'I know, I know.' Eve shook her head. 'I think I've got this impression in my head of this really perfect childhood that I want them to have. I want them frolicking in fields, not eating Krispy Kremes and cheese made into straws. The times I frolicked are etched in my memory. I loved frolicking.'

'I've never the heard the word frolic used so often,' Jessica mused. 'I think it's pretty safe to say that I never frolicked.'

Libby frowned at what Eve had said. 'But you didn't frolic all the time, did you? Your parents were pretty temperamental.'

'That's what I'm saying,' Eve replied. 'The moments spent frolicking were the great bits.'

'Well, maybe instead of frolicking, just be a good parent all the time,' said Jessica, but Eve twitched her face as if she'd missed the point.

'Do you frolic quite a lot at the moment?' Libby asked, thinking that actually Jessica had made quite a good point.

'We frolic a fair bit.' Eve nodded, readjusting the pebbles underneath her so she was more comfortable. 'I probably get a bit panicked that we don't frolic enough and that can take the edge off the frolicking. Forced frolicking is less enjoyable.'

'Frolic,' said Jessica. 'It's such a weird word.'

'You know, I could take them,' Libby said, almost before she'd run through the thought in her head.

'The kids?' Eve looked confused.

'Yeah,' Libby said, a bit less confident. 'I mean, they could stay here. Frolic in the lemon grove. You know, if you wanted. Give the two of you a break.'

'Oh, I couldn't ask you to do that, Lib.' Eve shook her head, the expression on her face suggesting the idea was so preposterous it was amusing.

'No, maybe not,' said Libby, feeling foolish for even offering and rolling away to lie on her back again.

Eve sat up on her elbows. The sun seemed to sizzle on the water in the silence before she said, 'Dex looks good doesn't he? Very fit.'

Libby wanted to have a look but her dented pride made her stay facing the other way.

'He's become a jogger,' Jessica said. 'Jogs to work at like seven in the morning.'

'It's paid off,' said Eve.

Libby really wanted to look.

'I can hear you, you know?' Dex called over.

Eve slunk down, embarrassed.

Libby sniggered.

After a couple more seconds' silence, while Eve got her confidence back, Libby heard her say to Jessica, 'Ask Bruno what he's thinking about. I bet it'll be funny.'

'No, you ask him,' said Jessica.

'Bruno?'

'Darling Eve?' he said.

'What are you thinking about?'

'The lovely Ms Jessica,' he said without a moment's hesitation.

Dex guffawed.

Libby sat up to see Jessica's whole body flush crimson at the same time as Miles strolled back from his exploration on the rocks. He smirked, clearly knowing down to the exact molecule how the statement would make Jessica feel.

Libby watched as Jessica rolled onto her tummy so she could bury her head in her folded-up t-shirt. She realised then that Jessica's lack of relationships wasn't to do with a lower tolerance. It was more to do with the six-foot, Ralph Lauren clad bloke suddenly blocking out the sun.

EVE

The skinny-dipping had done what skinny-dipping probably always did. It had broken down the barriers. Cemented the gang. Given them a shared experience of daring and laughter and awkward nakedness. When Libby had suggested cocktails on the Limoncello terrace it had gone without saying that Bruno should join them. Jessica had tried to suggest that maybe he had too much to do at the bar but Bruno was one of them now—a fellow momentary nudist—and he couldn't be brushed aside.

'So you were in the Olympics?' Dex asked, trotting with Jimmy and Miles next to their new hero.

'I was,' Bruno agreed.

'What for?' asked Miles.

'Sailing.'

'You get a medal?' Jimmy asked.

Bruno nodded. 'Seven.'

'Seven!' Jimmy repeated, stunned.

'All gold?' asked Miles

Jessica rolled her eyes.

'The seven are gold,' Bruno said. 'I have two bronze.'

'But those don't count?' Eve asked with a laugh.

Bruno shrugged. 'I like to win.'

Eve watched him glance momentarily to his right to see if Jessica was listening. Jessica however had deliberately turned away to show she wasn't interested and had quickened her pace to catch up with Libby.

'This guy's a hero,' said Dex. 'A bona fide Olympic hero.'

The light was dimming, the clouds starting to gather and cool the evening air. Eve considered that she would quite like a cardigan to throw over her previously sun-warmed shoulders as she watched Libby and Jessica fall into step together. She felt a bit out of kilter with the girls. When she'd been skinny-dipping, she'd watched them on the rock before they ran into the water together. Watched their conversation and the obvious closeness of it and felt a surge of jealousy. She had wanted to know what they were saying, what it was that convinced them both to take the plunge.

She'd have liked to have run in with the two of them; felt their protection either side of her. Striping naked and high-tailing it into the surf two kids down the line wasn't Eve's idea of a jolly time but she had forced herself to do it, spurred on by the image of her young, carefree self, brown as a berry, happily whipping her clothes off whatever the scenario.

Later, when they'd been chatting on the beach, Eve had found herself deliberately being a touch aloof. And yet as soon as she had rejected Libby's offer to look after her kids she had wanted to take it back. The fantasy that at some point in the future it might happen, her children frolicking as she had done in the lemon groves of the Limoncello was a beautiful thought and one that, had she just said thank you to Libby, might have been a giant step to the re-bonding of their friendship. Envy had got the better of her.

She kicked some loose pebbles on the boardwalk and listened to them bounce onto the beach.

That was always the way. She was a grass is greener kind of girl and it drove Peter mad. Someone else's kids were always happier, their house cleaner, their Christmas tree bushier, their dinner parties funnier, their holidays hotter, their lives shinier. She didn't just scroll through Libby's Instagram with envy, she scrolled through everyone's with a green tint in her eye. If someone had made a funny comment she'd go back days later and see how the conversation had developed, sometimes she'd go on the pages of people who had liked other people in the village's photos—getting deeper and deeper into the network of their friends and family—coming up for air amazed that so much time had passed. On Facebook she liked to see how people she went to school with had chosen to decorate their homes, zooming in on the photos of kids baking cakes or painting pictures just so she could see the home furnishings in the background. She wanted to know everything about everyone, almost as if she could then find out where she fit. Where she could rank her own life and see if it was all OK. Because she used to know, she used to get endless validation, when she was the young, angelic blonde with the fairy wings in the field, or the messy-haired boho beauty who had all the boys mesmerised, or the slightly more groomed, pencil skirt wearing exec shooting up the ranks in the office. But now she was tired all the time, and her hair was more beige, and her shoulders were a bit rounded and her back ached. Now she worked from home so didn't strut into the office in a new pair of black leather leggings. Somewhere along the line she had lost her confidence and in turn her ability to judge herself.

Perhaps, she thought as she strolled along, the easing of the pain in her back had nothing whatsoever to do with not hefting the kids about but was actually because of a break from her phone. With no Peter to call or text and limited WiFi away from the hotel she had it on her only for emergencies. She was on an enforced break from her love affair with anything and everything social media. Gone was her obsessive refreshing. And her constant checking.

As she climbed the steps to the terrace, pink-tinged, a touch chilly, and nicely tired, she looked at Jimmy in front of her. His body was lithe and relaxed, his laugh at Bruno's stories loud and echoing. She wondered if a certain portion of his freedom came simply from the fact he didn't own a mobile phone. He was completely free to go off on his boat, uncaring of who was posting what online. Then she tried to imagine him sitting with a cup of tea on the prow of his boat scrolling through a Facebook account while buffeted by the waves, with dolphins gliding past and the sun setting on the horizon, and realised that maybe it was more that even if he did have a phone, he was too busy *doing* things to use it.

'What's everyone drinking?' Libby asked.

'I'll have a beer,' said Dex, pulling out one of the heavy white wrought iron chairs. Miles, Jessica, Bruno, and Jimmy nodded in agreement as they each took their seats, Jessica between Dex and Jimmy, then Miles and Bruno to Dex's right.

Eve said, 'What was it we always used to drink here, Libby?' in an attempt to make up for her shortness with her earlier.

'Negronis.'

'Oh yeah!' Eve nodded her head, about to take the vacant chair next to Bruno. 'Yeah, I'll have one of them.'

Jimmy looked puzzled. 'What's a Negroni?' he said as he pushed out the chair next to him with his foot, nodding for Eve to sit down there instead.

Libby had to think about it for a minute. 'Campari. Vermouth. And gin, I think.'

'Urgh,' said Jessica. 'Campari tastes like earwax.'

Miles snorted a laugh, which made Jessica blush.

Eve nodded. 'There's definitely an earwaxy quality, but I like it.'

'D'you know it's actually made from chinotto,' said Libby. 'There are some trees in the lemon grove— you'll notice them, they're like tiny oranges.' She paused, seemed to be checking if people were listening or not before carrying on. Eve wondered where that habit had come from. Probably from Jake talking over her for years.

'Are they nice?' Eve asked.

Libby seemed almost surprised that someone had been listening, when in fact they'd all been listening.

'Well, kind of. Not really. They can be.' Libby laughed at her own garbling and paused to get her words in order. 'When I came here when I was little we'd soak the fruit in sea water and boil it in syrup because it's too bitter to eat. Stay there, I've got a jar of them inside.' Libby jogged quickly into the bar and came back with a big glass jar crammed full of little round fruits. 'They've been preserved in maraschino. It's how they always used to be eaten,' she said passing the jar round so they could pluck out an orange each. 'Aunt Silvia said they used to say, tough skin, soft heart. Like her, she thought.'

They all took bites, varying from the tentative— Jessica, to the in the mouth whole—Jimmy.

When Bruno had finished he said, 'The chinotto. The Ms Jessica of the fruits.'

They all sniggered. Jessica went bright red.

Dex saved her in his own inimitable style by leaning his elbows on the table and saying, 'I don't understand this whole earwax thing. How do you know what earwax tastes like?'

'Oh, come on!' said Jimmy, sitting back with a laugh. 'You're telling me you've never tasted your own earwax?'

'Absolutely not!' said Dex, aghast. 'Have you?' he said to the rest of the group as a whole.

Jessica shrugged. 'I don't think I've done it on purpose, but I know what it tastes like so I must have done.'

'I have,' said Miles.

'Me, I have,' added Bruno.

'That's disgusting,' said Dex.

'Do it now,' Jimmy goaded.

'No way.'

'Go on.'

'Jimmy.' Dex shook his head, pushing back his chair to stand up as Jimmy grinned up at him. 'I am no longer susceptible to that type of immature pack animal antic. I am a grown man. If I wish to taste my own earwax I will do it in the comfort of my own room, perhaps later this evening when I've gone to bed.'

Eve smiled as she chewed her fingernail.

Jimmy sat back, chuckling.

'Now I'm going to help Ms Libby with the drinks.'

Libby smiled. 'Thank you.'

'You are most welcome.'

As they disappeared into the hotel, Jimmy leant forward and swept the fallen olive leaves off the table before glancing back at Eve. 'Are you cold?' he said, nodding at the goosebumps on her arms.

She shrugged. 'Sort of. I think I caught the sun.'

'You want me to get you a sweater?'

She laughed. 'No. No, it's OK. I'm not that cold.' She paused, and he looked down at the hem of his shorts. 'Thanks, though,' she said and he nodded.

Behind them the sun was hovering over the lake like a nervous swimmer dipping a toe into the water. The swallows and house martins were arching in the sky while the cicadas made the lemon grove hiss.

After a second Jimmy said, 'Hey, I'm sorry about what I said earlier. You know about how I wished you'd come on the cycle. It was a stupid thing to say. Too much sun I think.'

Eve felt unexpectedly crestfallen. She shrugged as if it didn't matter at all.

Jimmy's eyes crinkled up at the sides. 'Don't look like that.' He laughed. 'I'm not saying I didn't mean it, just that I shouldn't have said it. It's the past. No one should try and change that. You might have come, hated your bike, and flown home.' He shrugged. 'Who knows what might have happened?'

'I might have come, loved my bike, and seen the world,' Eve said, then almost without thinking added, 'I might be living on a boat right now.'

Jimmy laughed. 'Maybe.' Then he sat back with his hands behind his head and closed his eyes for a moment. 'It would be a fun life, you and me on a boat. Just the sea for company.'

'And my two children,' said Eve, trying not to think of Peter in all this, at home in the cottage on his own, finally able to finish the *West Wing* boxsets that he'd been trying to get her to watch for the last three years.

Jimmy didn't reply about the children. He just stayed with his eyes shut, the last of the sun flickering over his closed lids.

'So what's your boat lady like? CeeCee?' Eve asked.

'Nice,' said Jimmy. Then he stretched his arms up to the sky and down again.

Eve wanted to ask more about their relationship but the drinks came. Libby with the Negronis—one for her, one for Eve—and Dex with five bottles of beer.

'You had the same,' Eve said, taking her drink from Libby.

Libby shrugged as if it was nothing, when really it was definitely something. 'Yeah, I haven't had one for years.'

Eve smiled around her straw. As did Libby.

Then Jimmy leant over and whispered, 'Hey, do you want to go for a walk? Watch the sun set?'

Eve sat back, her shared Campari moment with Libby over. She tucked her hair behind her ear, then took another sip of her drink as she decided how to reply.

'I, er…' she said, unsure. Then got her phone out of her pocket to see if Peter had texted. Nothing. She put it away again.

'Checking to see if you're allowed?' Jimmy said lightly.

Eve looked at him, brows raised.

He sat back, held his hands up, and said, 'Sorry, that was unfair.'

'Hey, Eve, you liking your earwax?' Dex called across the table.

'Very much,' she said with a laugh. 'Here, try it.' She held out the glass to Dex who took a sip and grimaced.

Jimmy leant over again and whispered, 'Come on, the sun's about to set.'

Eve half turned. She was trying to listen to Dex as well who was gradually getting a taste for the Campari. She met Jimmy's eye. She didn't want to leave because it was fun, but she also really did want to go. To watch the sun set with Jimmy was the kind of thing she wondered about as she lay in bed at home listening to the rain. It was where the grass wasn't just greener, it was lush and dewy and soft like a pillow.

'Let's go,' said Jimmy, nudging her chair. Then he downed his beer and stood up.

Eve got up more tentatively. Conscious of everyone turning to watch.

'Where are you two going?' Jessica asked, eyes narrowed, intrigued by the turn of events.

'To see the sun,' said Jimmy, loping away down the steps.

'Can we come?' Dex asked.

'No,' said Jimmy and taking Eve's hand in his pulled her along behind him.

She turned only briefly to see the faces of the others. Her eye caught Libby's and, expecting to see annoyance, she was surprised to see almost sympathy.

JESSICA

The sky dipped into an inky blue as they chatted on the terrace. Bats fluttered and dived, black butterflies in the night; the sound of the lake rattling the pebbles on the shore drifted into the silence left by the cicadas. The breeze made the air smell of lemons.

Dex and Miles were talking about the design agency.

'Congratulations on the award,' Miles said, leaning forward to clink his beer with Dex's and then stretching a touch further to make Jessica pick up her bottle and do the same.

She met his eye infinitesimally before taking a sip.

'What was it? Agency of the Year? It's really impressive. You'll be opening an office in New York soon,' Miles said, pushing the topic, still leaning forward, clearly trying to get Jessica engaged.

Dex tipped his chair back so he was rocking on the two back legs to give Miles better access to Jessica.

'That's exactly what I keep saying,' said Dex.

Jessica lifted her beer bottle to her lips. 'Maybe,' she said forcing herself to make eye contact again.

Miles nodded, seemingly satisfied, and sat back in his chair.

The conversation moved on to talking about Bruno's bar and the renovations to the once dilapidated boathouse.

Jessica excused herself to go and get a sweater.

'Oh, can you get me one?' Libby asked as she was on the threshold of the hotel. Jessica nodded, wondering if it was a ploy to make sure she came back out.

In her room she went into the bathroom to wash her face. And stayed, bent over, her elbows on the brown tiled surface, water dripping from her nose and chin into the sink as she stared down at the plug hole.

'Come on, Jessica,' she said out loud.

Then she got one of the fluffy white towels and stood with it muffling her face.

She could see them all in New York, walking into Dex's parents' apartment—all gaudy and gold, with floor to ceiling tasselled drapes, a grand piano, and a mural of cherubs painted on the ceiling. Sightseeing down Fifth Avenue. Strolling through Chelsea with take-out coffees and cinnamon buns. Staring at the Statue of Liberty on the Staten Island Ferry. Everything taking them a step closer to the day of the wedding. Miles and Flo's schedule had been so busy that there had been talk of not being able to meet as a group, which made Jessica's heart lurch. Caught between wanting it all to go ahead without her knowing anything about it and the pounding adrenaline that this was her last chance. This was the moment that he might come to his senses. That he might finally *see* her. Prior to the trip Jessica had spent her pittance salary on a whole heap of new clothes. She'd had her hair professionally straightened. She'd bought new make-up. Her brokeness as a result seemed worth it just for this snippet of a chance that now wasn't going to happen.

Then Dex had got a call to say that they could squeeze in a catch up the evening before the big day, meeting at a bar in Soho.

Jessica had looked perfect. Immaculate.

Flo and Miles had turned up looking shattered, Flo in grey tracksuit bottoms and a big, baggy, pale pink jumper, so huge it sloped off her shoulder revealing a honeycomb tan.

'I got so stressed I had to take a holiday to calm down,' she'd laughed when Jake had commented on her colour.

Jessica couldn't work out how Flo managed to do it. How every time Jessica went one way, Flo went the other and, without even trying, outdid her. In contrast to the tracksuit, Jessica felt buttoned up tight in skinny black trousers and a too-revealing green top. Flo's hair messily awry; Jessica's sleek and swept up with a tiny beehive. She wanted to go to the Ladies' and take all the pins out, mess it up, and scrunch it till the curls came back.

'You lot going out after?' asked Miles, clearly noting Jessica's outfit.

'No,' said Jake, 'just chilling at Dex's parents' place. Have you been there? Jesus, it's unbelievable. There's an actual cinema.'

Jessica had stared down at her drink. She'd felt Miles watching.

The drinks had flowed. She'd started to get light-headed, drinking more than usual. She'd heard her voice getting louder. Then a song had come on that she and Miles adored, had lain on his bed for hours listening to it on repeat, over and over. She hadn't heard it for years. She caught his eye and he smiled. He started to sing along softly; she joined in. Not loud, just above a hum. Word for word. Not a song anyone else would know. She loved it; felt her body tingle; felt for one second the familiarity and connection that they had shared for the pre-Flo years. And suddenly she didn't want Miles to notice her get-up and her new look, she just wanted this. A little moment to treasure.

'Oh god, please, no singing. You're so embarrassing,' said Flo, bashing Miles on the arm. 'I can't take him anywhere,' she'd laughed.

Jessica had snapped. 'Why? Why can't you just piss off for a minute?'

The whole table had stared at her, and the one next to them.

Flo had sat back, stunned like she'd been slapped.

'Why do you always have to take everything? You won, for fuck's sake. Why can't you just let us have this one thing? This one little thing? It was nothing to do with you. Just piss off,' she'd said almost shouting, standing up all in a hurry, knocking her drink, trying to get her bag, knowing she was about to cry. Immediately regretting her outburst. Red-faced with brewing embarrassment. 'You won,' she'd said again in a mutter under her breath. 'You sodding won, you stupid cow.' And then she had left, pushing her way past the rubber-necking onlookers on the adjacent table.

The moment she had left the bar she'd hated herself. Shame pooled inside her like honey, sticky and warm and inescapable. She couldn't believe she'd said it; couldn't believe she'd been so mean on the eve of their wedding. Couldn't believe the fury that had been growing inside her, and for what? Had she really expected Miles to jump up and say, 'How could I have been so blind? I choose Jessica.' But that was exactly what she had wanted. And a tiny part of her was holding out the hope of hearing his footsteps on the pavement behind her, ready to grab her arm and spin her round and tell her she was his.

But there had been no sound of footsteps. Just the hiss of car brakes, laughter and chat in snippets from the opening and closing of restaurant doors, her own stupid new high heels clicking on the sidewalk, and the hundred mile an hour thumping of her mortified heart.

Stepping back out on the Limoncello terrace, Jessica chucked Libby a cardigan. 'Is that one OK?' she asked.

Libby nodded as she slipped it on.

'You've been ages,' said Dex.

'No I haven't.' Jessica heard the defensive snap in her voice.

Dex raised a brow.

Miles glanced over, eyes thoughtful as he watched her.

There were more drinks on the table.

'We got you another beer,' said Libby.

'Thanks,' Jessica said, trying her best to soften her voice.

She reached forward to grab the new bottle and unexpectedly caught Bruno's eye. He was watching her with his calm, untroubled self-assurance. A tiny flicker of competition, challenge, in his eyes.

She arched a brow at him in question.

A hidden smile toyed on his lips. He was leaning back, ankle of one leg crossed over his knee, the lines by his eyes as deep as ravines.

The thought popped into her head that he knew nothing about her. Nothing about all of their past together as friends. He was a completely clean slate. In the flicker of the outside light he looked easy, raggedly attractive, uncomplicated.

'You need help tomorrow?' he said to Libby, breaking off eye contact with Jessica to ask the question.

'Oh, definitely.' Libby nodded. 'I always need help at the moment.'

'Then I will help,' he said, taking a swig of beer.

Jessica laughed without even thinking about it. Caught off guard by his decisiveness. No dilly dallying, no maybes or polite are you sures, just exactly what he thought. He turned back to look at her; she could just make out the wink in the darkness. To her surprise it made her want to giggle. It made her feel like there was a bubble of light inside her desperate to float to the surface.

'Anyone fancy a swim?' asked Dex, finishing his beer and smacking it down on the table.

'No chance,' Libby said, her feet tucked up underneath her on her chair, her cardigan wrapped tight around her.

'I'll swim,' said Miles.

'Good man.' Dex clapped and started to stand up.

'You're drunk, you might drown,' said Jessica.

'We're not going to drown. I'm not that pissed.' Dex shook his head. 'And if you're worried you can come and watch.'

Jessica stood up with an unexpected sway, taking her beer with her, quite keen suddenly for an adventure. Anything that kept her fixed in the present.

'You coming, Libby?' Miles asked.

Libby made a face. 'I suppose so. Bruno?'

'I'm going back that way anyway.'

Dex clapped his hands. 'Right then, let's go!'

EVE

Eve let Jimmy lead the way through the lemon grove down to the water's edge. Every step she could smell the chinotto mingling with the lemon.

She paused for a second. 'That's it.' The chinotto was the little kick her fragrance needed.

'What's it? What are you doing?' Jimmy asked at her sudden stop.

'Nothing.' Eve shook her head. 'Nothing,' she said again when he looked at her, curious, so he shrugged and carried on.

Eve followed behind without really thinking about it, her mind filling with a cacophony of smells and scents. She could see the bottle even. It wasn't going to be lemons, they were just a big, blowsy distraction, it was all about this little chinotto and her lovely pine trees.

The tangy bitterness seeped into her as the loose stones and branches crunched underfoot. She was imagining the white box printed with bright little oranges. She was thinking of the colour of it in the bottle—an amber hue to the liquid. She was thinking about marketing—about whether anyone would understand the word chinotto or if she would need 'orange' in there somewhere.

All this she was thinking about instead of thinking about the fact she was walking down to the water's edge with Jimmy.

As a little girl, every time she'd been left alone with the other festival goers or partiers in their group, when her parents went off to do whatever it was they did to be free, she would employ this same technique. She would be able to fill her mind so full with other thoughts that she didn't have to worry about who she was left with and whether they would ever come back. The year they took her to Roskilde Festival in Copenhagen and both spun out for twelve hours on some bad mushrooms, Eve had sat in the tent with the two of them being alternately sick and wildly tripping. As they clawed at giant ants on their legs then laughed at the whiskers sprouting from her cheeks, Eve planned her entire seventh birthday party in her head complete with a possible trip to the petting zoo and a five-tiered Victoria sponge.

Now, as Jimmy had his arm around her shoulders and was pointing to where the last rays of the sinking sun were bouncing off the white boathouse walls, Eve had her entire new fragrance range packaged up and ready for the shelves.

'I've missed having you in my life,' Jimmy said as only a fingernail width of sun was peeking out above the lake. 'I've missed your independence. I liked how we lived side by side. Stupidly, I didn't realise that that doesn't happen a lot—not expecting anything of each other—just being.'

His hand moved from her shoulder down her back, settling on her waist. His fingers felt warm through her t-shirt.

Eve thought about the times she had lain on his bed, the two of them entwined, laughing about their night, acting as mirrors for the other's arrogance and good looks, getting high off their own self-adoration. And they would kiss and touch and fall asleep. Living like two little caterpillars zipped in the same cocoon.

Of course they expected nothing of each other, she thought; they got everything they needed from elsewhere and just poured it into their shared pool. You could do that when you were twenty-one and ravishing.

She wanted to say, 'But you can't do that when you have kids, Jimmy.' You can't do that when you want something more. Some sense of the other person wanting to mesh as well as walk side by side.

The sun was just a whisper now.

She could feel the pressure of his hand on her hip, moving her round so they were face to face.

She had kissed him a hundred times for fun. But she had never stood opposite him and kissed him properly, never as a moment. Never serious.

And this was serious. Suddenly really serious. This was her marriage and her children. This was succumbing to a youthful addiction, acting on a zing of electricity that made her body shiver, stepping into the excitement of a first kiss after kissing the same person for five years, basking in the glow of feeling beautiful again.

His eyes looked almost white in the moonlight.

She thought about what Jimmy was looking for in a person. Had always looked for—no ties, no labels. Criteria so rigid for something that was meant to be so freeing. Was that independence, she wondered, desperately wanting one's other half to comply?

When he stepped forward she could feel the heat of his whole body against her. He smelt the same as he always had. Of skin and soap and the earth.

'Ow, shit!' Jimmy jumped away, bashing at his leg. 'Something's just bitten me. Jesus.' He swiped his hand against his skin, then held it there for a second, recovering from the shock and pain. 'The little shit.'

Eve stayed where she was. Holding in a snigger. She watched as he grimaced, breathed out slowly and then, shaking himself, stood up and said, 'OK, I'm OK now.'

'You think you should see a doctor?' she asked.

'No, no, it's fine,' he said, really serious. 'Just some bug. Probably just a massive mozzie. It's fine. I'm fine.' He stepped closer again; reached forward and took her hand again in his.

An image of Peter's wry half-laugh came into her head. He would have assumed the moment had gone the minute he'd yelped from the insect bite.

Jimmy leant forward to kiss her.

JESSICA

They traipsed through the lemon grove in single file, Dex using his phone as a torch to lead the way, then Miles, Libby, Jessica, and Bruno at the back.

At one point Bruno leant forward and whispered to Jessica, 'Can I ask you again if you want to see my boat?'

Jessica felt a soft smile inside her. 'You can ask me,' she said, glancing over her shoulder. 'I might not answer.'

She couldn't see Bruno's face in the darkness but she could hear the smile in his voice. 'I will ask you. Later,' he said.

'Can anyone see Eve and Jimmy?' Libby asked.

'No,' Dex shouted, up at the front. 'They might be on the beach.'

But when they got to the beach it was deserted. Just the cool navy water lapping against the grey moonlit pebbles.

Dex dipped his toe in. 'Ooh, it's cold.'

Libby took a seat on one of the rocks.

Jessica stood back on the boardwalk and watched as Miles and Dex stripped down to their underwear. Miles turned and placed his folded pile of clothes at Libby's feet saying, 'Guard these with your life.' For the first time Jessica noticed a hint of an American twang to his voice.

Libby laughed. 'Aye aye, sir.'

As she looked from the pile of neatly folded Ralph Lauren chinos and white linen shirt to Miles running into the water, Jessica experienced a strange sense of mounting freedom. It was as if she had been clutching something tight in her hand for years without realising and was finally beginning to let her fingers unfurl.

She realised that he had been looking, always, for someone like Flo, someone who would give him the confidence to go for his dreams—show him new dreams—rather than someone like her who wanted to squirrel them away in a dark room and exist in their own little world away from the real one.

She looked at Dex powering through the water, front crawl; she thought about their big glass Agency of the Year Award.

It had taken Dex no more than fifteen minutes to find her in New York. She'd walked in a straight line from the Soho bar, sniffing back snot and tears and wishing that she wasn't wearing new boots because to make it all worse she now had big blisters on her heels.

'Wait, wait, wait,' he'd said, putting his hands on her shoulders.

'Go away, Dex.'

'Yeah right, like I'm going to go away and leave you walking the streets of New York on your own.'

She'd carried on walking. It was cold. Her coat was too flimsy. She'd wiped her face with her sleeve. Dex had fallen into step next to her and handed her a tissue.

'Well, you certainly told Flo, didn't you?' he said after a few minutes' silence.

'Shut up, it was awful. I was horrible. I'm such an idiot.'

'Nah, don't worry about it.'

She'd stopped walking and given him a look.

He shrugged. 'OK, worry about it a bit, but, come on, it's Flo. She can take it.'

Jessica started up again, the blisters on her feet burning. 'I've never done anything like that. I've never said anything like that to anyone. I feel shit. I don't know what to do. I can't go to the wedding.'

'Sure you can.'

She shook her head. 'No way.'

Then, when they reached an intersection and had to wait for the lights to change, she had suddenly covered her face with her hands and stepped back into the shadow of a doorway and cried.

It had taken Dex quite by shock; he was halfway across the road before he realised she wasn't with him and he jogged back and wrapped his arms around her in a hug that smelt of Hugo Boss and warm wool.

She closed her eyes and sobbed into her hands pressed against his jumper.

'Oh god, Dex, why am I such an idiot? I got all dressed up. I'm such an idiot.'

'Don't beat yourself up,' he said with a laugh. 'I think you look beautiful.'

'You do?' She looked up at him all twinkling, vibrant blue eyes and floppy blond hair, and said, 'Do you think we're going to have sex?'

Dex guffawed, holding her even tighter. 'No,' he said, looking down at her. 'As much as I would love to have sex with you Jessica, a) I can't have sex with someone that I know is in love with one of my best mates, and b) you're my friend and sex will get in the way and I don't really have enough female friends to waste the ones I have got.'

Jessica covered her face again with her hands and sighed. 'And because *you're* in love with someone else?'

Dex went silent for a second then frowned. 'How do you know that?'

'I'm very observant,' she said. 'I see you looking at her.'

Dex sighed. 'Well, it'll never be, so…'

'It might be.'

He scoffed. 'It's never going to be. She's taken.'

It had suddenly occurred to Jessica that Dex was living through the exact same anguish that she was, except he was less inclined to make a scene in a New York pub. 'Is that why you don't really date any more?'

'I date.'

'Sleeping with people isn't dating.'

'See, Jessica, that's where you've been going wrong all these years,' he said with a laugh, trying to lighten the tone and change the subject.

'It *is* why you don't date, isn't it? God, I totally hadn't put two and two together,' she said, quite triumphant. 'See, I'm not just a pretty face,' she added with the first laugh since the incident.

Dex raised a brow. 'Right now, honey bunch, I'm afraid you're not even that.'

She gasped and thwacked him on the arm but had then found a mirror in her bag and cringed at the sight of herself, all mascara streaked and blotchy faced.

'Come on, there's a diner up here I love. I'll take you for…' He glanced at his watch. 'An early breakfast.'

Dex had then taken off his coat and draped it over her shoulders and together they walked two blocks to the Waverly Diner, Dex pretending he wasn't freezing in just his shirt. They'd nabbed the last available booth and had eaten grilled cheese sandwiches with pickles and slaw on the side and drunk black coffees in thick white mugs while outside people strutted through the night.

'Why did you come after me?' she asked.

He paused mid-chew, swallowed, and said, 'Pity.' Then he laughed when she covered her face with her hands and added, 'Admiration.'

She snorted into her coffee. 'I'm a disaster. I've just blown my friendship with Miles, insulted his bride…' She paused, ran her hand through her hair, pulling it out of its stupid up-do, then said, 'I don't know what I'm going to do, Dex. I hate my job, I earn no money. I thought I'd be someone, you know? I worked so hard to get to this point and it just feels like I'm nowhere.'

'Are you kidding? You…' Dex put his cup down on the table and stared at her. 'You're brilliant at what you do. You create things. Amazing things. Me—it's me that's nowhere.'

'You're not nowhere,' she scoffed. 'You're rich.'

He raised his brows as if that was verging on agreement with what he'd said.

'I didn't mean it like that. I meant you can do anything you want. You can talk the talk, you're in.'

'Nah.' He shook his head. 'It's all hot air.' A waiter came over to refill their coffees and when he'd gone Dex had added, 'You have *actual* talent.'

Jessica wrapped her hands around her coffee and slumped back against the booth. 'Yeah, but talent's no good if you can't sell yourself.'

'You're very saleable, Jessica.'

She glanced up. 'You think? You think I'm saleable?'

'I could sell you.'

Just then a New Yorker in the booth behind them popped his head over the partition and said, 'So why don't you start a business already? Jesus. I'm trying to enjoy my eggs over here.'

Jessica giggled into her coffee.

Dex cocked his head and said, 'Not a bad shout, mate.'

The New Yorker sat back down with a stream of grumbled muttering.

'How about it, Jessica? You can be in the office creating it, I'll go out and sell it.'

She narrowed her eyes, unsure if he was being serious or not.

Dex had sat forward and held up the napkin for her to see the name of the restaurant printed in black on white. 'Want to start the Waverly Design Agency?'

Now as she watched Dex and Miles splashing around in the pitch black water it occurred to her that the right one had come after her in New York. That she had lost one thing but gained something that before this holiday she wouldn't have realised was better. Through Dex she had found a place in the world where she fit.

She heard the crunch of pebbles underfoot as Bruno came to stand by her side, hands in his pockets. She could feel him watching her and glanced his way. The contours of his face were lit by the moon. His eyes always slightly laughing. His smile knowing. With his wide, broad chest and his knackered old sailing t-shirt he looked dauntless, immune, wicked, encompassing.

He met her eyes. 'You want to come and see my boat?'

She could smell the lemons in the air. See the moon reflected in lines of white on the lapping water. Hear the stillness of the pine forest. Jessica nodded.

One corner of Bruno's mouth tipped up in a smile. He touched her back gently to point her in the direction of the boathouse jetty. 'You are OK here on your own, Libby?' he asked.

Libby, clearly startled by the turn of events, whipped her head round and said, 'Yes, absolutely yes, I'll be fine. Yes. Of course.'

Jessica was hiding a smile as she glanced from Libby to the gleaming moon-white wood of the boardwalk up ahead.

'OK, let's go,' said Bruno, touching her briefly once more on the upper arm and after that just strolling easily by her side.

LIBBY

Libby couldn't sleep. She lay awake thinking about everything she needed to do in the hotel and then remembered the bills she'd stuffed in some random cubbyhole by the bar. She got up and walked tentatively down the corridor in the silent darkness. Passing the other rooms, she wondered who was sleeping in their own bed and who wasn't. She hadn't seen Eve come home, or Jimmy.

Downstairs she turned on a side light and went to retrieve the envelopes, chucking them on the desk in the office before turning off the light and heading back to the stairs.

When a figure blocked her path at the bottom step she almost screamed.

'It's me, it's me, Libby. It's OK.'

As she caught her breath she saw Miles's face start to appear as her eyes adjusted to the darkness.

'What are you doing down here?' she whisper-hissed. 'You almost killed me.'

Miles was half-laughing. 'Sorry. I'm sorry. I had a work call and the reception's crap in my room.'

'Jesus.' Libby had her hand on her chest. 'I'm only just recovering.'

Miles leant back against the wall, smiling as he waited for her to get back to normal.

'I'm OK now,' she said.

'I'm sorry.'

She nodded. There was a pause where everything seemed to heighten, the sound of her breathing, the hum of a fan. Libby was suddenly really aware that she was just in her vest and lacy satin shorts and Miles was wearing only chequered pyjama bottoms.

'OK, shall we go back to bed,' she said, then cringed when she heard what she'd said.

'After you.' He gestured for her to lead the way.

'Thanks,' she said, awkwardly moving to get ahead of him and then conscious of the smallness of her shorts as he strolled behind her.

'You OK?' he asked midway up the stairs. 'Why are you up?'

'I couldn't sleep.'

'Why not?'

'Just general worries,' she said, trying to make it sound light and breezy.

She turned to look back at him over her shoulder when he didn't reply.

Miles was closer than she'd expected.

Libby swallowed.

They reached the landing.

'How are you doing without Jake?' Miles asked.

'OK,' she said.

'He was crazy, you know?' Miles said. 'For doing what he did.'

She tried to shrug it off.

The only light in the corridor was a sliver of moonlight through the edge of the blinds. Otherwise it was black. They were two shadows in darker shadow. She could hear him breathing, could feel the heat of him.

She felt his hand touch her shoulder before she had a chance to say goodnight and walk away down the corridor. This was wrong.

'We can't do this,' Libby said. 'What about Flo?'

Miles shook his head. 'Just...' He paused. 'Just go with it.'

She shook her head at the same time as wondering when the last time she'd been kissed was. The type of kiss that left her reeling, breathless, wide-eyed. She knew Miles would kiss well.

She couldn't remember the last time Jake had kissed her. Kissed her in a way that wasn't just goodnight. That made her feel wanted. Sexy. Enough.

She was still thinking, still procrastinating, still hesitating, when Miles leant forward and kissed her. Kissed her in exactly the way she knew he would kiss her. In a frenzy of clashing teeth, hot lips, and hands in hair.

And suddenly it felt like everything, including their marriages, was from another life and they were in a bubble far, far away. The darkness made it all less real.

He pushed open her bedroom door and backed her in, his arm firm around her waist, his mouth never leaving hers, and then kicked the door shut behind them.

*

Libby hadn't slept so well in months. Years even. She yawned and rolled over and opened her eyes to see Miles, draped in a sheet, snoring softly.

'Oh shit,' she said, slapping her hand over her mouth.

Before she had a chance to do any more there was a loud banging on her bedroom door.

'Ms Price! Ms Price!' Giulia's voice was calling along with the knocking.

Libby, suddenly wide awake, jogged over to the door and, wrapping her robe tight around her, opened it just enough to peer her head out into the corridor. 'Yes,' she said, trying to smooth down her hair as she spoke.

'The hotel inspector is here.'

'What hotel inspector? Oh shit!' Libby covered her mouth with her hand. The door swung open slightly. She saw Giulia catch a glimpse of Miles who was now sitting up in bed, topless. Libby grabbed hold of the door and pulled it half shut again. 'Shit,' she said again. 'Why is he here?'

'I think he has come to inspect,' Giulia said dryly. 'What you want to do?'

Libby scratched her head. 'I don't know, I'm thinking. I can't give him a tour because the rooms look like shit. Oh shit.'

Giulia raised a brow at the swearing. 'You could do your club,' she said.

Libby frowned. Then thought about it. 'I *could* do my club, you're right. OK. Good. You give him coffee and I'll get everyone up. Right. Yes. We can do this,' she said, shutting the door as Giulia disappeared down the stairs to get a coffee for the hotel inspector who, stupidly, she'd envisioned arriving mid-season when they could laugh over biscotti in the lovingly manicured garden and marvel over the light in the freshly painted bedrooms.

'You have to get up,' she said to Miles, frantically gathering up clothes so she could shower and get dressed in the bathroom, not wanting him to see her naked. 'You have to creep out though, I don't want anyone seeing.'

Miles rubbed his eyes. 'What's going on?'

'The hotel inspector's here.'

'What does that mean?' Miles asked, sleepily pulling on his pyjama bottoms.

'That we have to look good, and we don't look good. So we, I, need to wake everyone up and you need to go. Oh my goodness.' Libby put her hand up against her forehead.

'Calm down, Libby. I'm sure it'll be OK. He can't close you down or anything can he?'

'No, he's not that type of inspector but he's from one of the best websites. Oh god, why didn't I open the letter.' She thought about the envelopes chucked casually on her office desk before the kissing frenzy.

'You need my help?' Miles asked.

'Only in ignoring the fact that this...' said Libby, pointing between the two of them, 'ever happened.'

Miles snorted a laugh. 'OK, no problem,' he said, walking over to her, putting his hand behind her neck and kissing the top of her head before strolling casually out of the door. 'I'll help get everyone up.'

*

It was one of those mornings when the world itself seemed to have forgotten to wake up. The air was completely still, the sun's rays suspended like glitter. The leaves of the lemon grove sat waxy and motionless, the water in the distance was a cool sweep of calm blue, even the wasps basked silently in the haze. Overhead the sky was a delicate white wisp, as if someone had got up early and wrapped it in candyfloss.

In contrast, the group slunk outside, puffy eyed and reeking of hangover fumes. Coffee mugs in hand they ambled down the garden path, eyes averted, no one bothering with small talk except Libby who was trying to chirpily chat up the humourless hotel inspector Frank and Dex who was doing his best to help.

'So you've been to the Limoncello before?' Dex asked, strolling along with his coffee.

'Yes,' Frank replied, his disdainful gaze sweeping over the butchered shrubbery. 'I liked the food. And I liked Silvia. But it was not quite right for us.'

Libby nodded. 'Well, I hope you like what we're doing with the place,' she said with a cheerful little laugh.

He paused at the outhouse and looked up. 'I don't like gimmicks.'

'Oh well, the Sunshine and Biscotti Club is definitely not a gimmick,' she said. 'It's about bringing people together through food. Through the shared experience of baking and cooking, chatting outside in the sunshine, learning together. It's an experience.'

As she spoke Libby looked around at the group congregating behind their workstations.

Eve's unbrushed hair fell over her eyes, and her clothes looked like she'd just chucked on whatever had been on the floor when Miles had knocked on her door; Jimmy stood, hands behind his back, barefoot, dressed in black shorts frayed at the knee and an old blue t-shirt, the neck pulled out of shape, chest puffed cockily, eyes not meeting anyone's; Jessica flitted up and down at the back, unsettled, sunglasses on; Dex was doing his best but he couldn't erase the tired, hungover look on his face. Only Bruno stood completely at ease, arms crossed casually over his chest, beaming a smile like the cat who'd got the cream.

Libby cut her gaze short before she got to Miles; this was no time for distractions. Her brain was already compartmentalising, creating a clear distinction between daytime Miles and night-time Miles. The latter, in the light of day, seeming as unreal as a very enjoyable dream.

'OK, so today as you can see we're welcoming Frank King to the group. Hi, Frank,' she said, pulling on her apron, and beaming at him. 'Frank works for the exceptionally popular website Hidden Gems. He's here today to have a look at the Limoncello, and we hope he'll be impressed with all the additions we're making.'

Frank's lip twitched in a half sneer.

'Lovely,' Libby went on. 'Perhaps you'd like to take a seat…' She gestured to a chair by the fireplace. 'And you can observe the Sunshine and Biscotti Club. You know it's an offshoot of the blog and the very successful Rainbows and Roast Beef Supper Clubs that we used to hold in the UK. Always sold out,' she said. 'Always a waiting list.'

Frank nodded, face impassive, then reached down into his bag and got his notebook and pencil out.

Libby was about to go on when she heard Dex call over to her. 'Libby, can you just come here a minute, I think there's something wrong with my bench.'

She frowned. 'What's wrong with your bench?' she said, glaring at him to stop causing trouble.

'I don't know. I need you to come and check.'

She rolled her eyes, then turned to Frank, gave him a big smile and said, 'I'll just be a minute.'

Frank sat back in his chair. 'Take all the time you need,' he drawled.

'What?' she hissed when she got to Dex who was bending down examining his oven.

'Calm down,' he said, opening and shutting the oven door.

'What's wrong with your bench?' she said, annoyed.

'There's nothing wrong with my bench,' he said in a calm whisper. 'I'm just telling you to calm down. You're trying too hard. Take a deep breath and believe in yourself.'

Libby swallowed.

Dex raised his brows, checking that his point had sunk in. 'OK?'

Libby nodded.

'Well, I think that's fixed it,' Dex said, slamming the oven shut and standing up. 'Thank you, Libby.'

'You're welcome, Dex,' she said, straightening herself up, smoothing down her apron, and walking as calmly as she could back up to the front.

'Right,' she said, glancing momentarily at Frank before clearing her throat and saying to the group as confidently as she could, 'Today we're going to think about dessert, but to keep you all on your toes—we're going to throw in a bit of competition.' She looked at Frank and felt herself panic when he didn't seem to be listening, then she caught Dex's eye and he winked, and she made herself take a breath and continue. 'The restaurant is open tonight and we always offer the guests a selection of desserts from the trolley—a much loved tradition of the Limoncello—but usually with a bit of a twist on the classics. So my speciality is a lemon tiramisu cake.'

Frank scribbled something down. She glanced over and lost her concentration.

Dex coughed.

Eve jumped in. 'We tasted that the other night. Delicious.'

Frank glanced up.

'It really was fabulous,' Eve said, nodding effusively in his direction.

Libby silently thanked Eve while scrabbling to pick up the thread of her concentration. 'Yes and, erm, Giulia makes the most delicious Budino al Cioccolato, which is a boozy chocolate pot and our chef, Dino, makes pears baked in marsala, which are sensational.' She exhaled; felt herself start to relax a touch. 'Now what I want to do with the group is for everyone to make their own dessert and the best will go on the dessert trolley and be served to the guests. Judged, I hope, by Frank.' She looked at Frank who glanced up from his notepad and shrugged a shoulder. 'Lovely,' she said. 'So that's exciting isn't it?' She smiled a big wide smile and added, 'It's a competition.'

Jimmy's hand shot up.

'Yes, Jimmy.'

'I don't know how to make a dessert.'

Libby nodded. 'Yes, yes I know that. That's why if you look at your benches you'll find a stack of really simple recipes that create the base of anything you might want to make. So there's a plain sponge, a panna cotta, a really classic torta di nocciole, which is an Italian hazelnut cake, and lots more, so have a flick through. What I want you to do is put your own twist on these traditional recipes. There's loads of ingredients at the back that will hopefully inspire you.' She pointed towards the shelves bursting with produce and then looked to see if Frank had looked up, which he hadn't. 'Or if you want you can take a little stroll round the property, have a smell of the air, a taste of the herbs. You know I make a thyme and lemon cake that came from just being here. There are prickly pears on the cactus out there, you might want to add them to a cheesecake? It's totally up to you.'

Jimmy remained unconvinced. 'It sounds very difficult.'

'I promise, Jimmy, it's not difficult. And I'll be here to help you.'

'I just feel that I'm at an unfair disadvantage. Don't you, Dex?' Jimmy said, a teenage whine to his voice.

'Me?' Dex said, surprised. 'Why are you singling me out?'

'Because you're shit at this too.' Jimmy made a face as if that were obvious.

Libby frowned and made big eyes at him to be nice. Jimmy just shrugged sullenly. She looked over at Eve to see if she thought his behaviour was odd, but Eve didn't look up.

Bruno was rolling his sleeves up. 'Sounds excellent to me,' he said, rubbing his hands ready to begin. Disregarding all the recipes he started pouring flour into a bowl.

Libby's eyes widened. 'Do you know what you're doing, Bruno?'

Dex peered over.

'Oh, yes,' Bruno said. 'I can bake.'

Jessica glanced up, either surprised by the news or impressed, it was hard to tell with her sunglasses on, but then she quickly looked back down again when Bruno turned to see if she had heard.

'OK, well, take ten minutes or so—unless you're Bruno—before you begin to study the recipes. I'm going to be up here making my tiramisu cake so ask me anything at any point that you need help with. I'll wander round as well just to check that all's OK. Any questions now?'

No one said anything; they just shook their heads and started skimming through the stack of laminated recipes.

'Another coffee, Frank?' she asked.

'No, I still have some of this,' Frank said, holding up his cup, a slight hint of mockery in his voice.

Libby went back to her bench and took a moment to perch on her stool and pull herself together. She was beginning to get into the swing of things. Beginning to quite enjoy herself. This felt like the real deal rather than some haphazard practice run.

Then she stole a quick glance at Miles, who was lounging against his bench waiting for the others to pick their ingredients from the back of the room, a touch of amusement to his normally impassive expression, and had a sudden unnerving flash of that same smile as when he'd brushed the strap of her vest off her shoulder. She could feel the warmth of his hand against her bare skin.

Stop it. She shook her head. She wondered if this was how Jake felt with the women he'd met on the internet. Carrying images of them in his head all the time he was here with Libby.

'Jimmy, it's not a supermarket,' she heard Jessica say, and looked up to see Jimmy struggling to stack jars of glacé cherries, candied peel, raisins, lemons, and tubs of ricotta in his arms.

'I'm making something with a lot of ingredients.' He sniffed.

'Yeah, a great big mess.' Dex laughed.

Eve, who'd been watching Jimmy with a small frown on her face, backed away and said, 'I might just pop outside for some ingredients.'

Jimmy glanced up from over his stack of produce.

Libby looked between the two of them. Eve wouldn't meet her eye and, picking up a bowl, she nipped out of the room, messy blonde hair shielding her face.

Outside the sun was burning the grass to white. The cicada inferno hummed in through the open doors. One of the local cats stalked past, its tail curling round the leg of a pink chair.

Libby saw Miles's reflection in the glass and wondered if he would knock on her door tonight. The idea made her stomach tighten. Like she was falling further into chaos.

Dex put his hand up. 'I think I need help,' he said.

'No kidding,' muttered Jimmy.

'What's up?' asked Libby, striding over, pleased to have some distraction.

'I don't know how one separates an egg.'

Libby had to hold in a smile.

'Yeah, you know, I might watch as well,' said Jimmy, with feigned nonchalance.

Bruno paused where he was scooping his cake mix into a tin. 'You boys don't know how to cook?' he asked, surprised.

Dex shook his head. 'Always had a cook.'

Jimmy shrugged.

'Such clichés,' said Bruno with a shake of his head. 'You should be able to do these things. They are life.' He turned back to the mixture he was scooping out. 'Can you chop wood? Can you sew?'

'I can sew.' Jimmy held up a hand. 'I *can* actually sew.'

Bruno nodded. 'It's a start.'

At the back Jessica had paused, her hand on her spoon, and was listening with the hint of a smile on her face.

'Jessica can't cook either,' muttered Dex, clearly on the defensive, unable to cook, sew, or chop wood.

'Jessica?' Bruno turned round, a hint of disappointment in his voice.

'I can cook,' Jessica said, whipping off her sunglasses, expression defensive.

'No, you can't,' Dex scoffed.

'Shut up, Dex.'

'She can't cook,' Dex said to Bruno.

Bruno was watching Jessica as she made a face to suggest Dex had no idea what he was talking about and busied herself melting her chocolate in a saucepan.

'You need a *bain marie*,' Bruno said, nodding towards the pan.

Jessica paused. She looked up to see if anyone else knew what Bruno was talking about. Dex and Jimmy looked clueless.

'You need to melt it over boiling water, otherwise it will burn,' Libby said.

Eve came back in, arms laden with pine cones and branches, the jar of maraschino soaked chinotto, and one of the small fresh little fruits in her hand. 'Can I use this?' she asked, nodding towards the jar.

Libby nodded, wondering quite what she was going to do with all the other stuff.

'Thanks,' Eve said, tumbling her wares down on her bench.

In the corner, Frank's interest was piqued.

Jimmy's eyes had followed Eve into the room like the Mona Lisa. 'You cooking up pine?' he asked.

Eve shrugged, pushing her hair out of her eyes. 'I'm thinking about it.'

Libby got the impression this was the first time they'd spoken all morning. She itched to know what had happened between them on their sunset stroll.

'Libby.' Dex's hand shot up again. 'What's self-raising flour and do we have any?'

Bruno stood up from where he was kneeling in front of his oven watching his cake rise. 'Dex, man, you know nothing.'

Dex held his hands wide, guilty as charged.

Libby liked Bruno. He had an air about him, a command that seemed to allow him to rise above normal conventions; to get away with wearing too tight twenty-year-old t-shirts and driving a big motorbike dressed in just an old war helmet, leather gloves, and his swimming shorts. To saunter with a self-confidence that without question he was the sexiest man alive. To give off an aura that he'd eat you alive in bed. He could pull it off simply because he didn't seem to care.

Libby cared too much, she knew she did. Cared not only what her friends thought of her, but what her public thought. She spent her life second guessing, smoothing over, worrying. That was why it had been so surprising she'd let anything happen with Miles. What about Flo? What if Jessica had seen them? What if Jake somehow found out? Yet lying together she had experienced the calmest sleep and it had felt like an obvious solution. Not for the long term, but for the now. As if someone had said, 'Here, this will help,' like handing her a cup of tea and a chocolate digestive.

Outside on the small outhouse patio Eve had set fire to her pine, catching the smoke in the now empty chinotto and maraschino glass jar. A woody, sweet, sticky smell infused the air along with the crackle of the branch as it almost refused to burn, its yellow sap dripping as it smoked.

Frank had gone over to watch in the doorway. 'What are you doing?' he asked.

Eve looked up and smiled at him, her hair now held back from her face with a makeshift tea towel bandana, her cheeks pink from the heat, her first smile of the day on her lips. 'I have no idea,' she said, and went back to trying to bottle the pine smoke.

Libby watched. When the jar was full Eve slid the lid on, the remains of the maraschino and chinotto dripping down the insides like a witch's brew. Carrying it carefully back to her work surface, Eve flicked on the kettle and then started to chop up the remaining unburnt pine needles. With the water boiled she made what looked to Libby like pine needle tea.

'This is unfair,' said Dex. 'Eve does things like this for work. She's got a flavour advantage.'

Jimmy paused in his dicing of candied orange peel. 'She does? You do?' he said, looking across at Eve. 'What's this got to do with your work? I thought you worked in marketing?'

Everyone in the room paused. All except Bruno who was filling another cake tin with a new mixture.

Dex was sporting an expression of stunned amusement. Jessica half laughed, half scoffed, almost as if it was to be expected. 'That's what happens if you only think about yourself, Jimmy,' she said.

Jimmy glared at her.

Jessica slipped her sunglasses back on and returned to her whisking with a smile twitching on her lips.

Frank was sitting back in his chair and glanced up from his notebook.

'I make perfume, Jimmy,' Eve said after a second or two, her expression seeming lighter, freer, as if it had just dawned on her that she had moved on from the Eve she was when she knew Jimmy. 'I started the business after I had the kids.'

'Oh.' Jimmy didn't look up from his chopping. 'I didn't know that.'

'I thought you did,' she said.

'Well I didn't,' he replied sulkily as if it were somehow as much her fault as his.

Libby thought she might have seen the corner of Eve's mouth quirk, as if the conversation had been with one of her kids.

Frank beckoned Libby over. 'Do I know the perfume?'

'Probably.' Libby nodded. '*Eve, With Love*. The logo's white and yellow.'

'I might have heard of it,' Frank said, narrowing his eyes, thinking, then he added, 'I like this,' he waved his hand at Eve's bench, 'creative freedom. Very nice. Could anyone do this?'

Libby nodded. 'Of course.'

Frank shrugged. 'I was expecting more of a school cookery lesson. More regimented,' he said. 'But this is interesting.'

Libby felt both a sudden wash of pride for Eve and an annoyance at her own orderliness as she went back to her bench. She spent the next few minutes vaguely concentrating on her lemon tiramisu cake but mostly watching Eve.

Her fragrance business had begun after their friendship had begun to fizzle. Libby had liked the odd Instagram photo showing the bottles on shop shelves, but she'd never appreciated what a success Eve had made.

Now as she watched her mid-creation, she noticed how Eve seemed to come back to life as she worked. The vibrancy made her hair shine, the concentration relaxed her face, her shoulders seemed to soften—she looked fresher, younger, cleverer.

Libby had harboured a fear when she'd seen her outside burning the pine that this new energy had come as a result of kissing Jimmy but now, after their exchange, she wasn't so sure. It seemed instead to come from an innate confidence as a direct result of Eve's work. She saw on her face how Libby herself felt when she was in the middle of a new recipe. Running on instinct. She wondered if she looked equally relaxed.

Eve mixed the few precious drops yielded from trying to squeeze the hard little fresh chinotto with a splash of the maraschino preserving juice and wafer thin slices of the marinated chinotto fruit. Then she pummelled the mixture with the end of a rolling pin like a cocktail waiter, squashing out all the flavours, before sieving the juice into a bowl. She took the tiniest sip of the pine needle tea for a taste and added a slosh to the mixture. After another taste she frowned, glanced up, and caught Libby watching.

'All good?' Libby asked, trying to pretend she hadn't been staring. Jimmy was doing the same.

'It's missing something,' Eve said. 'An earthiness.'

'Mud?' said Dex.

'Very helpful,' Eve replied.

'Figs?' said Libby.

'Maybe. But none of them are ripe yet.' Eve was unconvinced.

Then Bruno walked over to her bench and picked up the bowl of chinotto, maraschino and pine and gave it a sniff. He paused for a moment, seemingly rolling the smell over in his mind before saying, 'Cherry.'

'Cherry!' said Eve, smacking her palm down on the table. 'Of course, cherry.'

'There's a tree out there. Come, I'll help you,' Bruno said, ushering Eve forward.

At the back of the room, Jessica laid her spoon down on the table and, as Eve and Bruno walked outside, came round and had a sniff of Eve's mixture. She stood, seemingly trying to determine whether Bruno was some kind of maverick or just said things with the right amount of confidence to make people believe him. Jimmy came over for a sniff as well and when he did Dex nipped round to have a peer in Jimmy's bowl.

'Oi, get back to your own bench,' said Jimmy, dashing back to cover his bowl protectively with his arm as if it was a school test.

'I'm not copying you, don't panic,' Dex snorted.

'Well, stop nosing around my bench then,' Jimmy replied.

Dex raised both brows in a look of complete derision and went back to his own dubious creation.

'Miles, what are you making?' he called over Jimmy's head.

'New York cheesecake,' Miles said, glancing over his shoulder. 'And it'll taste better than whatever you're making, believe me.'

Dex laughed. 'I don't think so, mate, mine's looking pre-tty good.'

Miles huffed a laugh as if that was complete nonsense.

The room had started to get stuffy. Condensation was steaming up the windows; the ovens were pumping out heat; the fridges were humming. The air was thick with the smell of chocolate and sugar and pine smoke.

Bruno's oven timer bleeped and Dex, Miles, and Jimmy exchanged a look before Jimmy sidled over and turned it off.

Libby looked up from the cream she was whipping. 'What are you doing? You can't turn it off without telling him.'

'It's his cake,' said Jimmy with a sly grin. 'He should be on top of it.'

'Oh for goodness' sake,' Libby sighed. 'You're such babies.'

As she walked over to the door and called out, 'Bruno, your cake's ready,' all the boys were sniggering together, and it felt suddenly like old times.

Whatever messes they were making individually, as a group they were wrapped once again in the blanket of familiarity, stupid jokes, and the easy laughs of camaraderie.

*

As Bruno jogged in eating a cherry to pull an exquisite smelling chocolate cake out of the oven, Jimmy, Miles, and Dex exchanged a sigh. There followed a period of about ten minutes when Libby thought it was all going to play out beautifully. The group were diligently working away, the element of competition pushing all thoughts of hangovers out of the way, Bruno was creating bake after bake, Dex and Jimmy seemed engrossed, and her own lemon tiramisu cake was shaping up perfectly.

But then Frank stood up from his chair and went for a little stroll between the benches. He sniffed Eve's mixture, dipped his little finger in Miles's, peered at

Jessica's, and then stopped up short at Dex's and said, 'Ms Price, I believe you might have a problem.'

Libby winced and hurried over at the same time as Dex who'd been outside having a cup of tea.

'Admiring my mixture?' Dex said as he strode over. 'Oh shit,' he added, as he stared down into the bubbling inferno that was meant to be his cake. There was then an explosion in his oven that made Eve yelp, and they all crouched down to see what looked like a volcano in his cake tin.

'What did you do?' Libby asked, tentatively opening the oven door.

'Well, I wanted it to rise,' Dex said, sheepishly trying to put the lids back on empty baking soda and baking powder pots.

'You put the whole lot in?' Libby frowned, holding the volcano cake at arm's length. 'And the lemons?' she said.

Dex nodded.

'Dex, it's all reacting with the acid. Oh god, and it's still going.'

They all gathered round to watch the mixture in Dex's bowl frothing out like *The Little Shop of Horrors*.

'You take that, I'll take this,' Libby said, chivvying him on. 'Let's get it outside.'

On the grass the concoction continued to spew forth in the burning heat, the volcano cake sitting on the little patio like a school science experiment. Poor Dex stayed outside, looking forlornly at his ruined masterpiece.

Miles was next out of the running; the cream cheese of his cheesecake was overbeaten and inedible. Frank was suitably unimpressed.

Then it was Jessica's turn. 'Libby, I think something might have gone a bit wrong back here,' she said, biting down on her thumbnail.

Libby momentarily squeezed her eyes shut as Frank led the way, now seemingly enjoying this cacophony of disasters.

'She's put the grill on,' said Frank, getting to the ruined cake first.

'Oh no, did I?' Jessica covered her flushed cheeks with her hands. 'How stupid.'

'That's OK, that's OK.' Libby tried to usher Frank out of the way, riled by his complete lack of tact. 'It's OK. It's fine to make mistakes, that's what this is all about. We'll reset the oven and just slice this burnt bit off the top. Then you can cook it again.'

'But it's completely flat,' said Jessica.

'So whip up some cream, pick some cherries, and we'll turn it into a flan.'

Frank peered over, intrigued, as Libby helped Jessica attempt to rescue the cake. And when they'd made the best of what they had, Jessica was clearly delighted. 'I've never made anything before really,' she said, staring proudly at her flat, cherry covered cake flan. 'It's OK, isn't it?' she said to Frank, who had to concede that it wasn't a complete write off.

Things picked up with Bruno's triple-layered chocolate Italian cream cake that glistened with thick creamy icing and was liberally sprinkled with pecans and coconut. Bruno's chest was puffed out like a preening lion as he cut Frank a slice.

'Looks very nice,' said Frank, the compliment prised from his mouth. 'A good texture,' he added after a forkful. 'Very pleasant.'

But pleasant wasn't what Bruno was looking for and, pulling the cake swiftly away from where Frank was standing said, 'I think it is excellent. What is wrong with it?'

Frank, a little startled, said, 'Nothing—it's good.'

'Well,' said Bruno, crossing his arms over his chest. 'Say it is good, yes? Better say it is excellent.'

Libby cut in before either of them could say any more. 'OK, let's move on to Jimmy. Thank you, Bruno—a very good cake,' she said, and Bruno said something in Italian that obviously wasn't positive. 'Right, Jimmy, are you ready?'

'Am I ready?' said Jimmy cockily, and brought out a four-tiered creation that he'd put together in secret underneath his bench while sitting cross-legged on the floor.

Libby had to cover her mouth when she saw it in an attempt to hide an unexpected snigger.

'Christ, Jimmy, that's an eyesore,' shouted Dex from the garden, standing up to come in and have a look.

'You're just jealous,' scoffed Jimmy, proudly displaying his cake, each tier vibrantly dyed with half a bottle of food colouring so it looked like a traffic light. The top tier he'd cut to resemble the hotel, with little marzipan shutters on wonkily carved out windows, and big lumps of green icing had been plonked around the tiers to look like trees.

Jessica came round to have a look. 'Well, I mean, you've got to get marks for effort.'

'What's wrong with it?' Jimmy asked, clueless as to the extent of his monstrosity.

'Nothing, Jimmy.' Libby shook her head. 'It's a triumph.'

Frank cut a massive slice, knocking one of the lumpen trees to the floor, and tasted a forkful. 'It's…' he paused, 'interesting.'

Jimmy gave a whoop, taking that as confirmation of his genius, and said, 'Your guests will love it, Libby.'

There was no chance the iced monstrosity was going on Libby's dessert trolley, she'd make sure Bruno beat him even if she had to prise his chocolate cake out of his disgruntled arms, but then Eve's oven timer pinged and they all turned to look as she brought out an ugly brown wrinkly fruit cake.

Jimmy chortled.

'Well, it's not going to win on looks, is it?' said Eve, staring deprecatingly down at her cooling bake.

'Let's taste it,' said Libby, and cut out a wedge that she split into three for her, Frank, and Eve.

Frank ate his first, nibbling like a mouse then almost immediately stuffing the whole chunk into his mouth.

As Libby took a bite she watched as Frank closed his eyes and stood stock still as though the world had paused on its axis. He barely looked like he was breathing and when he opened his eyes again he seemed to have momentarily forgotten where he was.

Then the flavour hit Libby and she was no longer able to look at anyone, just savour the soft, buttery warmth of the maraschino and chinotto, as she felt herself walking through pine forests in the morning sun. 'It's incredible,' she whispered.

'It is?' said Eve.

'It is,' said Frank, instinctively reaching forward for another bite, all his bravado gone.

Suddenly everyone was clamouring for a taste of her cake, except poor Jimmy who was trying to prop up his increasingly lopsided cake hotel.

'I would never have done that if it wasn't for this club.' Eve laughed. 'I haven't made anything in months.'

Libby looked over at her, flanked by Dex and Miles as they congratulated her on her brilliant bake, radiant, grinning just like old Eve, only better.

Frank stood back to write something down in his notebook and Eve said, 'I'm serious, you know? I literally haven't had the head space to create a thing. And I'll admit, I was sceptical, I never for one minute thought that I'd achieve it here, but there's something about it.' She glanced around the room. 'Something about this place gets into your soul.'

Libby listened, watching Frank nod intrigued, wishing she could believe what Eve was saying but unable to quite trust that it wasn't just part of a helpful PR campaign.

The judging complete, Eve victorious, they wrapped a slice of her cake up for Frank to take with him in his briefcase and then all went with him as he headed back up the garden path. His haughty veneer lessened as Dex made him smell the lemon scented air and admire the newly scrubbed terrace. Jessica pointed lovingly towards the pool area, Jimmy talked about his plans for the garden, and Eve continued to rave about how inspired she was, to the point that Libby was forced just to listen at the back.

Half of it, she knew, was egged up in an attempt to secure the hotel a place in the guide, but their enthusiasm was starting to conjure a sense of pride in her for the Limoncello that she hadn't experienced until now.

'I like what you're doing,' Frank said when they reached the lobby. 'Enough to come back when the renovations are complete.'

'Oh, that would be fantastic,' said Libby.

'Let me just say though, our customers demand something special in the places they stay. You have created that in the club, but my concern is that in here you're lacking the personal touches. What I always did like about the Limoncello was that it had something, dare I say, eclectic in its style. I assume these…' Frank pointed up at Jake's halogen spotlights, 'won't be here when I come again?'

She heard Eve stifle a snigger.

Libby nodded. 'No, absolutely not.'

'Good,' he said, sauntering towards the door. 'Otherwise I'd say you're on the right track.'

JESSICA

Jessica was quite relieved to be able to escape back to her pool patio area. Hiding from the sun in a sliver of shade from the olive trees, she was scrubbing the mildewed sunshade canvases. Already her fingers were like prunes from the soap suds. Watching the white come through the dirt as she scrubbed was like therapy. She kept thinking about her night with Bruno. How he'd held her hand as she stepped onto his boat. How he'd asked if she wanted to go swimming in the remains of the old boathouse. How she'd looked at him like he was mad, but he'd pulled his top off and dived in so she followed. Ducking under the cool black water to bypass the iron grates, she'd surfaced inside a cavernous, echoey old chamber, the reeds swirling like feathers round her body, the light flickering on old broken boats half exposed in the water, and the echo of wings fluttering.

'This is spooky,' she said.

'Spooky?' Bruno asked.

'Weird,' she said. 'Bit frightening.'

'You're frightened. Of me?' he said, swimming over, confused.

'No of ghosts and stuff.'

He laughed. 'You believe in ghosts?'

'It's hard not to in here,' she said, glancing up at the looming shadows.

'There's no such thing as ghosts,' he said, swimming away to the darkest, blackest part of the boathouse. 'Just the imagination. Fear playing tricks. Come over here.'

'No way.' Jessica clung tight to the side.

'Come on,' he called, a voice in the nothingness.

'No.'

He'd gone silent.

'Are you still there?' she asked.

He laughed.

A cloud drew over the moon dimming the last of the light.

She felt her heart thumping in her chest.

'What are you afraid of?' he called.

Letting go.

'Swimming into the dark with a strange man,' she shouted in the end when she couldn't persuade her fingers to loosen their grip.

Bruno laughed and swam his way back. 'I am not strange,' he said when he got up close. And then he kissed her, soft on the mouth, the black water licking around them.

Jessica had been woken up by the early morning sun as it shimmered low over the lake. To her shame she had slipped away, as she always did, from the possibility of an awkward morning encounter, leaving Bruno fast asleep, the sun's rays flickering on his face.

He had strolled into the outhouse for the morning's baking as if nothing whatsoever had happened between them. No meaningful looks, no stolen smiles. Just exactly as he always was.

She realised she should have been relieved but she wasn't. And it kept coming back, the feeling that she should have swum out into the darkness.

'Working hard out here, I see.' Miles's voice yanked her back to reality where she was sitting with a sopping wet sunshade on her lap and her hand in a bucket of cold soapy water.

'I was just…' She got confused, the silhouette of Miles blocking out the sun, invading her little haven of escape. 'I'm just cleaning these,' she said, standing up and shaking out the canvas to see how much more scrubbing it needed.

'Want some help?' he asked, sitting himself down on one of the loungers.

'I don't need any,' she said. 'Not if there's someone else who needs help more,' she added, then frowned, unsure whether she'd made sense. She was quite keen for Miles to go but also annoyingly exhilarated by his presence.

'No,' he said, lying back on the lounger with his eyes closed, hands behind his head, long body stretched out, legs crossed at the ankles. 'Jimmy's working like a demon in the garden, Dex is whitewashing the back wall, and Eve and Libby are inside. They sent me out here.'

He opened one eye and looked at her, the incessant cicadas counting down the seconds. Jessica pretended to inspect a patch of mould on the canvas.

'Have fun with Bruno last night?' Miles said after the pause, eyes closed again, a sweep of black lashes, chin pointing up to the sun.

Jessica felt a blush creep traitorously up her neck. 'It was fine.'

Miles's lips were smiling. 'Fine, eh?'

Jessica went over and got the brush, then scrubbed furiously at the patch she'd missed.

Miles sat up and grabbed the other canvas. 'You got another brush?' he asked.

'There's one in there,' she said, nodding towards the red bucket.

When he stood up to get it, it occurred to her that in the past she would have scurried over and got it for him. Probably dragging the bucket over as well so he didn't have to move.

Jessica watched him strolling over to get the other brush, the collar of his white polo shirt turned up, his low-riding khaki shorts revealing a strip of Calvin

Kleins. Was everything he owned khaki now? She missed the skinny black jeans and the huge holey grey jumpers, the rollies, the reefers, the bare feet, and the unwashed hair. It was like that whole other person had vanished.

He took his brush back to the sun lounger where he sat at the foot, elbows braced on his knees, and started working on the other canvas.

For minutes the only noise was of scrubbing and cicadas. And for Jessica the weight of their silence grew with every second that passed. There was so much that she wanted to say but in the end the only words she could force out were, 'What are you listening to nowadays?'

'Complete shit,' he replied without looking up.

Jessica laughed despite herself.

Miles laughed. His chest rose and fell. 'And I'm judging some awful TV show.'

'Yeah?' She paused her scrubbing to look his way. 'What's it called?'

'*So You Wanna Be in a Band,*' Miles said, glancing up, expression pained. 'I've sold out, Jessica.'

Jessica looked away. It was weird hearing him say her name.

'And you?' he asked after a pause. 'What are you listening to?'

'I don't know really.' She went over to the bucket to rinse her brush, then moved it closer so it was between the two of them. 'I stopped listening to anything a while back,' she said, soapy water drizzling along the floor as she went back to her canvas. 'Just a bit of Bach now when I work.' She glanced over at him. 'It's good for the synapses.'

He looked up with a frown. 'I told you that.'

She rolled her eyes. 'I know.'

He chuckled, realising he'd missed the point. The atmosphere between them lightened.

'I lied,' he said. 'I don't listen to all shit. I've got this little label of my own. Kind of a hobby. No profit. I fund it with the sell-out shit.' He batted a fly off his arm. 'There's some good stuff, I think. One girl actually who you'd love.' He paused. 'I think you'd love.'

'Yeah?' Jessica asked after too many seconds, intrigued to know what he thought her taste still was, surprised that he still aligned a sound to her.

Miles shrugged, going back to his canvas scrubbing. 'Yeah,' he said, without looking up again.

Jessica watched him work. She wanted to say something. She wanted to apologise—to him, to Flo—but the words were stuck inside her. They seemed so little, so pointless now, yet at the same time huge, as if time had pumped them up like a balloon.

They stayed there in silence, the monotonous hum of brush on canvas occasionally peppered with the sound of water sploshing in the bucket. The sun rained down, the cicadas an orchestra of violins, the pump of the pool gently bubbling. Jessica was hyper aware the whole time, wishing she could walk away but at the same time hoping they both stayed, her night with Bruno wrapped up like a treasure, a moment to escape to, to relieve the pressure of this.

LIBBY

'So you think I'm right?' Eve said, leaning against the wardrobe in one of the vacant bedrooms, looking up from her phone.

'I concede that there are merits in both styles,' Libby said, staring at a patch of peeling wallpaper.

'Oh come on, Libby!' said Eve, sliding her phone into her back pocket. 'It's OK to admit it. The white does not work.'

Libby didn't know what she thought any more. She'd liked the white. Jake had liked the white. But then she knew that Eve had a point. She understood where Frank was coming from when he said the décor wasn't unique enough in the lobby.

She went over and sat down on the bed, blowing her hair out of her eyes. 'I don't know, Eve. I think I've got to a point where I've lost all faith in my own vision.'

Eve came over and sat next to her on the bed. Not close. There was a metre or so between them. 'Did you trust your aunt?' Eve said.

'Sort of,' said Libby. 'It was always a bit of a state though, wasn't it?'

'It was ramshackle. That's good sometimes. This is your history, Libby.'

Libby looked up at the green and gold wallpaper flopping off the wall.

'OK, how about we go for a middle ground,' Eve said, standing up so she could point to the different walls. 'This one, where the paper is fine, we leave it. This one, where the paper is bad, we strip it, line it, paint it to match the main colour of the wallpaper, or just white so the wallpaper becomes a feature?'

Libby thought about it. 'That could be OK,' she said. 'But I don't know how to line a wall.'

'Oh, don't worry, I do.'

'How?'

'Well, when you're bored and alone in the countryside you learn all sorts of things,' Eve said, laughing.

'It can't be that bad living in the country,' Libby said, getting up from the bed so she could stand in the middle of the room and imagine what it might look like.

Eve was checking her phone again. 'No, it's not that bad,' she said, a faux lightness in her tone as she put her phone back in her pocket.

'What about the curtains?' Libby said, walking over to touch the decrepit velvet. 'I feel like they might disintegrate in my fingers.'

'I love the curtains,' said Eve.

'The curtains have to go. They smell.' Libby held one up to her nose and grimaced.

'Well, maybe we just go simple. If we're accenting the wall with the colour of the wallpaper, we have simple cotton curtains the same colour. If we're going for white, we go for simple white curtains. Personally I think we should do it on a room by room basis, depending on how bad the wallpaper is in each.'

'Where will the curtains come from?'

'I don't know. You're the one who lives here.'

'I can make curtains,' a voice said from the doorway. They both looked to see Giulia standing with some folded towels in her arms.

'You can?' Libby asked.

Giulia nodded. 'I can make them for you. There is no more of this white?' she asked, cautiously. 'No more of these blinds?' she added, pointing to the simple roller blinds Jake had installed.

Libby shook her head.

'Then I can make curtains for you,' she said, adding, 'you just tell me the colours,' before walking off with the towels.

Libby covered her shocked smile with her hand. 'Blimey,' she said. 'That's a turn up for the books.'

Eve was on her phone. 'Yeah,' she said, glancing up with a nod.

'OK, what is going on with your phone?'

'Nothing?' Eve frowned, clicking it off and putting it in her pocket.

'Something's going on.'

'Let's go and inspect the rooms,' Eve said, brushing past her as she headed for the door.

They started with Jessica's, the red room, immaculately made up, everything neatly folded away, just her laptop on the desk and her toiletries and make-up lined up on the dresser. It smelt clean like washing powder and shampoo.

Libby went over to the window. Outside it was sweltering. The butterflies fluttered like their wings might burn. Sprinkler water dripped from the plants like sweat trickling down their leaves. Jimmy was out there, sawing errant branches off the cherry tree under the blazing sun. Libby looked across at Eve who had clearly spotted him too.

'I think this is in pretty good shape,' Eve said, turning her back on the window. 'The wallpaper's nice, furniture's a bit dated but I think probably just getting rid of the wardrobe would be enough. There's drawers in the dressing table people can put their clothes in. And what do you think, cream curtains? I think if they were red it would be too much.'

Libby nodded, certain something was going on that Eve wasn't saying. 'Sounds good to me,' she said.

'OK, write cream down for Giulia,' Eve said, and they moved on to the next room.

Libby got her notepad out and started a list, all the time watching Eve's hand as it kept moving to her back pocket checking that her phone was still there. Libby had assumed it was something to do with Jimmy, but that didn't explain the phone.

*

Next was Miles's room and Libby forgot all about questioning Eve as she was hit by the scent of him. She tried not to look around as she headed over to the windows to examine the curtains. The wallpaper was black and gold, the curtains moth-eaten black velvet.

'The paper's bubbling here.' Eve went over and tapped on the far wall. 'You could do with a huge mirror in here, over the bed. You may as well ramp up the decadence.'

Libby couldn't look at the bed. 'There's one in the garage,' she said, staring outside, the sun blinding in her eyes.

'And the curtains I think will have to go,' Eve carried on, sticking her finger through a moth hole.

It was only going to get hotter. Libby could almost taste the sizzle bubbling in the air. The wisps of clouds burnt down to strands like aeroplane trails darting across the sky.

'You know there is something…' Eve started, coming to stand next to Libby, her phone in her hand.

But all Libby's senses were infused with Miles and she couldn't concentrate. 'Do think maybe we should go into the next room?' she said.

Eve nodded, visibly clamming up as she turned to walk away, and Libby immediately regretted cutting her off.

It was Eve's room next. The yellow room. Buttercup walls and heavy gold and cream brocade curtains. Eve's stuff everywhere, clothes scattered over chairs, books piled up on the bedside table, make-up spilling from her bag out onto the dresser.

Libby went over to study the old wallpaper, moving a heap of clothes so she could stand up on a chair to see how easily a corner peeled away. She wanted Eve to pick up the conversation but she was over by the curtains, examining the details.

'I think these are salvageable, just need a good wash. And, actually, this is one room where white might work quite well, don't you think?'

Libby nodded, trying to press the wallpaper that had peeled off like an orange back on the wall. Eve was back to being matter of fact; it seemed unlikely she was going to broach the subject of her phone again, so, concentrating on the wallpaper, her back turned intentionally so there was no threat of eye contact, Libby said, 'What was it you were saying? About there being something?'

Eve was inspecting the wardrobe and the old desk. 'Oh, it's nothing,' she said, waving her hand.

Libby stayed where she was on the chair, still not turning to look, and waited. She could hear Eve checking the curtains again. Heard her pause by the window and maybe look outside. Was she looking at Jimmy?

She heard Eve sigh.

'Basically I've hacked into Peter's emails,' she said, and Libby swung round on her chair, unsure if she'd heard correctly.

'You've done what? Why?'

'Because I'm stupid. Because I was feeling quite good, you know, with the cake win. I haven't had any creative inspiration for months, Libby, and suddenly I was completely alive with it. I knew exactly what I was doing.' Eve ran her hands through her hair, holding it back from her face and then letting it flop down again. 'And I suppose I thought that I wanted to tell Peter. I wanted to talk to him about it, but we're not talking to each other so I couldn't,' she said, perching up on the window ledge. Libby stood down from her chair and sat on it instead. Eve carried on. 'So—he's written this script that at one point he wanted me to read and I thought if I went into his emails and got it, it would be a nice thing to do, you know, to read it. And almost be a way of talking to him.'

'Right?' Libby said, uncertain, still stuck on the email hacking part of the story. Jake would never let her near his emails—even his phone. They had this massive row once when he said it was an invasion of his privacy and she said that if he had nothing to hide he shouldn't mind. He said it wasn't about having anything to hide; privacy was a basic human right. She'd been won round. It transpired he had something to hide.

Eve pulled her phone out of her back pocket and tapped the screen a couple of times to bring it back to life. 'So I found emails to her.'

'Who?'

Eve sighed. 'The bloody supply teacher.'

Libby frowned, stood up from the chair, and moved over to where Eve was sitting on the window ledge to look at the phone. 'Eve, has Peter had an affair?'

'No.' Eve shook her head. 'Not as such. It's an almost affair. He found himself nearly doing something.'

'Why did he tell you?'

Eve exhaled slowly. 'I don't know. Because he can't keep a secret? He tells me everything.'

Libby watched her stare at the phone screen again before slipping it back into her pocket. She could feel the sun on her back as she perched herself up next to Eve, could smell the lemons and the petrol of Jimmy's chainsaw. She thought how Jake never told her anything. How she was always the last to know. Catch-ups with his group of mates were usually spent with Libby trying to get hold of all the gossip he never told her, while Jake was off talking with his big, wide, flirting eyes that sucked women in like her Dyson. Children were born, marriages ended, houses sold, without Libby having the faintest clue. The idea of having a partner who told her everything was almost unimaginable.

'What about Jimmy?' Libby found herself saying before she could help it. Knowing she was stirring but her relationship envy getting the better of her.

Eve glanced up, eyebrows drawn. 'What about Jimmy?' she said.

'You and Jimmy. Last night,' Libby said, angling her head towards where Jimmy had moved onto the rangy olives.

Eve's expression was like she might hiss at her. 'Nothing happened with Jimmy last night.'

Libby sat back into the corner of the window sill, pulling her legs up and wrapping her arms around them. 'So where did you go?'

Eve jumped down, defensive. 'Just to the water. To look at the sunset. That was all.'

Libby watched her. Eve held her gaze. Challenging, intimidating. Libby wondered whether to push it or leave it there—with her unbelieving. She left it. 'Fair enough,' she said, immediately annoyed with herself for copping out, then, sliding herself off the ledge as well added, 'Next room?'

Next was Jimmy's—the oldest room of the lot, orange walls with garish curtains. The furniture all needed replacing.

'I don't want to be in here,' said Eve. 'I think we can safely just say new curtains, new everything.'

Libby nodded.

They backed out, closing the door, and went on to the next. Dex's. Harrods green walls, a massive wooden sleigh bed in the centre, brown blanket curtains. Dex's laptop was in one corner, his open suitcase in the other. It smelt of expensive aftershave and warm wool as the sun streamed through the half-drawn blanket curtains.

'It's calm in here, isn't it?' said Eve, seeming surprised. She sat down on the side of the bed. 'Curtains are hideous, though.'

Libby smiled; she walked over, ran her hand over them and then went to sit next to Eve on the bed. 'So these emails?' she asked. 'Have you read them?'

'No.' Eve shook her head, then reached up to tuck her hair behind her ears.

'And they work together?'

'Yes.'

'So they could be work emails?'

Eve scoffed.

Libby sighed and leant back, the palms of her hands resting on the crisp white sheets.

'I think I should read them,' Eve said.

Libby sucked in her top lip, stared over to the brown curtains, the sun peeping through the weave of the wool like a chequerboard. She had wondered quite often if she was glad she had found out about the affair website. Or whether actually she would have been perfectly happy carrying on with her nice life as it was. Comfortable, pleased, happy most of the time. Lonely sometimes.

But wasn't that better than what a lot of people had?

It hadn't been a surprise when Jimmy had said there were other affairs. She knew. Somewhere down there she knew. Jake bored easily. He had this restless energy about him that built and built. His self-worth was so heavily tied up in what people—women—thought about him that it seemed as if he needed to go out every few months and get his fix. And he'd come back relaxed again, less angry, calmer. Happier. Had she minded? Of course she had. Had it stripped away layers of her own self-worth? Of course it had. But was she happier now? Now that he was gone.

'I don't think you should read them,' Libby said.

Eve had got her phone out again. Her eyes flicked up. 'You don't?'

'No.'

Libby had met Peter only a couple of times but both times he had made her laugh. Out loud. He had talked to her as a person. He hadn't flirted, he hadn't talked about himself all night, he had asked questions and he had listened to the answers, and Libby had found herself envious of Eve for having him in her life. She had been envious that Eve, who had always been so flighty, so adored, so coquettish, had grown up to get this guy. This man who listened.

Libby bit her lip. 'Peter told you nothing happened, yes?'

Eve narrowed her eyes and nodded.

'He told you something almost happened but it didn't,' Libby clarified, toying with the sheet beneath her fingers. She sat up straight. 'Eve, all those emails will do is either confirm or deny what he's said. And if they confirm it, and they're flirty and close, they're going to make you mad. They'll make it all more visceral. And all of it much worse.' She re-tied her hair for something to do with her hands and said, 'He's told you that something almost happened but he stopped it. That's all you need to know. If you trust him.' Libby tightened her ponytail and brought her hands down to rest on her knees, watching Eve throughout. 'In the same way you told me nothing happened with Jimmy. I'd bet that something almost did though.'

Eve barely flinched. A flicker in her eyes. As fast as a hummingbird's wing but it was there all the same.

'But you say you stopped it,' Libby carried on.

'I did stop it.'

'And I believe you, because you are my friend and I trust you. But I will never know, Eve, I will never know. And that's how trust works. That's the whole point.'

Eve pressed her lips together and lowered her phone a fraction as she thought about it.

'At the very least,' Libby said, moving to stand up, feeling that maybe yes, she herself was happier. Because suddenly she could give advice without the voice in her head saying 'that's rich coming from you.' 'I'm imagining you sure as hell wouldn't want Peter seeing the lead up to you putting a stop to it.'

Eve's jaw dropped, indignant, but her reply was stalled when Dex pushed the door open and, seeing them both sitting on his bed, smiled broadly and said, 'To what do I owe this pleasure?'

Libby laughed. 'Don't get excited, Dex, it's just new curtains.'

EVE

Eve couldn't believe it when she woke up at six in the morning. They'd been up until gone midnight painting and papering, all of them, even Jimmy who abandoned the garden when the light went. Jessica and Dex had come back from the local hardware store with everything they needed, including more plastic boilersuits, so they resembled a gang of CSI as they stripped old wallpaper, pasted up lining paper, sanded the newly revealed parquet flooring, and painted skirting boards as the lining paper dried. To their surprise, Giulia had brought up beers and then steered her way through the dust and mess to take measurements for the curtains.

It had been fun. All of them working; focused on their individual jobs. No eye contact, no time for any meaningful chat. Just old memories and funny stories that left them sniggering into their sandpaper. They'd always had fun as a group. It made her think of all the parties they used to throw, people dancing up on the roof in the summer or arriving, dusted with snow, in the winter surprised to have something so classy as the mulled wine Libby had insisted on preparing while the boys just rolled in a beer keg. The best bits were when everyone else had gone to sleep, drunkenly squished into the living room like sardines, while they sat together on the stairwell with a bottle of ice cold vodka that Dex kept in the freezer, talking, stuffing down pancakes that Libby knocked up, reminiscing about the hours just gone, laughing, getting shouted at by the neighbours, whisper giggling, Eve always a bit cold or needing the loo but never wanting to get up and leave because there was magic in the moment, just the seven of them.

To Eve's surprise, when they finished the renovations that night ready to crawl into their respective rooms, dusty, muscles aching, hot, sweaty, and satisfyingly bone tired, Dex said, 'Wait,' and disappeared downstairs, returning with a bottle of ice cold vodka. And without a moment's hesitation they all found their places, leaning against half painted walls and dust-sheet draped chairs, all of them clearly silently reminiscing about the same thing. And Eve found herself really needing the loo but she stayed exactly where she was because it was magic.

But now Eve was wide awake. The sun was up, grinning with the promise of exquisite ferocity. She went over to the open window and looked down the garden to the outhouse. She thought about how good she had felt when Frank the journalist had tasted her cake. She hadn't thought it would mean quite as much as it did but it was like a validation of her talent at exactly the time she needed it.

She felt a mounting urge to make another; to get dressed and go down to her workstation and perfect the flavour. Instead she got back into bed. It was stupid to start baking at six a.m.

But, as she lay with her eyes shut, Eve was hit by an equally strong urge to read Peter's emails. Temptation buzzed through her like the bees in the lemon trees.

So she got up, got dressed, and headed outside. Wearing a grey cotton skirt, yellow vest, and no shoes she felt like a local, especially with the scarf tying her hair back. She imagined herself living here, frolicking about in the heat. Then she stopped herself, pausing for a moment by the pink chairs and table, and made herself acknowledge that it was another dream, another greener grass. She looked back at the hotel. No. She didn't want to live here; she saw the stress Libby was under, she just wanted to be on holiday here, exactly as she was, not wishing it was something else.

Opening the outhouse door she felt like a burglar. No one aware she was there; her feet silent on the concrete floor. Time seemed to still as she worked—steeping the smashed pine needles for different lengths of time to test the best strength, slicing the chinotto thinner, testing the addition of a maraschino and lemon syrup drizzled down holes she made in the oven-fresh cake, sampling her different bakes as she sat on a stool and looked out at the garden. She could almost hear the prickly pear cactuses groaning as the heat began to build.

She saw Libby before Libby saw her.

'Oh, hi!' Libby stopped up short in the doorway.

'Hi,' said Eve, sliding off her stool and going back to her workbench. 'I'm just practising some stuff.'

'Great, that's great,' said Libby, walking over to her own bench. 'I didn't expect anyone else to be up. But that's great. That's what this place is meant to be for. Do whatever you like. That's great.'

Eve could tell she had hoped the place would be empty by the slight flush on the tips of her cheeks. 'I won't get in your way,' she said.

'No no, not at all.' Libby waved a hand. 'I didn't think you would. I was just going to practise some bakes.'

'Yeah, go ahead,' said Eve. 'I have stuff I'd like to do.'

'OK.' Libby nodded.

'OK.' Eve nodded.

For half an hour or so they didn't talk. Not a word. Just worked in concentrated silence. Neither of them referred to yesterday's conversation about Peter; acting almost as professional colleagues rather than friends.

Giulia appeared to ask Libby a question and then returned with a tray of piping hot coffee that she poured into little cups and put on each of their workstations with a biscotti. Her respect for the pair of them was growing with their diligence.

Outside the sun was hard and sharp. Inside it was still relatively cool and smelt of lemons and coffee, sticky pine sap and grated chocolate. As she put another cake in the oven, Eve found that she didn't want to leave, didn't want this to be the end of her session; her urge to work on her own ideas was still unsatisfied. The others had started to wake up. She'd seen Jimmy walk past with a towel over his shoulder, off for some mindful meditation. Dex was reading a book on one of the pink chairs.

'I can take your cake out if you like. When it's ready,' Libby said. 'If you wanted to go.'

Eve frowned. 'Why would I want to leave?'

'Oh, I just thought you were done. That's all. No need to go if you aren't ready to go. Carry on.'

'Do you want me to go?' Eve asked, head cocked, trying to work out what was going on.

'No, no, of course not. I was just going to record a new video, that's all.' Libby shrugged as if it were nothing.

'You can record your video with me here. I won't make any noise.'

Libby made a face to say no.

'Really,' said Eve, 'I won't get in your way. Or I can absolutely go and leave you to it.'

'No, this is your time, your holiday. I don't want you to have to go or be quiet. No.' Libby shook her head, emphatic.

'Honestly,' Eve pressed, 'do it. Otherwise I'll leave.'

'No.' Libby paused. 'It's embarrassing.'

'What is?'

'Being watched.'

'But you post it online.'

'After loads of edits.'

Eve made a face as if this was ridiculous. 'Libby, I know what you look like. And anyway, I'm going to be concentrating on my stuff. Please. Don't not do it because of me.'

Libby winced; Eve knew she had won. Libby couldn't bear the idea of someone not doing something because of her. She was a people pleaser. Of course Eve could see why recording in front of someone would be embarrassing, but part of her wanted to see Libby suffer the same way she'd made her twist with guilt at her comments about Jimmy in Dex's bedroom.

'OK,' Libby said in the end, and walked over to the corner of the room where she pulled open a drawer to retrieve her make-up bag and a small mirror that she propped up on the shelf.

A little smug, Eve trotted out to the garden and picked a few more of the small, hard, chinotto oranges and the only ripe fig, then with a tea towel wrapped round her hand and a kitchen knife, went to saw a couple of the huge red prickly pears from the prickly cactus. She dropped one when a spine jabbed through the folded tea towel, and the fruit, so fat and ripe, bounced like a tennis ball. As she followed after it, walking half-crouched through the grass, she looked up to see Libby doing her hair in the little mirror. She watched her pin the final curl in place then liberally douse with clouds of hairspray. Eve reached for the escaped prickly pear, intrigued. It hadn't all been goading; she'd always actually quite wanted to see Libby record, impressed by her success. She'd seen the wink to camera after a guilty forkful of raspberry swirled pavlova supposedly baked for a dinner party that night; now she wanted to know what it was like behind the scenes.

Eve walked back into the outhouse trying to prise a cactus needle out of her finger with her teeth. Libby was gathering up the mirror and her make-up bag and, after a quick double-check of her face, hair, red and white striped vest top and necklace, shut them back in the drawer. When she turned ready to go back to her workbench, Eve forgot all about the needle in her finger.

'Blimey,' she said, 'I almost didn't recognise you.'

Libby's make-up was caked on like a flight attendant—glossy red lipstick, liner outside the line of her lips to add faux plump, dark blusher streaks on her cheekbones, thick black eyeliner swishes, and lashings of mascara top and bottom. She'd piled her hair on top of her head and styled it with pin curls, her fringe swept to one side half covering one eye. A diamond solitaire pendant that she hadn't been wearing earlier glinted round her neck, along with a couple of other simple gold chains. It took Eve a second to notice she'd also slipped her big emerald engagement ring back on.

'This is what I wear,' said Libby, a touch too brightly. 'For the camera.'

'You look stunning,' said Eve. 'It just looks like a lot of work.'

'No. It's easy now,' Libby said, getting a selection of bowls out from a cupboard—all the beautiful earthenware Eve had seen on the blog.

'Like a uniform,' said Eve.

Libby shrugged.

Eve went back to her bench and got on with removing her prickly pear splinters then peeling and sieving the fruit to get rid of the hard seeds, all the while trying not to stare in fascination at Libby who was busy weighing out ingredients.

The prickly pear pulp smelt like fresh cut grass and sherbet and needed something to slice through the sweetness. She squeezed in a few drops of her chinotto orange and a bit of fresh fig and tasted it, shut her eyes and let the flavour infuse her, then she put the bowl down and went to the larder of herbs and spices, dried fruits, flavourings, anything and everything, and stared at it while her brain got to work plotting, planning, imagining.

She glanced up at one point to see Libby mouthing to the camera, lifting up bowls and showing the contents mechanically like a Barbie doll. Then she'd scuttle round, rewind, watch, adjust, change the bowl, and do it again. It looked exhausting.

When Libby looked up and caught her watching Eve grabbed the nearest ingredient to hand and strode back to her bench, trying to seem indifferent to the minutiae of video preparations.

It wasn't until Eve got back to her workstation that she looked down and saw what it was that she had picked up.

Liquorice.

Eve never ate liquorice.

All it reminded her of was the slowly hardening Liquorice Allsorts in a cut glass bowl in the centre of her grandparents' coffee table in the good living room. The one they saved for best. The one she never went into when she stayed with them, but was always used if she was there with her parents, visiting for lunch. Her dad would fidget uncomfortably on the hard, unused sofa, itching to go out for a fag. Her mum would defensively bat away questions about taking responsibility for Eve. About growing up, acting like adults. Her grandparents would ask what they did in all the 'together-time' they needed just the two of them. Eve would sense her dad's body tense like clay cracking and drying in the sun until he'd snap and stand, patting every pocket to find his Golden Virginia. And her grandfather would sigh, and her mother would stalk out, and her grandmother would stand up to make tea, and Eve's hand would creep forward, scoop up as many Liquorice Allsorts as she could get and stuff them all in her mouth till she could hardly breathe.

Libby had started filming again.

Eve silently grated the bitter, salty liquorice. Then she dipped her finger into the shavings and brought it up to her mouth. It smelt like stuffy living room and tobacco. But then she touched her finger on her tongue and tasted salt, smoke, fire, and mud, like she'd fallen to the centre of the earth. She dabbed her other finger into the chinotto, fig, and prickly pear mix, tried the two together and a rocket went off in her brain. The taste of waves crashing over her head and tumbling her through the surf.

She almost laughed at the potency. Whether it would work as a fragrance, who knew, but there was an unexpected alchemy in the combination that made magic in her mouth.

Eve glanced up and realised Libby was wrapping up. To camera she licked her spoon, said, 'Mm, just scrumptious,' then dropped it in the hand-thrown white bowl and did the same beaming fake smile she always did in every photo they'd ever taken of her.

Libby hated being snapped unawares. She'd always manage to pose in the split second it took for the camera shutter to close.

But Eve remembered one photo of her, taken on the terrace of the Limoncello, Libby really laughing at a story told by her aunt. She hadn't known Eve was watching and the snap was of her mid-toothy guffaw— double-chinned, eyes closed, hair wet from swimming. Eve considered it the most beautiful photograph she'd ever seen of Libby.

Libby had self-consciously grimaced at the copy Eve had had printed. Over her shoulder Jake had laughingly agreed that she looked hideous. Eve had been left fuming, aware that that was the moment she would lose Libby to him. And then to the many blog followers who fell in love with the perfect version of Libby as well.

'OK, I'm done now,' said Libby, packing her stuff away, wiping her lipstick off with a cleansing wipe and then her eye make-up.

'Yeah, me too,' said Eve. 'I'll just clear all this away.'

'OK.' Libby nodded, her jewellery back in the drawer, her hair loose again. 'Well,' she said. 'I'll see you back upstairs.'

'Yep.' Eve nodded.

'Lots to do today,' Libby added, her face back to normal but the big fake smile she gave Eve as she walked out of the door still the same.

JESSICA

Jessica's arm ached. She had never rollered a wall before. Her skin was speckled with paint, all different colours like a rainbow of freckles. The shower water was almost black with dust and dirt when she scrubbed her skin. She found the renovations quite invigorating. She'd loved that it brought them together on the same everyday level that living together had. She liked it when their different iPhones were plugged into the speakers and she heard songs she hadn't heard for years, so clearly aligned with the playlist owner. She liked the way the tea and coffee tasted familiarly different depending on which one of them made it—Jimmy always adding too much milk, Miles never enough. She liked that after ravenously scooping up spaghetti and parmesan at lunch Dex would try and squeeze in a small snooze while Libby would have them straight back to it. The only problem through it all was Jessica's brain—her thoughts, unoccupied by emails and work, in moments of silence could tunnel into a Miles and Flo spiral or drift into anxiety about Bruno, trying to interpret his nonchalance, trying to align it with her own, but also wanting his to be equally uncertain. She'd be happily reminiscing about him kissing her in the boathouse when someone would say, 'More paint, Jessica?' and she'd have to remember that they lived countries apart, annoyed with herself for giving it any thought at all.

When Libby mentioned that there was live music that night at Bruno's bar and everyone decided to stroll down after dinner, Jessica refused to acknowledge the butterflies in her stomach. When they arrived and she heard the sound of Bruno's laugh, and looked over to the bar to see him chatting with a couple of women, she swallowed down a surge of proprietorial jealousy. But as they walked under the fairy lit trees, past busy tables and kids running to jump in the lake, the sun setting behind them, she found herself wondering what was so funny, what he'd said to make them laugh so much. Annoyingly, as they reached their table, she glanced back over her shoulder for another look and he caught her, his eyes meeting hers with amused confidence. Jessica of course immediately looked away.

'The place is packed,' Jimmy said as he sat down. 'I didn't know this many people lived here.'

Libby pointed over to the makeshift stage on the jetty where a group of five old men were playing gypsy jazz wearing white suits and fedora hats as the last of the sun gilded the gently lapping waves behind them. 'It's this lot,' she said. 'They've been going since I was little. It's an institution.'

'Wow,' said Eve, standing up in her seat to get a better view. 'And look, there's people dancing.'

As they were all craning their necks for a view of the band and the bopping locals, Bruno strolled over, stopping with his hand resting on the back of Jessica's chair. 'Everyone all right? You have a drink?'

They shook their heads. Jessica didn't turn round.

'My staff are useless,' Bruno said with a shake of his head. 'What can I get you?'

When he'd taken their order he nodded towards the band and said, 'Anyone can join in, feel free.'

Dex bashed Miles on the arm and said, 'Now's your chance, buddy.'

Miles rolled his eyes. 'Unlikely, Dex,' he said.

'Why not, you should.' Eve leant forward, smiling.

Miles turned round to look at the band. A woman in her seventies was just taking the microphone from the main singer who stood back and counted them in with his fingers clicking for the start of her song. Miles looked back, vaguely intrigued, but said, 'There's no way I'm going on stage.'

'You should,' Eve urged. 'You don't have to sing. Just to play.'

One of the hipsters brought a tray of beers over and handed them out with a sullen frown like he was doing them a favour.

'Thanks,' said Dex; the guy ignored him.

Miles took a swig of beer. 'I'd maybe play. But it's been years. And I'd have to be pretty drunk.'

'Well then,' said Jimmy, lifting his beer in a toast. 'Let's get pretty drunk.'

They got pretty drunk. The alcohol flowed in rivers. There were trays of shots handed round, more beers; Negronis. Even a bottle of champagne at one point that Dex decided to order.

When Dex then dragged Libby up to dance and Eve asked Miles, presumably to prevent any awkwardness with Jimmy who sloped off to the bar on his own, Jessica found herself suddenly alone at the table, a sea of glasses and little candles in front of her.

'Everything all right?' she heard Bruno say as he pulled out the chair next to her.

'Yes, fine,' she said, all her sense suddenly alert.

Bruno nodded, leant back in his seat, his hands behind his head, and looked over at the band. 'They are good, no?'

'Yeah, they're great.'

'You not having fun?'

'No, I am.'

'Why don't you dance?'

'I don't have anyone to dance with.'

Bruno immediately started to stand up. 'I'll dance with you.'

'No, no, no.' Jessica shook her head. 'I didn't mean I wanted to dance.'

Bruno looked confused and sat back down again. 'Why don't you dance?'

'I don't really like dancing.'

'Why not?'

She shrugged.

Bruno narrowed his eyes as he studied her. 'You think people are looking at you?'

'No!' Jessica shook her head. But that was exactly what she thought.

Bruno didn't say anything for a second. Then he sat forward, his elbows on his knees, his fingers steepled under his chin, and said, 'You know no one is looking at you, don't you?'

'Thanks a lot,' said Jessica with a half-laugh.

Bruno sighed. 'I don't mean it like that. I mean they are looking at themselves.'

Out on the lake a couple of kids dive-bombed into the water, upsetting a group of white ducks that quacked and flapped then resettled further out.

'You see that duck?' Bruno said, pointing to the group.

'Which one?' Jessica asked.

Bruno laughed. 'Exactly. To him he is the centre of the world. To you he's a duck. And you don't even know which one.'

Jessica looked at the white ducks. All indistinguishable in the evening light.

'But let's say people do watch you.' Bruno bit down on a smile as he sat back. 'So they see you dance. So what? It is just one more thing that has happened in their lives.'

Jessica turned to look at him, leaning back in his chair with languid confidence, ankle crossed over his knee, while his bar buzzed with people wanting drinks, food, service. 'Does nothing faze you?'

'Faze?' He frowned, not understanding.

'Worry. You know? Get anxious.'

'No.' He shook his head, blank as to why it should. 'What's the point? It's easy, no? This worry. Safe.' He watched her for a moment. 'Like a blanket for the babies,' he said. 'You come and find me if you want to dance,' he said, then winked and strolled away, someone calling his name from another table, waving him over for a drink.

Jessica stared after him, slightly affronted. Unsure that she was happy to have her years of worry belittled.

It occurred to her then that all her panic over what had happened that evening in New York with Flo had centred on herself. On it having the reaction she had wanted it to have. Of it leaving Flo hurt and upset and ruining their wedding eve. When actually, it was quite possible that it was just—how had Bruno put it? *One more thing that happened in her life.* Massive to Jessica. Inconsequential to Flo.

She wondered suddenly what the rest of them had done when Dex had come looking for her. Flo probably hadn't cried, she'd probably more likely made a face. Been shocked momentarily. Maybe there'd been a moment of silence when they'd all cringed and when Miles had apologised; rather than needing comfort Flo had probably said something like, 'So she's in love with you, we all know that.'

Jessica had always thought of it as a terrible upsetting moment but possibly it had been more one of pity. For her.

She raised a hand to her forehead and shut her eyes for a second, suddenly mortified. They'd probably all bundled into a cab and gone for Chinese food. Flo loved Chinese food. Miles with his arm tight around her. They'd probably got a bit more pissed than previously intended and laughed over fortune cookies, Jessica inadvertently making the night before their wedding more memorable, more fun, more close than the wedding itself. And the next day when Jessica had been walking the streets of New York by herself, staring vacantly into shop windows and wishing she had someone to talk to, they had probably all just been having an amazing time. Libby or Dex maybe giving her half a second's thought, but otherwise it would have been all champagne and laughter. If she'd just apologised at the time it all would have been over years ago. But she hadn't because she couldn't. Because it had been her life and in her head it had been huge.

EVE

Eve broke off her dance with Miles when her phone rang. She looked at her screen to see Peter's email address asking if she wanted to FaceTime. Excusing herself from Miles she jogged to the entrance of the bar and, checking her watch to see that it was nine in the UK, too late for the kids to call, she answered it with a flush of excitement that it was Peter calling.

'Hi, Mummy!' Maisey and Noah shouted.

Eve immediately sobered up. 'What are you doing up?' she asked, surreptitiously trying to check her hair and make-up in the little FaceTime picture in the corner of the screen to make sure she didn't look drunk.

'You look pretty, Mummy,' Maisey said. 'All dotty.'

The compliment momentarily distracted her and she looked at herself properly for the first time since she'd arrived in Italy. Saw the freckles and the caramel skin, hair blonder from the sun, cheeks flushed with alcohol and dancing. At a push, she thought she could possibly be described as pretty, especially by a five-year-old who regularly told passers-by that her mother was a princess.

Noah nudged Maisey out of the way and, flicking the ring pull of a can of Coke, said, 'Daddy's been very grumpy.'

'Really?' Eve asked surprised, frowning at the Coke. 'Where is Daddy?'

'Out,' said Maisey. 'Granny's here.'

Eve saw her mother-in-law in the background, who explained that Peter apparently had some function at the school, while shaking oven chips out of a packet.

'You're eating very late,' Eve said.

'I think he's forgotten how to laugh,' Noah said.

The mother-in-law paused with the chips.

'I don't think he's forgotten, honey bunch,' Eve said, trying her hardest not to say anything about the saturated fat in oven chips. 'He's just maybe not finding anything really funny at the moment. Maybe you'll have to dress up as Shrek. He always finds that funny. You can use my pillow for the padding.'

Noah's eyes lit up. 'OK, Mummy,' he said, then added, 'Guess what?'

'What?' Eve wasn't sure she wanted to know.

'I'm having Coca-Cola with my tea, Mummy,' said Noah, holding the can to the screen. 'And Maisey's having bubblegum flavoured lemonade.'

Emily gleefully lifted a luminous blue drink to the camera.

'We were allowed to choose whatever we wanted, Mummy, it was great. And we're having Angel Delight for pudding.'

Before Eve could say anything she was cut off by the mother-in-law taking the iPad and saying a quick goodbye before switching her off.

Angel Delight!

She never let the kids have Angel Delight. Let alone Coke or lemonade with their tea.

She paused for a moment, struck by the memory of how much she used to love Angel Delight.

Her dad would make it and add a dash of rum to the mix. They'd snuggle up under blankets on the sofa on trips in the campervan. It was always cold, condensation dripping down the inside of the windows, and it smelt of damp, but they'd listen to the radio and he'd smoke and laugh and she'd feel the rumble of his chest under her head. It was always the getting there that Eve loved. The journey. Once they arrived, that was when the trouble always began.

'Hey, you all right?' Eve turned to see Libby had come out to find her. 'I saw you run off with your phone. Just,' Libby shrugged, 'thought I'd check you were OK.'

Eve nodded. 'Yeah fine. It was just the kids, FaceTiming.'

'They OK?'

'High on sugar.'

Libby laughed.

They stayed where they were for a second or two, Libby tapping her finger on the old beer barrel that propped the door open. 'Are you OK?' she said, tentative.

Eve nodded.

'Not too upset about the sugar?'

Eve laughed. 'Livid. But no.' She pushed her hair back off her face and tied it back with a band on her wrist. 'I was thinking about my dad, actually, and Angel Delight.'

Libby grimaced. 'I hated Angel Delight. We always had the pink one.'

Eve shook her head. 'No, we always had the chocolate. That was the good one.' She laughed, then stopped and took a breath in, glancing at the gravel on the floor, rolling it with the toe of her flip-flop. 'I suppose the thing is, I've never realised how similar my dad was to Jimmy.'

Libby leant her elbows on the beer barrel and rested her chin in her hands. 'You think?' she said, uncertain.

'Yeah.' Eve looked up and nodded. 'Just always out of reach. And you think it's because there's something deep there under the surface, some great philosophical thinking about life and the world and then one day you realise there's not that at all. They just don't like answering questions.' She rested her back against the white brick wall and shrugged. 'They don't like admitting that they're part of the organised world. Can't handle the fact that however much they try to believe they aren't conforming, really they are. They just pretend to themselves that they're not. All those festivals, all the drugs, it was just doing what thousands of other people did. Same with Jimmy on his boat. He's living it up on someone else's money. He's hardly a nomad is he?'

Libby sniggered.

Bruno came out to get something from his car and laughed when he saw them both. 'You are hiding from my band?' he said.

'Not at all,' Libby said. 'Just having a little pause.'

He nodded his head in understanding and, when he came back from his car, said, 'You need a drink?'

Libby and Eve looked at each other; both knew they'd probably already had enough but the moon was shining and the air was warm and a drink seemed like something that would prolong their pause nicely.

Eve said, 'A beer would be good.'

'Two beers,' said Bruno, and disappeared into the bar.

Libby swatted away a mosquito and then, fanning her face from the heat, sighed and tied her hair up in a knot on top of her head. 'How can it still be so hot?' she said.

Eve closed her eyes. 'I love it.'

Bruno came back out with the beers. 'Ladies. Enjoy,' he said putting them down on the beer barrel.

When Eve came over to pick hers up Libby said, 'And what about Peter. Is he like that?'

Eve took a long sip of the beer, wiped her mouth with the back of her hand and said, 'Not at all. I think that's what got me so hooked. He appeared and he made money and he worked hard and he got things done. He wasn't embarrassed or narcissistic or petty. He made all the others look like children.' She took another sip of beer. 'He just existed, you know? Confident in his own skin. And if he met Jimmy properly, I know he'd think he was a waster—which he probably is. But I think I have a soft spot for him because he's so like my dad. And really, I just think he doesn't want to grow up. He's holding on to this time that made him so happy—youth was his thing. It suited him.'

Libby had leant back against the door, her arms crossed in front of her, listening.

Libby was a good listener, Eve thought as she toyed with the label on her beer bottle. Always had been; always knew when to stay still, as though she knew the other person hadn't finished even if they thought they had. It worked because Eve went on to say, 'I mean, Peter, he could be more emotional, granted. But then where would that get us? He's solid, I'm emotional. Surely that's why it works, don't you think?'

'I don't know, Eve,' said Libby, taking a sip of her beer. 'They say opposites attract. Who knows what works in other people's relationships?'

Eve looked at her. 'That's what Jimmy said. He said people pick what they're looking for, that's why you should never get involved in other people's relationships.'

'When did he say that?'

Eve winced. 'When he was talking about you and Jake.'

Libby snorted. 'What an idiot.'

'Jimmy or Jake?'

'Both.'

They laughed. Both drank from their beer bottles. Above them the bats swooped in the sky and the stars glittered like rain.

'I suppose,' said Eve. 'The thing is, did I pick Peter because he wasn't like my dad or because I loved him?'

Libby frowned. 'Can't it be both?'

'I don't know, that's what I'm asking.'

Libby picked at the corner of her beer label and peeled a strip away. 'Why didn't you kiss Jimmy?' she asked.

Eve thought about it. 'Because he didn't laugh when he got stung just as we might have kissed. Peter would have laughed,' she said, paused, then added, 'My dad would have got annoyed.'

'What would you have done?' Libby asked.

'Panicked that it was some flesh eating spider that was going to kill me.'

Libby laughed.

Eve laughed.

Libby put her bottle down on the table. 'When you shut your eyes who do you see? Peter or Jimmy?'

'Oh Peter, definitely.'

'And you love him?'

Eve nodded. 'But something's happened, Libby. Something's happened to make us both almost unfaithful. I think we've ruined it. I mean, isn't that what you're meant to split up over?'

Libby shrugged. 'I think the thing you have to decide is whether the infidelity is the symptom or the cause.' She paused and thought about it for a second before carrying on. 'Say with Jake and me, it's the symptom. Our relationship is not working—it hasn't been working. I'm not even sure he loves me any more.'

'Do you love him?' Eve asked.

'I don't think my ego will let me say I love him,' Libby replied with a laugh, then she picked up her beer and took a swig before adding, 'maybe.'

Eve stared down at her feet.

'I've sort of lost my train of thought now,' said Libby. 'Oh yes. I think you've both lost your way a bit—and that's the cause—that's why he looked at the…?'

'Supply teacher.'

'The supply teacher. And why you looked at Jimmy,' Libby added. 'You needed resetting. To see what you had. Have. I bet it wasn't so clearly Peter when you closed your eyes before all this stuff with Jimmy.'

Eve swallowed. It occurred to her that maybe her problem was still that she was always waiting to arrive. Always waiting for trouble. The food, the picturesque country life, the bloody chickens, all of it just tying her tighter in knots as she waited and waited, failing to realise that she had arrived. Some time ago. And the trouble had come only as a result of her reluctance to accept the fact. To relax into her happiness. To accept that it was hers to enjoy.

Libby finished her beer, put the bottle down and said, 'I think you needed to understand each other's value. The proposed infidelity is a result of that. Oh god, maybe that makes it a symptom? And maybe Jake's was the cause?'

Eve laughed, playing with the label of her bottle, tearing little patterns into it.

'Whatever. Bollocks. Either way, it's not the same,' Libby carried on. 'Mine's shit because he actually sought out an affair. Yours is a hiccup.' She shrugged as if it were all that simple. 'Peter is a man. Jake thinks he's a man but really he's an eighteen-year-old on a permanent gap year.' She paused for a couple of seconds, sighed, and added, 'I would really like to have children.'

Eve's head shot up to look at her. 'Don't take him back because of that.'

Libby shook her head, her eyes sad.

Eve watched her shoulders rise and fall as she tried to steady her breathing. 'Libby, you will meet someone else. But just say you don't, Christ, you can adopt, you can go it alone, have mine on loan if you want—I can't believe I snubbed your offer before. I was being defensive, sorry.'

Libby's eyes widened a fraction at the apology and suddenly it was like they saw each other properly for the first time that holiday. Like they were finally speaking direct to each other rather than just saying words that skated over the surface like ice.

Eve reached over and touched Libby's hand where it rested on the barrel. 'Libby, don't make a decision based on something that isn't fundamentally about the two of you, that isn't about you being cherished. Because believe me, if there are cracks now, children will turn them into bloody great ravines.'

Libby took a deep breath and nodded. The church bell chimed. The music from the bar lulled as the band took a break.

'We should probably go back in,' Libby said, collecting up the two empty beer bottles, then putting them down so she could redo her hair and rub her cheeks. 'God, I must look a state,' she said, running her fingers under her eyes to sort her mascara.

Eve looked her up and down. 'I think you look nice like that.'

Libby scoffed.

'I'm serious, you do.'

'I bet I look dreadful. Drunk and emotional.'

Eve laughed. 'You look natural,' she said. Then after a pause added, 'You look like you.'

Libby raised her eyebrows suspecting Eve had a subtext.

Eve knew it would be safer not to say any more but instead said, 'You should do it on your blog, too, you know? Show a bit more of the natural you.'

Libby shook her head. 'I knew it was a mistake letting you watch,' she said with a half-laugh.

'I thought you looked amazing, Libby. I just don't feel like it's a hundred per cent you, that's all. More like, I don't know, who you think you should be.' She picked up the empty beer bottles. 'But then, what do I know about blogging?'

She looked at Libby, standing there with barely any make-up left after an evening drinking and dancing, hair messily tied in a knot on top of her head, eyes soft and a little sad, skin—like all of theirs—still speckled with paint, and thought of her made up like a china doll for the camera. Then she thought of Jake emailing the women on the website—strangers glammed up for profile shots, nothing real, no need to make a lifelong impression, just a quick, engineered affair. All gloss, all fake, all built on lies.

She wondered if Libby had ever thought the same thing and knew that she had. That was always their problem in the past—they knew too well what the other was thinking. There was no hiding.

That was probably why the friendship had fizzled out, because it made lying to oneself far too difficult.

'I'll think about it,' Libby said as she started to walk back inside. Eve knew she wouldn't.

And, as they walked back into the bar, side by side, in silence, it was hard to tell if they were a step closer or one step further apart.

JESSICA

The drinks didn't stop. Bruno brought them all shots and then there was more dancing. And suddenly, when Jessica looked up from where she was standing by the bar with Dex and Bruno, she saw Miles taking the stage with a couple of the old guys from the band.

'What's he doing?' she asked Dex.

'He's been lured by the guitar,' said Dex. 'And copious amounts of booze. You should go up and sing.'

'Oh get real.' Jessica snorted.

'Ms Jessica sings?' said Bruno, surprised.

'Oh yeah, pretty well actually.'

'Like you'd know,' Jessica said, shaking her head.

'I've heard you in the office. When you think no one can hear.'

She turned to Bruno. 'I don't sing in the office.'

Bruno shrugged. 'Fine with me if you did.'

And Jessica had to look away, feeling like she'd been caught out again for not being free-spirited enough. She shot Dex a look for being a stirrer and he sniggered.

On stage the sax player was counting them in and then a second later Miles was playing. Toe tapping, fingers strumming, smiling like he hadn't had such fun in years. There was a guy with a harmonica and another playing the double bass. Dex started to clap and Jimmy came over to join them, pointing at Miles and doing a wolf whistle. Miles laughed. Jessica felt herself staring at him, mesmerised. Like he was twenty-two again, face relaxed, eyes half closed, shoulders low.

Libby and Eve appeared and Dex pointed to the stage; they both gasped when they saw Miles, both clapped and cheered.

People were dancing. The harmonica guy did a solo. Some kids splashed in the water. And Jessica watched. Watched as Miles laughed, as his knee bobbed, as his head nodded along.

Then the song changed.

She felt Dex straighten up next to her.

Saw Miles's eyes flick open.

'Shit.' Libby covered her mouth.

'What?' Jessica frowned. 'What's wrong with this?'

'It was their first dance,' said Dex, running his hand through his hair with a frustrated sigh. 'At the wedding.'

Miles had stopped playing.

'Well, someone's got to do something,' said Jessica.

'Like what?' Dex held his hands wide.

Jimmy made a face. 'The guy's dying up there.'

Libby thwacked him on the chest.

'Oh, for god's sake.' Jessica huffed and suddenly she found herself striding through the crowds. The bass player was looking awkwardly at the saxophonist, trying their best as Miles strummed absently out of rhythm, his eyes fixed on a spot just at the edge of the jetty.

And then all of a sudden Jessica was standing at the mic and she could hear herself singing before her brain had registered that this might actually be about to happen. And she heard the bass player perk up and get his confidence back and the guy on the harmonica came and stood next to her and tried to get her all involved, while Jessica was having to use all her energy simply to stay where she was. But then after a few seconds she glanced over her shoulder and saw that Miles had pulled himself together and was back in the game; he met her eye and nodded and she looked back, her shoulders dropping with relief, but that was when it really hit her where she was and what she was doing. Over by the bar she could hear Dex and Jimmy cheering and saw Libby and Eve come over to dance. She wondered if she could slip away now that Miles was OK, but then she caught sight of Bruno, standing a few feet in front of the bar, arms crossed, watching her with pure delight, his eyes sparkling, his mouth smiling, and she felt her breath hitch in her throat and a tiny nugget of pride swell in her chest. And all the locals kept on dancing, and kept on drinking, half turning to look, half barely noticing that she was on the stage. And she felt suddenly like this was her swimming through the darkness. All those faces watching. All those ghosts. And it was both as terrifying and as liberating as she had imagined.

*

When the song ended the band took another break. Libby and the others crowded round to say lovely things about her singing and Miles stretched himself out and then said, 'Think I might go and get a drink.'

Dex and Jimmy went with him.

Jessica watched him walk away. Libby and Eve were still talking; she tried to listen and make the right noises but then had to excuse herself.

'I just need to cool down,' she said, fanning her face as if she were boiling. 'I'll be back in a sec.'

They nodded. Their attention diverted as the original band took their places again and practically the whole place got up out of their seats and crowded the dancefloor.

Jessica slipped away to the tables furthest from the bar and the music, shrouded in darkness, where she sat on the ground and dipped her bare legs into the water. In the distance the ducks floated, grey in the moonlight. She could feel the remains of her adrenaline make her hands start to shake as she rooted through her pockets for a piece of paper and called to one of the hipsters to borrow a biro.

As the water lapped, the reeds tangled soft around her feet and her instinct was to pull back, to move, but she couldn't, her whole being focused on this one task as she started to write.

Dear Flo,

I am sorry.

Not just about what I said before your wedding but for everything. And the fact I haven't said it until now.

When I heard about the car crash I was devastated that you were gone because you were so alive and vibrant and vital. I couldn't work out where all that energy could have gone. But awfully, shamefully, horribly, I wasn't sorry. Because you had taken something I loved. I loved him so much. I felt like I couldn't breathe for years. Every day I woke up and remembered I was missing something. And I realise that's what Miles must feel like every day he wakes up without you. I can see now, I know now, that he was never mine. Nor I suppose was he yours. I've realised people are theirs to do with as they please. I'm not in love with him any more. And I am truly sorry for what I said. And I am more sorry for what you have lost. Yours was a life that should have lived longer.

Jessica x

When she was finished she folded the piece of paper until it was half the size of a matchbox and threw it into the lake, watching it bob away like an origami boat. Then she stood up, wiped her eyes, brushed the water off her legs, and walked over to the bar to join the others.

LIBBY

They started later the next morning, blinding hangovers blighting the renovation progress. Jimmy had fallen asleep under the cherry tree and woken up with one half of his face sunburnt. Dex, Miles, and Libby carried on with the painting and sanding, while Eve and Jessica had been sent to the garage to sort through all the old previously discarded paintings, lighting, furniture, and knickknacks to see what might now be suitable for the revised interior design.

Giulia knocked tentatively on the door of Jimmy's room where they were painting all the walls sky blue. 'Ms Price,' she said, and when Libby turned she saw another red reminder bill in Giulia's hand.

'Oh, hang on,' she said, dropping her roller into the tray and jogging over to get the letter before Dex or Miles could see. 'Thank you, thanks,' she said, nodding to Giulia who gave her big eyes as a warning to get it paid.

Both men were watching when she glanced over her shoulder.

'Everything all right, Libby?' Dex asked.

'Fine. Fine, I just need to pop downstairs,' she said and took off to her office.

It was there, as she sat looking at the ever increasing pile of bills and quotes for work they'd requested, that she realised she hadn't paid it because in the back of her mind she'd assumed Jake would take care of it when he got back.

The thought caught her up short.

Did she really ever think that she wouldn't take Jake back? Even with Miles knocking softly on her door every night and slipping back to his own room at dawn, she had been living this gap in her life as temporary.

She realised that yes, she'd heard everything that everyone had said, and yes it made perfect sense, but when it really came down to it, she never had any intention of going it alone. The unpaid bills were surely testament to that.

As she sat fingering the brittle cellophane windows of the envelopes it occurred to her that she'd just been nodding along at advice—including her own—in an attempt to keep the peace.

She leant her elbows on the desk and rested her chin in her hands, looking up at all the files and papers on the shelves above her. Bulging box files that made her shudder. She didn't want to do this on her own.

Her eye landed on a slim black book that she recognised as her aunt's. It had always lived under the counter in the hallway. She slid it down from the shelf, opened it, and laughed when she saw what was in it. Lists and lists of people banned from the hotel bar, the reason, and for how long they weren't allowed in. It made her giggle as she turned the pages. Columns of names, half of them the same, half of them surnames she recognised from the village.

Her aunt was a great believer in the idea that people could change if they wanted to. That was why she never kicked anyone out for good. But as she sat looking at all the names, the reoffenders, Libby realised that she had spent all this time wondering what she'd do if Jake said he'd changed, that he was sorry, when all the while she should have been questioning whether she could. Whether change was in her nature. Whether indeed she had not just the courage but the inclination and the determination to go it alone.

She sat and thought about it for a moment then gradually her eyes started to scan the desk and files, looking for the ones that had Jake's passwords to their online business account; her hands started flicking quickly through the filing cabinet, working her way through all of the past transactions, trying to getting a handle on their incomings and outgoings. She found the files for invoices and the passwords, and looked through the folders at all the old bills.

And she realised that just opening the drawers, just logging into the accounts, made the weight she'd been dragging around a little less heavy.

She paid the most urgent bills and tried to get a grasp on their cash flow, then before heading back upstairs did a quick check of her emails.

And there it was. Just as she was starting to persuade herself that perhaps she did have the courage.

Lib,

Sweetheart. I'm in Whistler with a group of heli-skiers. They needed a medic to go on the trip—a fortuitous chance for a bit of soul-searching for me. There's nothing like watching the sunrise while at the top of a glacier to make one realise what a complete and utter prick one's been.

I know I have no right to even get in touch. But I've always thought it's worth taking a risk in life. So even if I'm relegated to Trash before you even read this then I still know it was worth trying.

God I'm an idiot. I look in the mirror and I just see an idiot staring back. An idiot who put a bullet through his perfect life. And the only reason I can come up with is that I must have been scared. It was all the change—the move, it's so isolated, there was a lot of pressure with the hotel— but away from it, from you, I see that I was completely wrong. (Hard for me to admit, as you can well imagine.)

I feel like half of my whole—like I'm only walking on one leg!

I love you.

I made a terrible mistake.

I need to be forgiven. I need to be loved by you for the rest of my life.

So I'm taking one more risk. My plane lands tomorrow lunchtime. I'm coming to get my wife back. I will fight for you, Libby Price.

Jake.

Libby had to go outside.

She closed her emails and got up, left the office, and walked out onto the terrace, ready to make a dash for the lemon groves before anyone saw her.

But Jimmy was sitting alone at a table in the far corner having a glass of water and escaping from the sun. One half of his face was an angry sunburnt red. He waved her over when she stepped outside.

In the distance the sun was settling into the late afternoon, resting heavy on the treetops waiting for bed.

'Doesn't look good, does it?' Jimmy said, pointing to his face.

Libby shook her head. She really wanted to be on her own. 'Have you put anything on it?'

'Your Giulia gave me some aloe vera.'

'That should help,' Libby said, wondering if it would be rude to leave him there and carry on to the lemon grove.

'You wanna sit down?' he asked.

'OK,' she said, as brightly as she could, snatching a fleeting longing glance at the dark shade of the lemon trees before pulling out a chair.

'You all right?' Jimmy asked, sitting forward and taking a sip of his water.

'Yeah, you?' she said.

'Well, apart from the face, yeah, good.' He nodded. They sat in silence for a second and just as it was starting to get awkward Jimmy said, 'So Jake's coming back.'

Libby frowned. How did Jimmy know?

'He emailed me earlier,' Jimmy said, reading her thoughts. 'Talking about doing some fishing before I fly out.'

They were friends. Libby knew they were friends, but really? He'd emailed about fishing? Completely confident that he was just going to slip back in, unquestioned. But then when had she ever given him cause to think that he wouldn't. She hadn't even thrown him out when she'd confronted him about the website because he'd got in there first by saying he would leave.

'That's OK with you? Yeah?' Jimmy asked, hand on his water glass about to raise it to his lips. 'I presumed he'd been in touch with you, too,' he said, taking a gulp then holding the cool glass up against his burning cheek.

'Yeah, yeah, absolutely.' Libby shrugged as if she was completely on board and knew exactly what was going on.

She felt Jimmy eyeing her with uncertainty and after a second or two he sat right forward and said, 'Look, Libby, I've been meaning to say, about what I said about Jake in the past—I'm really sorry that you heard that.'

She stared at him, half frowning, half unsure. 'Are you sorry I heard or sorry you didn't tell me?' she asked.

Jimmy opened his mouth to reply but changed his mind. Instead he put his hands in the pockets of his cargo trousers and sat back again, his face hardening ever so slightly. 'I'm sorry you heard,' he said. 'I would never want to intentionally hurt you.'

Libby narrowed her eyes. 'But you've hurt me by not telling me.'

'I couldn't have told you,' Jimmy said. 'It was never my place. If something's meant to happen in life, Libby, it'll happen. That's my philosophy.'

But it didn't sound like a philosophy at all. It sounded like a cop out. A way of shifting all responsibility away from oneself. And suddenly Libby realised that that was precisely how she had lived. She let the actions in her life be controlled by other people.

'Isn't that just sitting on the fence, Jimmy?' she said. Then added, almost as much to herself, 'When do you ever fight for anything?'

Jimmy held up his hands as though he was under attack. 'All right Libby, calm down.'

'I'm serious,' she said. 'If you just let it play out it means you never get down from the fence.'

Jimmy finished the rest of his water and stood up without answering. 'I'm going to go back to the garden,' he said.

Libby nodded. She watched him jog away, almost as fast as was polite, and felt the frustration of his passivity course through her.

She realised it must be what Eve thought about her when she talked about Jake and the blog.

Libby leant back in her chair with a sigh and looked across at the lemons, like fat little suns hanging among the waxy leaves. She stared at all the trunks, rows and rows like soldiers lining up for battle. She thought about her swims with her aunt, crunching through the grove to get there, surrounded by the sharp bitter scent of citrus. And she thought suddenly that she would do anything to save this. That she *wanted* to do it, even if it was alone. She would never let it go. It was a part of who she was. Their roots were her roots.

JESSICA

Jessica and Eve had sorted the paintings into piles. Ones that were too awful to see the light of day again they put in one pile and others that might possibly complement the new scheme they put into another pile, along with some old etched mirrors, their glass speckled with age, that Eve insisted would add a bit of vintage chic. There were two boxes of possible ornaments, vases, statues, and sidelights that had potential and a whole stack of other rubbish they had sorted through ready for the tip.

Jessica was filthy. Her face covered in black smears, her hair thick with dust, her top damp from the baking heat of the metal garage. Their hangovers sweated away. Outside it had gone from day to dusk without either of them really noticing. So when Eve suddenly stood up straight and said, 'I'm going for some air,' Jessica wasn't as surprised as she might have been to see Miles leaning against the doorframe.

'Hi,' she said, pushing her hair out of her eyes with the back of her hand.

'Hi,' he said, walking into the dark heat of the garage.

He came right over to where she was sitting on the floor, stacking a group of paintings ready to take them into the hotel. He rolled his lips together and looked at her for a second, then sat down on an old tea chest, elbows resting on his knees as he toyed with something between his fingers.

'The thing about throwing something into a lake,' he said, unfolding a water-damaged scrap of paper, 'is that it has nowhere to go. There's no current.'

Jessica swallowed. 'I hoped it might sink,' she said.

Miles shook his head.

'You weren't meant to read it,' Jessica said.

'No.' He looked up at her under thick dark lashes. 'But I'm glad I did.'

She stared back at him, a slight sickness rising in her chest.

'I didn't mean what I wrote about not being sorry,' she said.

'Yes, you did.' He nodded.

'I know,' she said, scratching her head then pushing her hair back again. 'I didn't know she was going to die. I can't believe it. I'm really sorry.'

'It was pretty difficult to read.' He looked up. 'Not least 'cos it was soaked with lake water,' he added with a half-smile.

She nodded.

The outside lights flicked on, casting them in yellow, Miles's face suddenly sharp and outlined but the expression in his eyes surprisingly gentle. 'But it's OK,' he said. 'This shouldn't still be hanging over you.'

And she nodded again. Almost unable to stop. Nod, nod, nodding. She stopped as soon as she realised she was still doing it.

He folded up the paper and gave it back to her. 'Thank you,' she said, stuffing it into the pocket of her shorts.

He stood up and walked back over to the door. 'Thank you as well,' he said, pausing in the doorway, 'for last night. For coming to my rescue.'

'It's the least I could do,' she said.

He shrugged a smile. 'Call it even?'

'I'm not sure it's quite the—'

'Jessica,' he said, resolute, 'call it even.' Then he walked away, back in the direction of the hotel.

LIBBY

The outhouse was spooky late at night.

Libby had helped clear up after the evening restaurant shift and then she'd left Giulia and Dino having cigarettes out the front before they went home; she headed through the hotel, out over the terrace, and down the path to the outhouse.

Eve, Jessica, Miles, Jimmy, and Dex had gone down to Bruno's for a drink. Half of her was jealous to be missing out, but she needed to do this and there was no other time.

It was cool inside the building, moonlit shadows of the trees dancing eerily on the concrete floor as she fumbled for the light switch in the dark. When she found it and turned it on the room was thrown into stark, electric brightness. The window turned straight to black, reflecting all the empty workstations back at her, the ghosts of their owners behind them. Eve's watch was still next to her mixer, Dex's jumper thrown over the back of his stool.

Refusing to be spooked, Libby went to the front and set her camera up on the tripod. Then she got a selection of bowls out. Not all the fancy ones from the cupboard but some of her normal everyday ones as well as the real beauties that she saved for camera. Then she opened the drawer in the corner and took her mirror out.

Standing it on the shelf, she stared at herself. Her eyes looked tired from the day's renovations, a hangover, and post-restaurant shift. Her mascara and liner were smudged, her foundation had barely survived, and her lips were back to their natural pink. She looked like her father.

Or maybe, she thought, she looked like her aunt.

The idea made her smile as she reached into the drawer and rummaged through all the various make-ups for a bronzer. The camera, however natural one wanted to be, was particularly unforgiving on paleness and she figured this was better one step at a time. She didn't want to give them all the shock of their lives.

Then she tied her hair up, all of it, scraped back from her face like she did when she went swimming, high on her head so it caught up her fringe.

She'd done the shift in a white shirt with a red vest underneath, so she took the shirt off, left the vest, and donned her white chef's apron. Then she reached forward and turned the camera on. No rehearsals except to check that she hadn't chopped half her head off, she said, 'So this is what I look like when I've just finished work.' She looked herself up and down and then back to the camera. 'I thought it was time for you to see the real me for a change. The actual, every day version, and this is she.' She paused; laughed. 'God, I'm actually quite nervous,' she said. 'I want you to get to know me for me. No more perfect staging to hide behind. It might all be a bit less slick but it will be real, and that, for me at the moment, feels like what's important.'

She paused, unsure how to carry on, deciding whether or not to say more but then looking down at the ingredients and realising it would be best to focus on what it was all about—the cooking.

'OK. Right. I was thinking maybe tonight, because I'm knackered, I'd just show you how to make a really simple chocolate cake.

'It's very easy. There's no twist. It's just really, really good chocolate cake. It's the one my mum used to make.'

In a bowl she mixed her dry ingredients, explaining the measurements as she went. Then went on to whisk her eggs with a fork and melt the butter and as she did she started to chat. Relaxed and calm with the camera. No longer spooked.

'There were six kids in our house growing up,' she said, 'and we didn't have a lot, but there was always a cake on a Friday when we came home from school. Always. And we'd come in, dump our stuff,

Blue Peter would be on the telly in the corner of the kitchen and we'd be sitting round the table ready, even before it came out of the oven. There was this restless anticipation in the air. Like we knew it was Friday which meant the weekend and we knew we could stay up later and—I mean usually the weekend meant absolute chaos but before it started, when it was just Friday night, it could be anything. It didn't matter. Because there was this piping hot cake and mugs of tea and no homework and without fail it was my favourite part of the week.'

It was the most she'd talked of her memories in years and she found herself unexpectedly proud. Felt the lightness of honesty in her tone. For a second she worried she might well up but she was nothing if not a professional and she certainly wouldn't be crying on camera, so she smiled and went on. 'It's nothing fancy, it's nothing flash, it's just melt-in-the-mouth rich, indulgent, chocolate heaven—exactly what you want from a cake. And if you want to make it taste even better, sit and stare at it for ten minutes as it cools,' she added with a laugh, a genuine laugh that she promised herself she wouldn't edit out however bad she looked.

The cake went wrong twice. The first time she didn't mix it long enough and there were white swirls of flour in her mixture as she scooped it into the tin so she heaped it back into the bowl, gave it another quick whisk by hand and said, 'It could possibly be over-whipped now, and I probably should have started again, but I don't really have time and I certainly can't see you having time so let's just cross our fingers.' The second time she took it out of the oven too early and then put it back in for too long and burnt the top. 'See,' she said, 'everyone makes mistakes. It's really just looking at how you salvage them. There you go, cake as a metaphor for life,' she said with a knowing smile. 'I know you know there have been ups and downs in my life recently, but this blog is meant to be about us creating stuff out of nothing. It's meant to be positive. I find baking and cooking a real haven. Somewhere I can escape to when it all gets too tough, and I think that quite a lot of you must feel that way too. I know I've stopped it being possible to make comments on what I do—and I really miss all your lovely comments—but it just got a bit personal for a while there and I wasn't ready for that, because that isn't why I do this. I will put the comments back, I promise. Very soon. But for now, I'm just going to show you *me*, and you can decide if you like it—then we can get to know each other again.'

She sliced the burnt top off the cake and then slathered it in chocolate butter cream icing, dipping wedges of the chopped off top into the bowl and eating them as she iced. 'Oh my god, even the burnt bits are amazing,' she said, as she slid her finished cake onto one of her vintage glass cake stands. 'This is how we ate it as kids. Nowadays I tend to cover it in cherries—

especially when they're in season, which they are now, so...' She went over and took the camera from the tripod. 'I thought you might like to come and pick them with me.'

It was only as she walked to the door that she saw Eve standing watching in the shadows, clearly trying to look as if she wasn't, but with the sweetest, proudest smile on the face.

'This is my friend Eve,' said Libby, pointing the camera in Eve's direction, who put her hand up to shield her face and laughed. 'She's going to help me pick cherries.'

EVE

The next morning Eve was sitting with Jessica on the terrace having home-baked lemon curd cornettos and espresso for breakfast. The weather had changed overnight and they'd woken up to a thick marshmallow grey sky and a forest of fog rising over the lake. All the locals had their woolly jumpers on. With only a couple of days left, Eve and Jessica were sticking fast to the holiday feel in their flip-flops and vests; the only concessions to the chill were Eve's jeans and Jessica's big cotton scarf. Despite the goosebumps they pretended they were warm enough.

Eve had just put a big mouthful of cornetto in her mouth, the curd dripping out and onto her chin, when she heard a familiar voice say, 'Eve.'

'Peter?' she said, looking around, shocked to see him walking through the maze of tables to get to theirs, dishevelled, travel worn, greasy haired, tired and a little grey.

'What are you doing here?' Eve said, standing up so quickly her chair teetered. 'Where are the kids?'

'With my mother,' Peter said, rolling his hand luggage case up to the spare chair and then moving to stand opposite Eve.

Jessica dabbed her mouth with her napkin and said, 'You know, I'll probably just leave you two. Erm…' She pointed towards the lemon grove and got up and left.

'Are they OK?' Eve asked. 'Do they know you're here?'

Peter nodded. 'Yeah. They love it. She bought them an Xbox.'

'Oh my god.'

He shrugged. 'They like it.'

Eve sat down.

Peter sat down.

Eve pushed her hair back behind her ear. 'Why are you here?' she said.

'To see you,' he said, then picked up a spare knife and tapped the end on the table for a second or two before looking back at her and adding, 'I missed you.'

Eve didn't know what to say. She felt like she'd just been pushed off a ledge and was sitting startled, legs akimbo. The obvious answer was to say that she missed him too and then they would hug and kiss and all would be OK, but she had to tell him about Jimmy.

'You look good,' Peter said, staring at her face like he hadn't seen it in years.

'You look really tired.'

'My plane was delayed on the runway for hours.'

She nodded. 'I have to tell you something because I almost read your emails and I didn't because you told me and I trust you and so for you to trust me I have to tell you…'

Jimmy stepped out onto the terrace with a plate of cornettos and a cappuccino. He had a newspaper under his arm and was dressed for meditation in his wide, baggy, grey tracksuit pants and black t-shirt. 'Hey, dude,' he said, nodding to Peter like they'd been mates for years.

Peter raised a hand in greeting and nodded.

'I nearly kissed Jimmy,' said Eve.

Jimmy stopped where he was.

'You what?' Peter asked.

'Jimmy. We nearly kissed. But we didn't. Nothing happened.'

Jimmy turned on his heel and walked straight back into the hotel.

Peter's tired face fell. To Eve he looked just like Noah. Like he might cry, but without the trembling lip.

JESSICA

Jessica arrived at the beach as the first drop of rain fell. Lightly to begin with, just tiny circles in the lake like a million fish coming up for air.

Miles was just coming out of the water, a silhouette in the mist. He saw her as he was reaching to get his towel and he jogged over to where she was standing on the boardwalk. His hair was blacker from the water, his eyelashes clumped from the moisture, his cheekbones sharp, his expression serious. The clouds behind him looked like thunder.

'You OK,' he said, 'with everything yesterday?'

Jessica nodded.

'Good,' he said. 'So we can be normal?'

'Yeah.' She swiped some rain out of her eyes. 'But I still feel like I should keep apologising to you, just again and again.'

'Well that's stupid,' he said, towelling himself dry despite the rain. 'It's over, it's past. I was annoyed with you for a bit but, Jessica, it's so small in the scale of things.'

She nodded. 'I know. I just made it big.'

He watched her. The rain pattered down around them.

'And I'm not in love with you any more. I'm really not,' she said into the silence. 'Just for the record. Just to clarify.'

He nodded. 'OK.'

The clouds got darker. Over the lake they were black, swooping down on the treetops like smoke.

'OK,' she said, nodding her head.

'OK,' he said, his mouth just tilting up into a smile.

She huffed a small laugh. 'OK.'

He grinned at her.

'Thank you,' she said.

'Don't apologise again.'

'OK.'

He laughed. 'OK.' Then he put one hand out and squeezed her arm before jogging back up to the hotel, the rain getting steadily heavier as he disappeared into the lemon grove.

She watched him long after he'd gone. Knowing that that was as good as it was ever going to get. And she was OK with that.

LIBBY

Libby,

I am coming back. But my plane's been cancelled. There's been a massive dump of snow. The guys want to go back up, make the most of it. I'm sort of tempted. Otherwise I'll just be waiting at the airport. I am coming back though, I promise. I am coming to get you! Just need to wait for the snow to melt. Nothing's flying. It's a relief not to be the one to blame, actually.

Keep a biscotti back for me.

J

EVE

Peter and Eve stayed out on the terrace even when it started to rain. Sheltered by the awning, they watched as the water dripped down from the canvas onto the patio.

'Did you want to kiss him?' Peter asked, after Giulia had brought them out fresh espressos and he'd been to the bathroom to get himself together.

'Yes,' Eve said, hands cupped around her coffee, wishing she had a jumper. 'Initially, yes.'

'But then?'

'Well,' she said. 'Then I realised he wasn't you.'

Peter paused as he was about to lift his cup up, and looked at her.

'Why didn't you kiss your girl?' Eve asked.

Peter gave a small shrug. 'Same reason.'

'What was that?' she asked.

He looked confused. 'That she wasn't you, obviously.'

'I just wanted you to say it.'

'Oh god.' He rolled his eyes and downed the espresso.

The rain got heavier still, hammering down on the awning. Miles appeared from the lemon grove wrapped in a towel and nodded a quick hello as he jogged through the pouring rain and into the hotel.

Eve looked at Peter's hand on the table. His strong, long fingered, cool hand. It felt like years since she'd held it.

She looked at her own hand on the handle of her coffee cup, wondered if she could make it move telepathically, overcoming the fear of rejection that kept it firmly where it was. To make it creep over and link with his. She saw her little finger waggle, almost imperceptibly.

Then the gate to the lemon grove opened again.

'Oh god, sorry.' Jimmy paused, one foot on the terrace, a towel slung over his head to shelter him from the rain, no top on, bronzed chest, tattoos glistening.

Peter visibly shrank into himself, obscured his face by feigning an interest in the geraniums in the window boxes.

Jimmy stayed where he was, stalled in his tracks.

Eve closed her eyes for a second.

Jimmy took an embarrassed step forward. 'Sorry, sorry, guys, I didn't think you'd still be out here.'

Giulia appeared at the terrace doors. 'You want drinks?' she asked, grimacing at the rain as it poured off the side of the awning.

Peter nodded, clearly happy with the distraction, and said, 'I'll have a beer.'

'I'll have a gin and tonic,' said Eve. It was almost eleven and the situation seemed to call for it.

Jimmy shook his head and slipped past them into the hotel.

'Did you talk to him about us?' Peter asked when he was gone.

Eve nodded.

'What did he say?'

'That we'd be happier if we moved back to the city.'

Peter snorted. 'Doesn't he live on a boat in the middle of nowhere?'

Giulia came out with the drinks and, after depositing them on the table, shivered and said, 'You wouldn't prefer inside?'

Eve shook her head.

Peter took a swig of his beer. 'It's not actually that bad advice. Moving back. I miss the city.' He put the bottle down then ran his hands through his hair. 'If I hadn't done anything would anything have happened between the two of you? I mean, was it retaliation or would it have happened anyway?'

Eve thought about it for a while. 'Possibly,' she said in the end with an apologetic wince. 'It may not have happened then. But I think maybe it needed to happen at some point.'

Peter's face hardened. 'You'll have to explain that to me.'

'I think maybe I had to do it. For old me. The one that got left behind. I think it's always been a "what if", you know? If I'd gone cycling would my life be different now? And I think what it's shown me is that I don't think it would be.'

'Well, you wouldn't have Noah and Maisey,' Peter said.

'That's what I'm saying,' said Eve. 'I think I would. I would have all this, as it is, because me and Jimmy, we were right for a bit of our lives—not all of them. I wanted something different. I wanted to find someone who was happy to love me. Who took pride in it. You just stood there and were like—I'm more than happy to love you.'

Peter frowned. 'I wasn't more than happy to. I wanted to.'

'I know. You were a man.'

'A man?' Peter snorted into his beer.

Eve shrugged. 'I just think we've lost sight of each other. I mean, I feel like I haven't seen your face for ages.'

'That's because you've been away.'

Eve sighed. 'No, I don't mean it like that. I mean like I'm always looking somewhere else—sorting the kids, checking you're sorting the kids, checking my emails—I want to look up more. At you. At everything. I want to know how you are and for you to know how I am.'

Peter looked at her and nodded.

Eve shrugged a shoulder as if she'd said her bit.

'You know you wouldn't have Noah and Maisey though, don't you? You know how it works? That it would have had to have been those specific sperm and eggs on that specific day, and it's pretty unlikely that it would have happened like that if you'd gone off cycling round the world. What? Don't look at me like that. I'm just saying. I'm just checking that you don't believe it's like fate or anything like that.'

'Oh god.' Eve shook her head. 'You're totally ruining the moment.'

'What, with sense?'

Out over the lake it started to thunder.

'Yes,' Eve said, exasperated.

Peter half-smiled around his beer. 'Well, you wanted a man, Eve. That's what you're going to get. Strong, practical sense.'

Eve looked at the droplets of condensation on her gin and tonic, could feel the smile starting in her eyes, the bubble of comfortable happiness, the feeling that she could exhale again.

LIBBY

Libby was staring out of the window of the outhouse waiting for a lull in the rain so she could dash back to the hotel when Dex came running up the path from the forest. His hair was plastered to his head, his clothes soaked through. She pulled open the door for him and shouted, 'You can come in here if you want.'

There was no telling him twice. Dex shot in, shaking the rain off, swearing about the weather. 'Who comes to Italy for the rain? There I was having this really nice morning reading my book and then suddenly it's pissing it down. What's it playing at?'

Libby laughed. 'Do you want a coffee?'

'No, I want two fingers of brandy and an open fire,' he said, pulling off his t-shirt and wringing it out into the sink. 'Is that my jumper?' he said, pointing to his workbench chair.

Libby, side-tracked for a second by the sight of Dex's bare, tanned chest and the muscles that Eve had been admiring on the beach, took a moment to nod that it was.

'Brilliant!' he said, going over to pull on his sweater.

Libby stopped staring and poured cheap cooking brandy into two tumblers.

'Ah, you're an angel,' he said as she handed him a glass, and sat down on Jimmy's chair.

Dex knocked it back in one gulp and then went to get the bottle. 'So, what are you doing hiding out in here? Looking, if I might say, a tad glum.'

Libby sighed a smile and handed Dex her phone so he could read the two emails from Jake.

'Oh god, he is complete idiot,' Dex said, handing her the phone back. 'Only Jake would mess up coming to win you back and still manage to get something in about how great the snow is.'

Libby laughed. 'I know.'

'He's just selfish, Libby. Always has been.'

She nodded.

'What are you going to write back?'

'Nothing,' she said.

Dex frowned.

'I'm going to ring him. I can't do this over email any more. It's ridiculous.'

Dex took a gulp of the brandy, involuntarily grimaced, and then said, 'So what are you going to do—in the long term?'

She toyed with the glass in her hand, swirling the liquid as she shrugged, and said, 'Be on my own for a bit.'

There was a pause. Dex nodded. The rain got heavier. Like ball bearings pelting the roof.

'Well, if you ever decide it's time for someone new,' Dex said. 'I am always available.'

Libby laughed; then looking at him properly realised he was serious.

'Yes, I know,' said Dex, with a resigned shake of his head. 'I have loved you for years, Libby. Probably since you interviewed me for the room.'

Libby frowned. 'No you haven't.' The brandy suddenly seemed really strong and the rain deafening.

Dex shrugged. 'It's OK though. I keep it tucked away in my pocket. I just thought I'd tell you because I'd be annoyed if I didn't. Then I'll put it back again,' he said with the softest smile she'd ever seen on Dex's face.

Libby didn't know what to do.

But it was OK because Dex did it for her by saying, 'Right, let's top these up, shall we?' and sloshing some more brandy into the glass. 'You can tell me exactly what you're going to say to Jake. Use me as practice.'

'I'm not really sure what I'm going to say yet.'

'What do you think you're going to say?'

'I don't know. Something about how he can't think he can just come back and think he can slot right in.'

'Yes,' Dex nodded. 'Good start.'

'This is weird.'

'No, no, keep going, it's good.'

'I don't know what I'm going to say next, Dex. I want to tell him that I don't think he should come back at all but I'm worried he'll just jump in and bulldoze me with his way of doing things.'

Dex looked at her for a second then took another swig of brandy, leant forward and said, 'I'll tell you what, Libby, if I was you I'd say something like… I am worth ten thousand times more than this, Jake. I am somebody magnificent who should be cherished and loved and laughed along with and there are a million good people out there better for me than you.' He paused, traced a line on the work surface with his finger, then looked up and added, 'Jake belittled the value of something priceless that was entrusted into his care. And that's unforgivable. You have to say to him that you want to be with someone who is certain with all their heart that you are enough.' He shrugged. 'That's what I'd say anyway,' he said with a smile and then drained his brandy.

Libby stared at him for a second, unable to reply, then had to look away because she could see in his eyes how much he wanted that someone to be him.

JESSICA

'Jessica!'

She was standing on the boardwalk in the pouring rain, staring out at the lake. She'd decided not to go back to the hotel in case they were all together, chatting in the warmth of the bar, and she couldn't face it just yet. This felt like a moment—one that perhaps she should mark with a baptism of torrential rain and lightning forking on the horizon.

'Jessica!' Bruno was walking towards her from the direction of the bar. 'What are you doing standing in the rain?'

She narrowed her eyes to focus through the sheets of misty water. 'Nothing. I'm fine, I'm just watching.'

'You're soaking.'

'I know, I'm fine. It's only water.'

He got closer, wiping the rain from his face and brushing it from his hair with his hand. 'I like your style.'

She shrugged as carelessly as she could, quite pleased with what he would assume to be her *laissez faire* attitude to weather.

He stopped next to her; the sky rumbled with thunder, and they both looked out to the horizon where the forks of lightning were moving further away into the distance, the clouds still tumbling down with darkness.

'You look very beautiful,' he said, and she turned, realising his gaze had moved from the horizon to her profile, and did a little snort to say he was being preposterous.

He shrugged to say that she was wrong and he was right, then he leant forward and kissed her.

Jessica took a step back, startled. 'No, no, no, you can't do that. You can't just walk up to someone and just kiss them. I might not want you to kiss me.'

'We've kissed before.'

'Yes, I know, but I might not want to kiss now,' she said, caught off guard.

He chuckled. 'But you do.'

'How do you know?' she asked, disbelieving.

'Because I see you. I see it in you. It's obvious.' His mouth lifted up into a cocky grin as he took a step back, clasping his hands behind his back.

She shook her head. 'That's ridiculous,' she said, ignoring the fact it had actually been quite exciting to be kissed so passionately in a rain storm on holiday. 'And,' she went on, 'a terrible answer. Feminists could write whole theses on why that's such a terrible, presumptuous answer.'

Bruno ran his hand through his hair to shake off some more of the rain and then said, 'Are you a feminist?' over another shudder of thunder.

'Yes.'

'As am I,' he said.

Jessica rolled her eyes, 'Oh please.'

'Of course I am,' he said. 'I believe one hundred per cent that we are all equal. Why not? Where would the fun be otherwise?'

She had to wipe her eyes to see him properly, could feel the water beading on her face and eyelashes and turning her hair to long corkscrew curls.

'Jessica, I wholeheartedly want you to ravish me,' he said, spreading his arms wide, eyes dancing behind sheets of rain.

She bit down on a traitorous smile at the sight of him. 'You are unbelievable.'

'Come,' he beckoned, 'come with me to the beach. It's the perfect weather for sex.'

'What?' Jessica choked.

'Come on. You are thinking too much.'

She paused. He was right. She was massively overthinking. She had never had sex on a beach and her hesitation made it obvious.

Bruno frowned. 'It's the beach,' he said. 'Surely everyone has had sex on a beach?'

She shook her head. What if someone saw? She glanced around at the deserted rain-soaked landscape.

'Ha.' He clapped his hands together. 'Even better. Come, let me relieve you of this sad injustice.'

She stood where she was, thinking about it. How did he do this? How did he make her feel like she had a little bird trapped inside her, fluttering, excited to be finally set free?

'OK,' she said, surprising both of them. 'But that's all this is. You know that? Yes. Just a holiday fling. No more.'

He shrugged as if it was of no consequence to him either way. 'If that feels better for you,' he said.

Jessica nodded, then, checking behind her to make sure no one was watching, stalked past him towards a gap in the rocks.

LIBBY

'The thing is, Jake, I want to be with someone who is certain with all their heart that I am enough. And for the moment,' Libby paused, swallowed, then said, 'I want that person to be me.'

There was a silence at the end of the line. Then she heard Jake clear his throat before saying, 'But what will I do?'

Libby looked out at the rain-soaked view, at the water rolling round the ripe red cherries and the sparrows sipping from the puddle in the centre of the pink metal table. 'You'll be free.'

'I suppose at a push I could go back to the army,' he said.

'Jake, listen to me,' Libby said, taking a step outside, the damp grass springy under her feet. 'You'll be free. You can do whatever you like. That's what you wanted.'

'I've got friends in London. Friends in a lot of places actually,' Jake said. 'Maybe I should take a leaf out of Jimmy's book and cycle round the world.'

Libby watched the rain dripping from the cactus spikes of the prickly pear. Smelt the sharp citrus of the glistening fat lemons. She didn't want to hear it. It was his story now, not hers. Maybe one day they might be friends but she didn't want to be his friend right now. She wanted him to go back to London, to live in the flat, and for their lawyers to work out all the rest.

One day there might even be time for forgiveness.

For now, she had a lake to swim in, fresh lemons to pick, a blog to rebrand, and a hotel to renovate.

EVE

'So, back to the city you say?' Peter sat back in his chair, the remains of the rain dripping down the corners of the awning into big puddles on the patio. 'Interesting.'

'It's an idea,' Eve said.

'Or an elaborate ploy to get rid of the chickens?' Peter replied.

'The chickens can come too if they have to.'

'Or we could just eat them.'

'No.' Eve leant forward and smacked him on the thigh. 'We can't eat them, they're pets. They've had a hard life.'

'No, we probably shouldn't. I think they'd be quite tough as well. We'll just have to hope that the whole battery-hen trauma finishes them off.'

'I can't believe we're having this chat. This is meant to be a seminal romantic moment and we're talking about eating our pet chickens.'

Peter nodded. 'I know, it's barbaric. Do you want me to do something to make it more romantic? Go down on one knee or something?'

'No, it's all wet.'

'I can if you like, I don't mind. I've been doing yoga, I've become very supple,' he said, moving as if to drop down to the floor.

Eve frowned. 'When have you been doing yoga?'

'At work. They have a teacher who comes in once a week to de-stress the kids and there's a staff lesson afterwards.'

Giulia came out to clear away the empties and asked if they wanted more drinks.

'We're going to be drunk at this rate,' Eve said, ordering another gin and tonic.

'It's raining on holiday. What else is there to do?'

'I didn't know that you did yoga.'

'No.' Peter shook his head. 'I didn't tell you, I don't know why. Too busy?'

'You should tell me stuff like that,' Eve said, looking seriously at him.

'I know. But I'm a man. We don't do small talk.'

She rolled her eyes. 'You can't use that as an excuse for everything now, you know?'

Peter laughed.

Giulia came out with their refills.

'I want to hear your trivia,' Eve said when she'd gone.

Peter looked at her for a second, sitting back in his chair. 'OK.'

Suddenly a bit shy, Eve took a sip of her drink and looked across at the ferocious sky. When she turned back to Peter she said, 'Go on then.'

'What? Do some yoga?'

'No, get down on one knee.'

Peter glanced around him. 'There might be people watching.'

'Who?' said Eve, sweeping her arm to take in the empty tables and the drenched terrace. 'You suggested it.'

'OK, OK, I'm going down,' he said, putting his beer back on the table and sliding himself onto the rain-soaked floor.

Next minute he had her hand in his and, gazing adoringly up at her, said, 'Will you marry me, Eve?'

Eve sniggered. 'I already have.'

'I know,' Peter said before pushing himself up so he could cup her face in his hands. 'And it makes me the luckiest man alive,' he said looking down at her, blue eyes sparkling, before leaning in to kiss her with lips that tasted of beer and rain with the sound of her heart thumping in her chest almost as loud as the cicadas.

'I read your script by the way,' she said when he had sat back down, her hand held tight in his like he was never letting go.

'And?' He looked like Noah again, vulnerably nervous.

'You're funnier than I gave you credit for.'

She saw the corner of his mouth tilt. 'You think I'm funny?'

'Yeah.'

'Well, you should have just said that from the start. All of this was completely unnecessary…' He waved a hand as if the last hour or so was nothing. 'You really think I'm funny?'

She nodded.

Peter's mouth stretched into the widest smile. 'She thinks I'm funny,' he said to Giulia, who had come out to wipe the rain off the tables; she gave him a look like she couldn't care less. 'She thinks I'm funny,' he said again to himself, and Eve watched him as he watched her and he said, 'I love you more than anyone else in the world.' Then added, 'Except maybe the kids, but they're half me so that stands to reason.'

LIBBY

When Miles knocked on Libby's door that night—all dark, brooding eyes and self-assured certainty—she thought just how easy it would be to push the door open and let him stalk inside.

But, unlike other nights, she stood instead with the door ajar and said, 'Miles, this isn't right. It's been very lovely, but it's not right.'

He raised a dark brow, surprised.

'We're just using each other,' she said. 'You don't fancy me.'

'I fancy you,' he said.

'Not like this you don't,' she said, and he frowned. 'We're never going to be together and I don't want to ruin us as friends.'

Miles listened, the hint of a smile on his lips.

Libby looked down at the floor, at her bare feet on the newly polished boards. 'The thing is, while it's been really fun, it's messing with what's starting to become clear to me, about my life and stuff,' she said, pushing her hair back from her face. 'That sounds bad, but it's not bad. It's been like this lovely bubble. But I think now it has to end. Now it's all a bit more real.'

Miles nodded. 'It would end tomorrow though, wouldn't it?' he said. 'I go back to the States and that'll be it done.'

'I know,' she said. 'But I feel like if it doesn't happen tonight then there's more chance of us just being friends. All of us. That's what I want it to end on.'

Miles bit down on his bottom lip, stared at her for a second, and then nodded. 'Fair enough,' he said. 'That's a good point.'

Part of her was desperate to ask him in. Just to smell him. He smelt so good. She remembered the teeth clashing and the taste of his lips. 'Are you mad?'

'Seriously?' He made a face. 'Of course I'm not mad. Just, maybe a bit frustrated,' he added with a laugh.

She smiled.

He reached up and touched her hair. 'Lib, this was one of the best things that could have happened to me this holiday.'

'Really?' she said, surprised. 'I've felt really guilty about Flo.'

'No, don't.' He shook his head. 'I've known I've had to move on for a while. In a funny kind of way I think she'd have approved.'

Libby snorted a laugh. 'I'm not so sure.'

He smiled. 'Maybe not. But no, I think she would. No, it's good. And good to end it as well. Very grown up, Libby. Well done.'

'Thanks.'

He nodded, then leant down and kissed her softly on the cheek, his hand resting on her shoulder. And as his lips were just touching her cheek she inhaled. For one last smell of him. So she could remember.

'Goodnight, Miles,' she said, stepping back.

'Night, Libby.' Their eyes met and his mouth split into a grin. 'If you find you need anything, I'm just there up the hall.'

'I'll bear that in mind,' she said with a smile, and closed the door.

EVE

Eve woke up when a note was pushed under the door of her bedroom.

She crept out of bed, careful not to wake Peter, and picked up the slip of A4.

It was from Jimmy to say he was leaving early to catch his plane. He asked her to thank Libby for her hospitality and then wished Eve well, saying how nice it had been to see her.

She read it and reached for the door handle, knowing there was time still to catch up with him. But then she pulled her hand away and stood for a second before turning to look at Peter, fast asleep, the dawn sunrise casting a soft haze of light in the room, the lemon scent drifting through the open windows, and she folded up the note, dropped it in the rubbish bin, and slipped back into bed.

She slept soundly for another hour until Libby knocked on her door and called, 'OK, we need to get going.'

They all assembled in the lobby, dressed for the last time in their boilersuits. Peter was more than happy that there weren't any spares.

'So, there's loads to do still and one day left to do it,' said Libby, her smile clearly strained as she looked down at her list. 'Jimmy's gone so we need someone to take over the garden. Peter? Do you know anything about gardening?'

Peter shook his head. 'I have tended to kill most plants I've ever owned.'

'Right.' Libby frowned. 'OK, forget the garden for the moment. We need the furniture we're not using taken out and the bits from the garage brought in. There are two rooms still to be painted, and…' She looked at the list. 'Oh god, there's the floors. There's three floors still to polish. The light fittings need changing. Shit. OK. No it's fine. It's fine. Then there's the terrace. Dex, that's pretty much done, isn't it?'

Dex made a face. 'Some of the tables could do with a sand and a paint.'

Libby brought her hands up to her temples. Eve could see the panic in her eyes. 'Oh, I forgot about them,' Libby said. 'Oh Jesus. OK, well, let's just get done what we can done.'

When Libby smiled her big fake smile at the group Eve had to look away. Which meant she was the first to see Bruno appear on the terrace. She watched him pause and turn to look at something, frown, and then make a gesture as if he was chivvying small children. Eve watched, intrigued.

'Ms Libby?' Bruno said, opening the terrace doors, summoning Libby's attention.

Libby turned. 'Oh, hi, Bruno.'

'Hello,' he said, as if pleasantries were by the by. 'I have brought you some help,' he said, then stood back and ushered in all his young hipster bar staff.

Libby's eyes widened. 'You don't have to do that, Bruno,' she said.

'Don't worry, it is good for them. They need to learn how to work,' he said, winking at the rest of them as his staff trouped in, unimpressed. 'We are at your service.'

Eve bit down on a smile as she watched them trying to maintain their cool as they all pressed up single file against the wall. Then she turned to see Libby quite overcome.

'Well erm,' Libby was consulting her list, confused and emotional. 'I wonder, maybe, erm…perhaps some of you could do the garden?' she asked.

Bruno threw his hands wide. 'I love the garden. I am very good with the garden.'

'Excellent.' Libby beamed.

Eve glanced at Jessica who rolled her eyes but couldn't hold back a smile.

Libby was just making more notes on her list, dividing up the work, when the front door opened and Giulia walked in carrying a massive heap of curtains.

'I bring these,' she said. 'My mother is working on the yellow ones and my aunt she is making the white ones.'

'Oh, I didn't know your family were—' Libby started, guiltily.

Giulia cut her off. 'My mother is eighty-two. She is very happy to have something to do. I am very happy for her to have something to do because it means that she doesn't spend her time telling me what to do. For these curtains, we all win,' Giulia said in her usual deadpan tone, and dumped the pile of new curtains on the floor in the lobby. Then she took a scarf out of her pocket, tied it round her hair, and said, 'Now I am ready for the painting. And,' she said, taking a step back and a quick look out of the front door, 'Dino is just arriving and he has brought friends and then my sister will come this afternoon with her husband and their son. So we have the full house.' She walked towards the group, rubbing her hands together.

Eve watched Libby. She was hesitating. Eve could see that she didn't quite know what to do or say. All her emotions—surprise, gratitude, uncertainty—were playing on her face. So when Giulia said, 'Well, where are we starting?' it was Eve who stepped forward, took the list from Libby's hand, and replied, 'We'll have one team bringing in from the garage, and one taking out from the bedrooms. If you prefer to paint stand over here.' She pointed to the bottom step of the staircase.

'Come on,' she said, ushering some of the reluctant hipsters forward. 'And we'll have sand and polishers stand here. Giulia, you're in charge of curtains and curtain hanging—take all the help you need. And Libby, I think you're going to have to oversee in general. Check that you're happy with which paintings go where and what lighting. Yes?'

Libby nodded, less shell-shocked, more touched, and slowly a smile began to spread over her previously anxiety riddled face. A real smile. A wide, double-chinned, toothy, excited, childish smile. One that made Eve lift up her phone and take a photo.

LIBBY

They worked tirelessly until well beyond sunset, like ants, lifting, lugging, hammering, and painting. And, when it was done, the Limoncello once again stood proud, ready and waiting to show itself off to guests. Ancient oil paintings hung next to fairy lights twinkling around white billowing curtains. Brass lampstands with fringed shades stood on upturned tea chests either side of freshly painted bedsteads. Old Indian kilim rugs were laid on newly polished herringbone parquet and in the lobby the strips of halogen lights had been replaced by the original wooden chandeliers, sanded back to the bare wood and rewired by jack-of-all-trades Dino.

It was old meets new. The same but different. For Libby, as she wandered the corridor in the middle of the night, poking her head proudly into the unoccupied rooms, and staring out at the moonlit garden, it felt like she finally understood why she'd been left this place: because she had the capacity to carry on its promise of great food and slightly erratic hospitality that was nothing if not interesting. It was her job to pick up the baton left by her aunt. To fill the Limoncello with these people that made her open her eyes wider and live her life better and laugh louder and remember that she was good enough on her own. And if she wasn't, they would be there to help her.

When she woke up the next morning she could barely believe that it was the last one. It made her sick to think about it. It was like the day they all moved out of the flats. A compulsory purchase order slapped on by the council meant they were forced to take their next steps. Libby and Jake got a flat together, Miles went with Flo to the States, Dex, Eve, and Jessica talked noncommittally about getting a place but Eve was already staying most nights at Peter's and ducked out of the trio to move in with him. Then Jessica got a job in North London and Dex categorically refused to move north of the river so they all went their separate ways. Their boxes all in different rented vans and boots of cars, they'd stood together on the pavement staring up at their soon to be demolished block, no one saying anything, the sun shining hard, reflecting off the windows and the dirty white paint.

One of her favourite memories was of laughing as she found herself tearing up and Dex putting his arm around her when Jake had scoffed that it was only a flat. It only occurred to her now that Dex must have loved her then. She had always remembered that hug, could still feel the warmth and the kindness of it.

Libby got up and opened the curtains, looking out at the sun-soaked garden and her outhouse. Like standing on that pavement outside the flats, she wanted her friends to stay beside her forever, but there were real Sunshine and Biscotti customers waiting—more than she knew how to handle after a flood of bookings post her chocolate cake blog—and she knew they were a safety net she had to let go.

So, as it was their last morning, Libby decided to end it as they began. Making biscotti.

The sun was shining. The sky was a huge blanket of blue, marked only by far off aeroplane tracks; insects danced in the heat and birds swooped to sip from the lake.

Everyone had taken their normal places in the outhouse except Bruno, who had moved across to Jimmy's old table so Peter could have his without it being symbolically awkward.

Eve had been glowing ever since Peter had arrived— from the freckles on her face, to the curl of her smile, to the shine on her hair—and proudly showed them all her liquorice, chinotto, and prickly pear combo, delighting in their eye-popping reactions.

Since Dex had confessed his feelings to Libby he'd acted like nothing had happened. He'd been exactly as he always was—exactly as he promised he'd be, laughing and joking as he decorated yesterday and now making the usual hash of his biscotti baking. Libby on the other hand found herself acting a little shy around him, more formal. All confused when she looked at him. When she went over to his bench as he was laying out his mixture she said lamely, 'Very good. Very uniform.'

Dex raised a brow and said, 'I will cherish that compliment forever.' Then he laughed as the lapse in concentration made him mess up the next one.

Libby smiled too slowly, hyperaware of how she was acting around him, and so backed away to carry on her stroll around the room. Bruno was making a snazzy trio of chocolate biscotti. Peter, slightly bemused at the fact he was making anything at all, had settled on a simple, plain biscotti, while Eve furiously grated liquorice and chinotto into her mix.

When Libby reached Miles and his tray of perfect lemon biscuits, she leaned on the bench and said, 'Those are beautiful biscotti.'

And Miles laughed. 'I had a very good teacher,' he said with a wink before getting diligently on with his bake.

Libby went and stood alone at the front of the room, watching them all.

Bruno looked around at everyone hard at work and said, 'So this is a yearly thing, yes? This reunion?'

Libby shook her head. 'I don't think so.'

'It would be a shame to only do it once when you have all come so far,' he said, and, after a pause, added, 'with the baking.'

Miles turned at his bench. 'Very perceptive, Bruno.'

Bruno laughed. 'I am very in touch with my emotions. Unlike you boys.' He glanced over his shoulder at Jessica. 'And girls.'

Jessica rolled her eyes. Dex snorted.

'I'll come back next year,' said Eve. 'I'd love to.'

'You would?' Libby said, surprised.

'Definitely.' Eve nodded.

'Well, you're more than welcome,' she said. 'Any time.'

'No, I don't want any time. I want our time,' said Dex. 'First week pre-season. That should be reserved for us.'

Libby laughed. 'I'll put it in the diary,' she said, wishing, but not quite believing, that it would happen.

*

When it came to waving them off in their taxis Libby found it so emotional she had to get straight back to work to distract herself. She headed for her office, determined to get more of a handle on the accounts, but found Giulia sitting in her seat.

'Oh.' Libby paused in the doorway.

'I just install a new system. My cousin owns a hotel in Florence. He tells me all about it. It is the best,' Giulia said, tapping away at the computer keys.

'Right.' Libby nodded. 'That sounds good.'

'Yes,' said Giulia. 'Here, I show you how to use it.' She patted the stool next to her and Libby duly went over and sat down.

'So, this is all the new bookings. Look, you are nearly full,' Giulia said, pointing to the little red squares all over the screen. 'There are some people asking for the winter. Are you doing your club in the winter?'

Libby shook her head. 'I don't know. I thought I'd see.'

'Well, you need to decide. Pronto.' She opened another page on the screen. 'And look here, you already have bookings into next summer.'

Giulia's hand stilled on the mouse.

Libby leant forward and narrowed her eyes at the screen. Four rooms booked out for the first week pre-season. All the surnames of her friends. Libby felt her mouth tilt into a half-smile. She put her hand to her chest.

When she looked at Giulia she expected her to roll her eyes at the tear Libby couldn't swipe away fast enough; she didn't expect the small, slightly hesitant pat on the back and the nod that might at a push be deemed as praise, in the right light.

EVE

They were so late for their plane. Eve and Peter's taxi had broken down on the way to the airport so, after furious phone calls and terrible Italian, they managed to get Jessica and Dex's cab to turn around and head back to pick them up. Miles had left earlier for his transatlantic flight. They all clambered in together, much to the annoyance of the driver who stood swearing and smoking at the side of the road as they tried to force all their luggage into the boot. In the end they all crammed into the beaten up old Merc with no air conditioning and a dangerously laconic driver. Eve spent the entire journey praying that she would live to see her kids again.

So when they finally pulled up at Departures she had never been more relieved to see an airport terminal; she was just taking a moment to stand on the pavement and catch her breath when she saw a familiar face watching from the revolving doorway.

'Jimmy?' she said, turning quickly to see if Peter and the others had seen.

Dex looked confused. 'What's he doing here? He left yesterday.'

Jessica shrugged, wary.

Peter, who was on his phone and hadn't heard, glanced up to see what the hold-up was. 'What's going on?'

'It's Jimmy,' said Eve. 'He's here.'

As she said it Jimmy seemed to pluck up his courage and started to walk with purpose towards them, his rucksack slung over his shoulder.

Dex took a step backwards to stand alongside Jessica. Peter took a step forward to be closer to Eve.

Eve didn't know what to do. She didn't want a scene. It was all going so well.

The air smelt of cigarette smoke, hot sun, and diesel fumes and was peppered with the sound of whistles, car horns, and the intermittent voice of the tannoy through the revolving door.

When Jimmy got closer he seemed to take a breath and brace himself, as if he'd been building up for hours to this moment. Eve could almost see the whiteness of nerves underneath his tan.

'Hi,' he said when he reached them, dropping his bag at his feet and pulling at the neck of his t-shirt as if it was too tight.

'All right, Jimmy?' Dex nodded.

Jimmy nodded.

'Why are you still here?' Eve said softly.

He took in a breath; he clearly didn't know what to do with his hands so he stuffed them in his pockets and said, 'I was waiting for you.'

Eve felt her whole body clench. 'Don't do this, Jimmy.'

Jimmy hesitated.

'There's no point fighting for me. I can't be with you, I'm sorry,' Eve said. 'This is about my family,' she said, turning to look at Peter. 'I love Peter and while I did once care so deeply about you it just wasn't the same. It wasn't this. I'm so sorry. I'm so sorry that you've waited. But, Jimmy—it will always be Peter. Always.'

Jimmy looked down at the floor.

Eve had her hand to her mouth, knowing she had just broken his heart. Wishing there was something else she could do, say, to make them all OK.

Jimmy took a moment, nodded, ran his hand over his mouth, then looked up. 'I was, err…' He bit down on his lip. 'I was actually err…waiting, because I wanted to talk to Peter,' he said.

Eve glanced at Peter, confused.

'Yeah.' Jimmy nodded a couple more times. 'Yeah, I didn't want to leave it how it was. You know? Without clearing the air.'

'Oh.' Eve frowned.

'Yeah. I err…·I didn't want there to be any animosity, you know, so we couldn't do this again. I was here thinking that it had been really fun and I didn't want to have been the one to screw it up. I'm really sorry, mate,' he said, turning to Peter.

Eve felt a creeping blush of embarrassment start to spread up her neck as she thought about everything she'd just said. She looked surreptitiously round to check the others' expressions and saw Jessica clearly holding in the giggles.

Peter was watching Jimmy, his eyes narrowed.

'It wasn't my place to do anything,' Jimmy went on. 'I knew she was married. I knew she had kids. I just suddenly saw what I'd missed.'

Eve wanted to step in and make some comment about how she was standing right there and that it hadn't all been in Jimmy's court but she knew enough to realise this wasn't the moment.

Peter nodded almost imperceptibly, clearly drawing the moment out to make Jimmy suffer.

'I think perhaps it was, you know, in the air— reunion, old times, all that kind of thing. But I would really like you not to hold it against me. You know, put it down to the heat. I was fully intending to just piss off but I realised, I don't know, that it needed an apology. So…' Jimmy stepped forward, his hand outstretched to shake. 'I'm sorry, mate.'

Peter looked from Jimmy to his proffered hand and waited a second longer than was polite, making it look like he might leave him hanging, then he drew his hand out of his pocket and reached forward to meet Jimmy's in a shake.

Jimmy blew out a breath of relief then laughed. 'Jesus, I thought I'd had it then.'

Peter shrugged a polite smile.

'I half expected you to deck me one,' Jimmy added, reaching into his pocket for a tissue so he could wipe the beads of nervous sweat from his forehead.

Peter shook his head then said, as if quoting someone, 'Only the person who is emotionally unfulfilled resorts to violence.'

Jimmy started to smile, surprised. 'You're studying mindfulness?'

Peter looked equally shocked that Jimmy had picked up on his reference. 'Only a bit, just as part of this initiative at work.'

'Really? That's really good. I'm really into it. Reading everything at the moment,' Jimmy said, and pulled a battered paperback out of his back pocket to show him. 'Right now I'm looking at developing emotional intelligence through mindfulness.'

'Nice, yeah,' Peter said, and reached to have a quick look at the book cover. 'I've got a book on that.'

'Really?'

'Yeah,' he said, handing Jimmy's book back. 'I mean, not much time to read it but I try to fit in a bit of daily meditation now. At work we have designated sessions.'

'That's really great.'

'You meditate?' Peter asked

Jimmy nodded. 'All the time.'

'Do you have a mantra.'

'Nah.'

'Oh I do. I really need it.'

Eve looked at them both, dumbfounded. 'What are you talking about? Peter, I didn't know you meditated?'

Jimmy made a guilty face as though he might have unwittingly started an argument.

'Yeah, it's part of the whole yoga thing,' Peter said to Eve.

'You do yoga?' Jimmy asked. 'What type?'

'Oh, I don't think we've got that far. It's called yoga as far as I know.'

Jimmy nodded, still impressed.

'Wait, wait,' said Eve. 'Just go back, you have a mantra? What's your mantra?'

Peter shook his head. 'Oh I can't tell you. We were each given our own personal one. You shouldn't tell anyone. It's yours and specific to you.'

'Oh, come on,' Eve scoffed. 'You can tell me.'

'No.' Peter shook his head.

'He's right,' said Jimmy. 'You should never feel you have to tell anyone your mantra.'

'Oh, for god's sake.' Eve sighed. Then, not quite sure she was happy with this turn of events and their buddy buddy-ness, said, 'We've got to get moving, we're going to miss our plane. Jimmy, it was nice to see you again to say goodbye.' She went over to give him a quick hug but he held up a hand to stop her.

'I'm actually booked on your flight as well,' he said, looking a fraction sheepish.

'You are?' Dex said, wheeling his and Jessica's luggage trolley up level with them.

'Yeah,' Jimmy said, nodding. 'I thought I should probably sort my shit out a bit in London. Can't live on a boat forever, can you?'

'What about CeeCee?' asked Jessica, her expression innocent, her eyes knowing.

'Who's CeeCee?' Dex asked with a frown.

'You remember—the owner of the boat,' Jessica said.

'Yeah, she's erm… She's err…' Jimmy scratched his head.

Jessica's mouth stretched into a grin. 'Sailed off without you?'

Jimmy shook his head from side to side. 'Something like that.'

Dex stifled a smile. 'So you need somewhere to stay?' he asked.

'Nah, mate, thanks.' Jimmy shook his head. 'I'm actually going to hook up with Jake.'

'Jake!' Eve's eyes widened.

'No kidding?' said Dex.

'Well…' Jimmy shrugged. 'Someone's gotta be there for him.'

No one said anything to agree.

'Like old times,' said Dex.

'Yeah.' Jimmy nodded. 'A whole new chapter. Young-ish, free and single,' he said, picking up his bag and turning to walk towards the revolving doors, the rest of them following behind with their trolleys. Then he glanced over his shoulder and said, 'Jealous?'

Jessica shook her head. 'Not one little bit.'

Eve looked down to hide her smile, hanging back so she could walk with Peter, his hand reaching over to link tight with hers as they walked through the airport doors.

JESSICA

Jessica had been back at work a week and already the holiday felt like a lifetime ago, relegated to a screensaver photo of the view out to the lake taken from Bruno's jetty.

She hadn't emailed Bruno even though she'd thought about him, instead filing the memory under 'holiday romance' and focusing on all the work she had to catch up on. She had made one fairly—for Jessica—monumental change, however, and moved her belongings out of her office and into a spare desk in the open plan, next to Dex's.

Dex watched, intrigued, a smirk on his lips as she carried her meagre box of possessions over.

'Well, this is a change,' he said.

'Don't make a big deal out of it,' Jessica warned.

Dex laughed and turned back to his computer.

She wasn't a hundred per cent sure of the change. There was no doubt she was more involved. Less reclusive. People started talking to her about more than just work and the foosball league. They asked about her holiday, about her lunch and her weekend and evening plans. She was slowly becoming part of the team. And, even though she was now subject to Dex's pitifully short attention span and semi-constant chat, being part of the team wasn't as horrendous as she thought.

But she missed her office. There was no doubt about that. Her cosy little corner that was all hers where she could block out the world. Another safety blanket, Bruno would say.

Bruno.

The thought of him made her roll her eyes and do a little shake of her head, but then, against her better judgement, smile a little as she opened a new document or checked her emails.

'Coming?' Dex asked.

They were having a meeting—in the new boardroom created out of Jessica's old office. The beanbag casual chat area was now fully relegated to the company archives.

The boardroom had a fridge stocked with Cokes and soft drinks, a bowl of fresh fruit on the table and, on Dex's insistence, a Nespresso machine with a tin of little individually wrapped biscotti.

Four of the design team were already seated and discussing the flavour nuances of the different coloured Nespresso pods when Jessica and Dex joined them. Dex made everyone coffees as if he was in an Italian café, adding a little spoon, sugar sachet, and biscotti to the saucers. Jessica watched amused as they all gleefully unwrapped their biscuits while she pulled her presentation up on the screen.

Becky, their junior designer, was just passing handouts round when there was a knock on the door and Bruno's grinning head appeared in the glass porthole.

'Oh my god,' Jessica whispered, hand frozen over her keyboard.

'Who's that?' asked Becky, frowning disparagingly at the excitable-looking imposter.

'Bruno!' Dex slammed his hands down on the table in delight.

Becky raised a brow at Jessica who found herself staring back at her blankly.

Bruno was in her office. Tanned face, thick dark hair, ancient green t-shirt under a beautifully cut grey suit, aviators hooked into his top pocket.

He stood in the doorway, all confident, cocky smile, his hands in his pockets pushing back the flaps of his jacket.

'What brings you to London?' Dex asked, standing next to him, clearly delighted by the turn of events and chucking Jessica a wink.

'I have come to take Ms Jessica for coffee.'

Jessica's eyes widened. She was completely at sea as to what to do. Half fizzing with excitement, half mortified, as she glanced around and saw all the designers staring at her.

She could feel her cheeks flushing beetroot as she stood up and said, 'I'm actually in the middle of a meeting,' knowing it was possibly the most ungrateful response she could have come up with but not knowing what else to say.

Dex frowned. But Bruno just shrugged. 'That's OK,' he said. 'I can wait.' He looked around. 'Play a little pinball,' he added.

'No,' she said ushering him out of the boardroom. 'No one plays it.'

Bruno frowned in confusion. 'Why not?'

'Because it's annoying. Look, you can't wait here,' she said quickly, her voice a whisper.

Giving up her office was one step; public displays of any kind of affection, feelings, or emotion, especially ones in the workplace, were another thing entirely. Things to be tackled further down the line.

'There's a coffee shop, two doors along, I'll meet you there,' she said, almost pushing him in her desperation to get him out of the building. 'Give me half an hour.'

She could feel Bruno taking in the panic in her eyes and the pinking of her cheeks. He glanced behind her to where everyone had paused at their computers. She could see them reflected in the window. All absorbing the scene, fascinated, and everyone in the meeting room transfixed, Dex grinning with delight.

Bruno turned back to Jessica, slipped his shades on, tucked his hands back in his pockets, and said, 'Take your time,' before strolling out of the building.

Jessica could barely concentrate on anything in the meeting. Her mind kept wandering to Bruno in London. Would he be able to find the coffee shop? Of course he would. He wasn't an idiot. What would he be saying? Oh god, why was he here? Dex kept trying to catch her eye. She refused.

When the meeting finished she watched the youngest design assistant scuttle over to her desk and start whispering with the other assistants, glancing repeatedly back in Jessica's direction. One of them giggled. Jessica felt her shoulders tense as she walked back to her computer. She hated being watched, couldn't remember how to put one foot in front of the other as she felt the meerkat heads all turn in her direction. When she finally reached her chair she sat down and clicked on her computer. She was about to put her headphones on to block them all out when Dex appeared, looming over her desk.

'What are you doing here?' he asked, annoyed.

'Checking my emails,' she said, a little curt.

'Get the hell out of here. There's a man waiting in a café for you. And, I might add, the most miserable café in the vicinity. You could at least have sent him to the pub.'

'I didn't think.'

'Stand up. Go.'

'Why is he here?'

'I have no idea.' Dex raised his hands. 'I can tell you now, though, he's not about to bloody ask you to marry him so there's nothing serious to worry about.'

'That's true.' She nodded. 'We'll probably just have a cappuccino and that'll be it.'

'Yes,' he said, taking a seat on the edge of her desk. 'Although possibly have an espresso. It's very uncool and un-Italian to order a cappuccino after midday.'

'Why is he here, Dex?'

'Go and find out. Jesus, Jessica. This could be fun. The Miles thing is over, thank god. Grow some balls.'

'You can talk,' she said in defence. 'I didn't see you telling Libby how you feel.'

Dex straightened up. 'I did actually.'

'You did?'

'Yes.' He looked around at all the surreptitious earwigging. 'Jesus, why did you give up your office?'

'You encouraged me to.'

'Well anyway, I told her.'

'And?'

'No.'

'No?'

'No.'

'OK?'

'OK.'

'Sure?'

'Sure.'

Jessica looked at him, trying to convey her sympathy in her eyes. He shrugged a shoulder as if it were nothing.

'It's fine,' he said. 'It's good. It's out now. Quite a relief really. And I'll tell you what, if I had the female equivalent of Bruno—a bona fide Olympic hero, Jessica—waiting for me in a café, I would be down there. In a flash.'

'Do you want me to ask him if he has a sister?'

Dex thought about it for a second then said, 'Not a bad shout, actually.'

Jessica smiled. 'You definitely think it's a no with Libby?'

'Don't change the subject.'

'I just don't know if it's right. Him and me.'

'Well, you shagged him twice. For you that's a bloody miracle. God knows what you'll do if you are sure it's right.'

Jessica sniggered.

'Seriously, Jessica.' Dex tapped the top of her computer as he stood up to leave. 'People don't wait forever.'

'Will you wait for Libby?'

He laughed. 'We're not talking about me,' he said and turned to go back to his desk.

She watched him walk away. Then she glanced behind her at the people pretending to work. As she turned back to her computer and her photo of the lake on the screen, a reel of images flashed through her head—she saw herself in the New York bar shouting at Flo, sitting in the diner with Dex, standing with Miles in the rain, and then right back to walking away from her parents' house with just her rucksack knowing if she ever went back it wouldn't be for years. She thought of answering the ad for a flatmate and meeting two naive idiot girls who giggled too much and having to beg them to let her stay. She thought of writing her apology to Flo. To Miles. Maybe even to herself.

So why? Why did she feel so watched? So judged? And why did she care so much? She glanced up at the young design assistants—all around the age she was when she moved in with Eve and Libby. What had she known about life then? How many people had she judged and found wanting?

What had she known?

Everything.

Nothing.

She had come so far. Too far to care so much what other people thought.

She bent down and picked up her bag.

When she stood up and shrugged on her jacket she half expected the whole office to burst into spontaneous applause. Instead junior designer Becky stood up and said, 'Will you be out long? We've got to go over those samples?'

As Jessica paused, completely out of the zone of answering work questions, Dex spun round in his chair and said, 'Leave it with me.'

And Jessica walked out, realising finally that no one really cared.

*

As she approached the café she saw Bruno sitting outside having a loud gesticulating chat with the moody owner. One ankle crossed over his opposite knee, leaning comfortably back in his chair, he was nodding and then jumping in as they talked, an espresso steaming on the table in front of him.

At the end of the road the sun was just peeking out from behind a skyscraper like a game of hide and seek, casting a few shafts of dusty light on the café tables and the shabby trees standing at intervals along the pavement.

The café owner was laughing. Nodding. Laughing again. Jessica had never seen him crack anything so much as a smile previously. Their exchanges had always been curt, perfunctory. Bruno, though, was in deep conversation, telling some wild involved story and the café owner had stopped his clearing up to listen, to frown, to smile, to clap, to belly laugh. Finished, Bruno sat back, arms crossed over his chest, proud as though his work was done.

Then he caught sight of Jessica and immediately his mouth stretched into a wide grin; he raised a hand and beckoned her over as if he owned the place.

'Jessica!' he shouted.

She walked over, a touch wary.

'This is her,' he said to the café owner. 'You know her?'

The café owner gave her a look up and down, acting like he didn't see her every day of the year, and shook his head.

Bruno frowned as if he couldn't believe it. 'Well, Jessica this is Lucas. Lucas, Jessica. Now you've met.'

They shook hands, Jessica half lamenting the loss of her coffee anonymity, half quite pleased that she might become one of those people who knew people—who made casual chat.

She sat down opposite Bruno, the sun on her back, and Lucas went inside to make her the espresso she ordered.

'So, why are you here?' she said once they were alone and immediately regretted her abruptness.

Bruno laughed. 'I came to take you for coffee.'

'All the way from Italy?' she said, incredulous.

He shrugged. 'It's only a few hours.'

She raised her brows.

'Like taking a bus,' he said with a cocky half-smile, and sat back as Lucas brought out the coffee.

'You came two hours on a plane to take me for coffee?'

Bruno nodded.

'But we agreed it was just a holiday fling.'

He pulled on his shades and gestured to the beaming sun as it slipped further out from behind the skyscraper. 'And I'm on holiday.'

Jessica shook her head and then sat back with her espresso, defeated.

'So are you pleased to see me?' he asked.

'I don't know.'

He laughed. 'I'm always pleased by your honesty.'

She felt herself getting warm and had to shrug off her jacket. 'I just don't want you to expect anything,' she said.

He held his hands wide. 'I expect nothing.'

'But you've come all this way.'

'For coffee,' he said. 'Very good coffee and very good company.'

'I haven't been good company so far.'

'Well, try harder.'

'I'm worried that you've had a wasted trip.'

He huffed a laugh. 'Don't worry so much.'

'I can't help it.'

'Yes you can.'

'You flew all the way here to see me—that's pressure.'

Bruno leant forward, resting his forearms on the table. 'OK, how about I say my sister lives here. I come over and see her quite a lot. Does that help?'

'Is it true?'

He laughed. 'You are very suspicious.'

'Did you come to see your sister this time?'

'No, I came to have coffee with you. But I will see my sister. If there's time.'

Jessica didn't say anything, just bought some time by sipping her coffee. Then she sat forward gesturing between the two of them and said, 'I just don't see how this would work.'

'Jessica…'

'What?'

'The sun is shining. We have half a coffee left. Just relax. Talk.'

'What about?'

'What was your meeting about?'

'It's a big rebrand we're doing. For a museum.'

'Interesting,' he said, getting comfy in his chair. 'Tell me about it.'

So she told him about the rebrand. And he asked questions. She told him about working with Dex. About setting Dex up with Bruno's sister which was impossible because she was happily married with three children. They talked about cappuccino etiquette and Bruno nodded seriously and said, 'Never after breakfast.' They talked about the Olympics, Italy, the bar. And they had more coffee. And then they strolled across London, along the Thames, over the river. They popped into the Tate; glanced at some art. Then they passed a pub and Jessica found herself suggesting a beer. When they walked inside she felt Bruno place his hand on the small of her back, not guiding her inside but almost letting her know he was there. And when she got the drinks and turned to the table she found herself glad that it was him sitting there. At no point in the afternoon had she had to think of what to say next or rehearse questions and answers in her head. She had chatted as she chatted to her friends—easily, calmly, wittily.

She looked at him. Short dark hair a bit messed, shoulders so wide they swallowed her up, eyes almost black under hooded lids. Eyes that saw everything, every detail of her, with a look that put her both completely at ease and shockingly on edge. A look she found herself already missing before he'd even gone.

As the sun dimmed outside and the pub began to fill with after-work drinkers it was on the tip of her tongue to suggest dinner. The urge took her completely by surprise but, just as she opened her mouth to ask, Bruno glanced at his watch and said, 'Time for me to go. I have a plane to catch.'

'Oh, OK.' Jessica hid her disappointment behind the relief of not having made the suggestion.

They walked out of the pub together weaving their way through tables, again his hand on her back at the door, again her liking the feel of it.

He paused in the street to glance around for a taxi, pulling his shades on. 'I'm actually here again in a few weeks,' he said.

'To see your sister?'

He laughed. 'Yes. But actually I have investments here.'

'You do?' she said, a touch too much enthusiasm in her voice.

He laughed again. 'You like that?'

She tried to reclaim her cool. 'It's interesting. Something else for you to come over for.'

He smiled. A taxi pulled up next to them. 'Interesting is good enough for me,' he said, opening the door.

Then to her surprise he slipped his arm around her waist and pulled her into a crushing great kiss.

She was just getting over the shock, her excited heart thumping like crazy, when he let her go and climbed into the taxi.

'I'll call you,' he said and, about to shut the door, added, 'and remember, don't think about it too much. Yes?'

Jessica nodded, still a bit breathless. She glanced round with a half-smile, disbelieving that she had just been kissed so passionately on the pavement in public and enjoyed it.

'Trust me. I never lose,' he said.

She nodded.

'Until next time, Jessica.'

'Until next time,' she said, and the taxi drove off in one direction and Jessica walked to the tube in the other, a secret smile playing on her lips all the way.

LIBBY

One year later

'So how's it been?' Miles asked.

'Crazy!' Libby replied.

Miles laughed. Then he turned to the woman next to him and said, 'Libby's one of those superstar bloggers now.'

'I am not,' Libby said, waving a hand for Miles's new girlfriend Chloe to ignore everything he was saying. 'It was a teeny weeny press whirlwind that I got caught up in. It was nothing. It was just about people who are "honest" online.'

'I believe the term is Social Media Realism,' said Jessica.

Libby shook her head, going over to throw open the outhouse windows because she was starting to get a little hot. The noise of the birds and the hum of the cicadas filled the space in the air. 'I was just an add on, they had much bigger people than me to focus on.'

Eve leant forward on her bench and said, 'Libby was in every magazine and newspaper in the UK. It wasn't that teeny weeny.'

Peter, who was sitting at the bench behind Eve, nodded. 'Even I read about it and I don't know about anyone famous.'

'I'm *not* famous.'

Chloe nodded, still impressed despite Libby's protestations.

'And did everyone see the Hidden Gems sticker on the front door?' Jessica said from the back. 'She got into the guide as well.'

'Congratulations,' said Miles with a proud grin.

'Frank came good,' laughed Libby. 'I think it was more to do with Giulia in the end, plying him with bowls of spaghetti vongole.'

'Don't believe a word of it. They all love Libby, the people who come here,' Jessica said. 'I'm always hearing them in the bar chatting about how she rescued their bake and how fabulous their dinner was.'

Miles turned. 'So you're here a lot, are you?'

Jessica shrugged, self-consciously pushing a curl behind her ear. 'A fair bit.'

'She's here all the time,' said Libby, pleased to have the focus moved onto someone else. 'Like once a month.'

Miles nodded as if he was pleased to hear that. Jessica nodded back. 'I like it,' she said. 'It's very calming.'

'She even has her own little desk set up at Bruno's bar,' said Libby with a big grin.

Jessica rolled her eyes as if she hadn't needed everyone to know that.

'Do you now?' said Eve, delight shining in her eyes. 'That sounds cosy.'

'It's *very* cosy,' said Libby.

'*Very* cosy, eh?' said Eve.

'OK you can stop now.' Jessica sighed.

They sniggered.

Jessica leant forward on her bench. 'And what about you two?' she said to Eve. 'How's the frolicking?'

Peter looked confused, as if he'd just been asked something about their sex life, but Eve laughed. 'The frolicking is fine. We have scheduled frolicking when we go back to the countryside to visit the chickens who are now living very happily with our old neighbour. And the children are with Peter's parents. I have no idea what they're doing but when they get home they will be drinking a lot of Nutribullets to make up for it.'

'What the hell's a Nutribullet?' Jessica asked.

'It's a blender,' said Peter with a sigh; clearly he'd heard far too much about the subject.

'It's not just a blender,' said Eve. 'You can put the whole apple in stalk and all and it turns it into a drink.'

Jessica snorted. 'I can see why you need a holiday, Peter.'

Peter chuckled. 'It's not that bad. And at least we got rid of the chickens.'

'Yeah, otherwise Eve would have Nutribullet-ed them,' Jessica laughed.

Miles's girlfriend looked a bit shocked.

'Oh don't, I still feel really bad about the chickens,' Eve said. 'Maisey and Noah were really sad.'

'They weren't that sad,' said Peter. 'Nothing a trip to the fair didn't fix.'

'Yeah, and now we've got two bloody goldfish because of that,' Eve added. 'It never ends.'

Libby watched Eve as she talked, all wavy blonde hair and toothy smile, lounging back against Peter's bench. It struck her that she looked like a whole person. Solid. Rather than before when it was almost like her edges were blurry, parts of her almost see-through like a faded photograph.

'And are you still meditating?' she heard Jimmy ask Peter.

'Every day.' Peter nodded.

Eve rolled her eyes. 'He still won't tell me his mantra.'

'As it should be,' said Jimmy.

'How about you?' Peter asked.

'Yeah, it's all good.' Jimmy nodded, casting a quick glance at Libby before repeating. 'All good.'

'You can talk about him, Jimmy, it's OK,' Libby said, coming round from behind her bench and leaning against it, wanting at that moment to remove the barrier and bring herself further into the group.

'Well…' Jimmy shrugged. 'It's fun, you know? Just normal I guess. We've got a flat in Camden. It's what you'd expect I suppose, two blokes together.'

'And you think you'll stay there for a while?' Miles asked.

Jimmy made a face. 'Yeah, no, maybe. I don't know. I feel maybe, you know, maybe it's time…'

'Don't say you're going to say settle down,' said Jessica, 'please.'

Jimmy ummed and ahhed. 'Yeah, maybe, maybe I'm feeling the pull.'

'Oh my god,' Jessica laughed. 'So much for no labels and young-ish, free and single.'

Jimmy conceded a smile at himself. 'Well, it gets a bit lonely sometimes.'

Libby wondered if Jake felt the same. They'd had the odd text conversation, a few emails to work out how they would split their assets. She was ready to agree to anything as long as she got to keep the hotel but in the end it had all been much more amenable than she'd imagined. She had wondered if Jimmy had had anything to do with that, coming down off the fence in order to make Jake see her side of things. She wasn't sure but she suspected that was the case.

'Well you know, Jimmy,' she said. 'There's a lovely girl who comes from Florence with a yoga group at the end of the summer. You'll have to come back then.'

Jimmy cocked his head as he thought about it, as he looked at Libby with the realisation that this was a gesture to confirm the definiteness of their friendship. 'I might just do that,' he said with a smile.

'Good.' Libby nodded and went back round behind her bench.

'So what are we making today?' Jimmy asked, rolling up his sleeves.

'Well, I was thinking we should wait for Dex to arrive,' Libby said, peering out of the open windows of the outhouse. 'What time does his train get in?' she asked, checking her watch, thinking that he should be here by now.

Jessica glanced up. 'Oh, he's not coming,' she said. 'Something came up at work. Sorry, did I not tell you?'

Libby felt like her whole body had just pooled at her feet.

How could Dex not be coming? They'd emailed loads about it.

Now, as she heard that he wouldn't be there, it suddenly made her realise quite how much she'd been looking forward to him arriving. How when she pictured them all working in the outhouse or sitting on the terrace laughing it was his face that was the clearest, his voice the funniest, his smile the brightest, him that she was sitting next to in the garden as the sun set.

She was unexpectedly crestfallen.

'Oh,' she said. Then she nodded. 'OK. Right.' She looked down at the floor. Why did it feel like the whole week was suddenly in black and white? She looked out of the window at the blinding sunshine and blue, blue sky. 'That's OK. Right. Well, let's think about what we're going to make.' She'd completely forgotten what she had planned and walked over to her bench to take another look at her recipes.

As she was familiarising herself with the lemon panna cotta recipe that she usually knew by heart, the door slid open and Dex walked in, case slung over his shoulder, pale blue shirt rolled up at the sleeves, familiar self-assured glint in his eye. 'Just when you were starting to worry,' he said, doing a small bow and dumping his bag on the ground. 'I made it, safe and sound. The train, I'll have you know, is a god damn fine mode of transport.'

'Dex?' Libby looked up, confused, delighted.

'Don't sound so surprised,' he said with a bemused smile. 'You knew I was coming.'

'But Jessica—' Libby started then stopped and glanced to the back of the room where Jessica was leaning over her bench, her chin resting in her hands, enjoying the scene with a huge smile on her face.

'But Jessica what?' asked Dex, wary.

Libby shook her head, unable to believe she'd been so easily duped. So easily read. 'Nothing,' she said. 'Nothing. Just. I'm glad you're here,' she added, suddenly a touch shy.

Dex narrowed his eyes and looked at her for a second, trying to work out what was going on, what he'd missed.

But then the others all came forward to say hello. Eve bounding over for a hug, Jimmy slapping him on the back while Miles proudly introduced Chloe. Dex made all the right comments, said all the right greetings, but all the while Libby could see he was half distracted, glancing over to check that she was still waiting patiently to say hi.

'All right?' he said, when they were finally standing opposite each other.

'All right,' she said, nervous and excitedly shy.

'Sorry I'm late,' he said.

'That's no problem at all.' She shook her head.

In the background the noise of the others chatting seemed to fade away as he bent down to kiss her cheek. She smelt the warmth and the kindness of him. She wanted to somehow tell him something that she couldn't with everyone around. Something that had been waiting and building and finally seemed real now he'd walked back in the door. So she reached forward, tentatively at first, then with more confidence. And when her palm touched his, Dex was momentarily taken aback. But she laced her fingers tight through his for just a second and, giving his hand the quickest squeeze, whispered, 'I *really* am glad to see you.'

'You are?' he said, unsure.

'Yes. Very.' She nodded, biting down on the start of her smile as she looked up at him and saw a momentary flicker of surprised delight in his eyes.

'Well I'll be damned.'

With the sun beaming into the room, the cicadas humming through the open door, Dex strolled over to his bench, a massive grin on his face, and said, 'Right then, what are we baking? You'd better all watch out because I've been practising all year.'

* * * * *